Following
Gandalf

Following Gandalf

Epic Battles and Moral Victory
in *The Lord of the Rings*

Matthew T. Dickerson

Brazos Press

A Division of Baker Book House Co
Grand Rapids, Michigan 49516

Published by Brazos Press
a division of Baker Book House Company
P.O. Box 6287, Grand Rapids, MI 49516-6287
www.brazospress.com

Fifth printing, May 2004

Printed in the United States of America

Library of Congress Cataloging-in-Publication Data
Dickerson, Matthew T., 1963–
    Following Gandalf : epic battles and moral victory in The lord of the rings / Matthew T. Dickerson.
       p.   cm.
    Includes bibliographical references.
    ISBN 1-58743-085-1 (pbk.)
    1. Tolkien, J. R. R. (John Ronald Reuel), 1892–1973. Lord of the rings. 2. Epic literature, English—History and criticism. 3. Fantasy fiction, English—History and criticism. 4. Free will and determinism in literature. 5. Middle Earth (Imaginary place) 6. Battles in literature. 7. Courage in literature. 8. Ethics in literature. I. Title.
PR6039.032L63334 2003
823′.912—dc21   2003012190

Contents

117125

Contents

Acknowledgments

Thanks to Jonathan Evans and Greg Vigne for their careful readings of the early drafts of this book, and for their numerous helpful suggestions that followed. I don't know either of them half as well as I should like, and I can't thank them half as much as they deserve. This book bears many of their fingerprints.

Thanks also to Kathy Skubikowski for co-teaching with me a course on Myth Making: *Beowulf* and *The Lord of the Rings* during the time I was writing this book and for her insightful comments on a few early chapters of this book. Thanks to Tom Shippey for a thoroughly enjoyable interview. (Only wish I could have been in England too.) And thanks to the many Middlebury College students who have taken my courses on J. R. R. Tolkien over the past fifteen years, especially to Keith Kelly, who has already become more of a scholar than I on many areas of study near and dear to J. R. R. T.'s heart.

Thanks last, but also first (and foremost), to my wife, Deborah, who continued to encourage me to write during the eleven years between the publication of my first book and the contract for my second and third.

Matthew Dickerson

Reference Abbreviations

Throughout this book, I use the following abbreviations for referenced works.

Works by J. R. R. Tolkien

Page numbers to *The Hobbit* and *The Lord of the Rings* come from the Houghton Mifflin second paperback edition, with "Note on the Text" by Douglas A. Anderson, 1986. Page numbers to *The Silmarillion* come from the Ballantine Books first paperback edition, 1979 (twelfth printing, 1989). Other reference information is given below.

(FOTR)—*The Fellowship of the Ring*

(FS)—J. R. R. Tolkien, essay "On Fairy-Stories," in *The Monsters and the Critics, and Other Essays*, edited by Christopher Tolkien, Houghton Mifflin, 1984.

(Letters)—*The Letters of J. R. R. Tolkien*, selected and edited by Humphrey Carpenter with the assistance of Christopher Tolkien, Houghton Mifflin, 1981.

(MR)—J. R. R. Tolkien, *Morgoth's Ring: The Later Silmarillion, Part One*. Vol. 10, *The History of Middle-Earth*, edited by Christopher Tolkien, Houghton Mifflin, 1993.

(ROTK)—*The Return of the King*

(TH)—*The Hobbit*

(TL)—J. R. R. Tolkien, *Tree and Leaf,* Houghton Mifflin, 1989.

(TS)—*The Silmarillion*

(TT)—*The Two Towers*

Other Sources Relevant to J. R. R. Tolkien

(B)—*Beowulf.* Norton Critical Edition. J. F. Tuso, ed. Translated by E. T. Donaldson, W. W. Norton, 1975.

(Ca)—Carpenter, Humphrey, *J. R. R. Tolkien: A Biography,* Houghton Mifflin, 1977.

(Ki)—Kilby, Clyde, *Tolkien and The Silmarillion,* Harold Shaw Publishers, 1976.

(Pu)—Purtill, Richard, *J. R. R. Tolkien: Myth, Morality, and Religion,* Harper & Row, 1984.

(Sh)—Shippey, T. A., *J. R. R. Tolkien: Author of the Century,* Houghton Mifflin, 2000.

Note: All Scripture citations come from the Douay-Rheims Catholic edition commonly in use during the lifetime of J. R. R. Tolkien.

Introduction

There comes a moment in *The Lord of the Rings* when the story has taken one of its darkest turns. The Fellowship is at its most fractured. Boromir is dead. Aragorn, with Legolas and Gimli, has gone against hope into the Paths of the Dead. Frodo has been bitten by Shelob and captured by Orcs and sits alone as a prisoner in a tower in Cirith Ungol. Sam is alone at the very gates of Mordor. Merry has been left alone with Théoden. Gandalf and Pippin have gone ahead to Minas Tirith, where Gandalf is beginning to see evidence of Denethor's fall into despair. Gondor is expecting a siege, and none are sure whether any help will arrive from Rohan or from the south. The Nazgûl have taken to the air on deadly steeds. Faramir has not yet returned to his home city. And the morning that has no dawn is fast approaching. In short, the world is full of evil tidings, and hope has waned to its lowest point. It is, as Gandalf tells Denethor, a "dark hour" (ROTK, p. 26). Yet as Pippin and Gandalf return from their first meeting with Denethor, the young Hobbit notices something interesting in the wizard.

> Pippin glanced in some wonder at the face now close beside his own, for the sound of that laugh had been gay and merry. Yet in the wizard's face he saw at first only lines of care and sorrow; though as he looked more intently he perceived that under all

11

there was a great joy: a fountain of mirth enough to set a kingdom laughing, were it to gush forth. (ROTK, p. 31)

Tolkien is painting for the reader a very intriguing picture
of Gandalf. Reading this passage, we wonder with Pippin
how the wizard can have so much joy in the midst of such
darkness. How do we explain it? Is Gandalf completely deluded
and unable to see reality or to understand the depths of the
coming darkness? Or does he actually take pleasure in all the
evil tidings, as Wormtongue suggests at one point? Or is there
something else going on? Could it be the case that Gandalf has
some sort of wisdom or knowledge that penetrates beyond
what is visible to everybody else—the desperation of the situation that is so evident to Pippin and Denethor—and enables
the wizard to take hope and joy in something invisible that is
nonetheless real and true? This third possibility, of course, is
the correct one, as Tolkien shows us. Gandalf is aware that
there is both a seen world and an unseen world; reality includes
both a material plane and a spiritual plane. Furthermore, these
two planes touch upon each other and affect each other. What
happens in the spiritual plane affects what happens in the
material plane, and vice versa. And Gandalf, with the eyes of
wisdom, is one of those characters who sees the unseen. His
sight extends into the spiritual, as well as the material, reality. He is a little like the Elf-lord Glorfindel, of whom he says
to Frodo, "Those who have dwelt in the Blessed Realm live at
once in both worlds, and against both the Seen and the Unseen
they have great power. . . . You saw [Glorfindel] for a moment
as he is upon the other side" (FOTR, p. 235).

This book is an exploration of a single theme—or rather a
collection of tightly related themes—in the Middle-earth writings of J. R. R. Tolkien. Over the course of about fifteen years
of teaching college classes and lecturing on Tolkien and his
writing, I have found that with nearly any topic I have chosen to explore or have been invited to address, invariably the
exploration has somehow led back to touch on one particular
theme: the reality and importance of human free will.

In his most recent book, *J. R. R. Tolkien: Author of the Century*, T. A. Shippey correctly, persuasively, and insightfully (as well as enjoyably) argues that philology (the study of language) is at the center of Tolkien's Middle-earth writing, in its inspiration and purpose, as well as in the actual carrying out of that purpose in the final work. That is to say, Tolkien's work is not only philologically centered, but consciously so. Understanding this leads us to a deeper understanding and appreciation for what Tolkien has accomplished. As has been pointed out by Shippey (and by Humphrey Carpenter and by J. R. R. Tolkien himself), Tolkien's philological studies—"the inner life, the life of the mind, the world of Tolkien's work"—was not only his academic pursuit but also "his hobby, his private amusement, his ruling passion." Indeed, he "refused to distinguish the two" (Sh, p. xi). It should not be surprising, then, that this academic study not only should find its way into *The Lord of the Rings*, but would actually be behind it from the start, and would so thoroughly run through it. What makes it surprising, I suppose, is that Tolkien could begin with such academic roots and accomplish something that so many nonacademics have found so enjoyable.

The point of this book, however, is that Tolkien's deep philosophical and theological convictions also course thoroughly through the veins of his work. In particular, Tolkien's understanding of Man (male and female) as having been created in the image of a Creator—and thus not only being endowed with the possibility of real moral choice, but being given the corresponding responsibility that goes with it—is the central theme in his writing. Of his own work, Tolkien wrote: "I think a primary 'fact' about my work [is that] it is all of a piece, and *fundamentally linguistic* in inspiration. . . . The invention of languages is the foundation. The 'stories' were made rather to provide a world for the languages than the reverse" (Letters, p. 219). Whether Tolkien also *consciously* set out to undergird his writings with his philosophical and spiritual beliefs and presuppositions—his *weltanschauung*, or "worldview"—in the same way that he had consciously set out to engage in a work of philological significance is not my main point (though I will give some evidence about Tolkien's intent as well as the result). His worldview was so thoroughly ingrained in him (as was his philology) that he could not help its becoming central to his writings.

There is yet another similarity between the philological significance of Tolkien's writing and the theological/philosophical: in both cases Tolkien's views were considerably at odds with the prevailing view of the cultural elite of his day and age. With regard to his philological views, Shippey wrote: "Tolkien was the holder of several highly personal if not heretical views about language" (Sh, p. xiv). Neither his views nor his popular writing received the approval of his colleagues in academia. Likewise, Tolkien's basic philosophical beliefs were also in contradiction to the prevailing materialist presuppositions[1] of modernism as well as the relativism of postmodernism, especially with respect to his views on human free will and objective morality. Just a few quotes from important twentieth-century thinkers will suffice to illustrate this. Bertrand Russell, in his essay "Has Religion Made Useful Contributions to Civilization?" (published as part of his well-known collection *Why I Am Not A Christian*), wrote:

> Materialists used the laws of physics to show, or attempt to show, that the movements of human bodies are mechanically determined, and that consequently everything we say and every change of position that we effect fall *outside* the sphere of any possible free will. . . . If, when a man writes a poem or commits a murder, the bodily movements involved in his act result solely from physical causes, it would seem absurd to put up a statue to him in the one case and to hang him in the other. . . .
>
> My own belief is that . . . the physicists will in time discover [these] laws governing minute phenomena, although these

---

1. The word *materialism* has two definitions. The first refers to the belief that all that exists is the "material," or physical, universe. The second refers simply to a greedy desire to acquire more material (without interest for intellectual or spiritual concerns). I am using the term in the first of those two senses: the deeper philosophical sense. Under the beliefs of materialism, physical reality is the only reality—there is nothing spiritual or supernatural—and thus all phenomena can be explained purely by physical processes.

laws may differ very considerably from those of traditional physics. . . .

Whatever may be thought about it as a matter of ultimate metaphysics, it is quite clear that nobody believes in [free will] anymore.[2]

In the same essay, Russell went on to say:

When a man acts in ways that annoy us we wish to think him wicked, and we refuse to face the fact that his annoying behavior is a result of antecedent clauses which, if you follow them long enough, will take you beyond the moment of his birth and therefore to events for which he cannot be held responsible by any stretch of the imagination.[3]

In short, Russell is absolutely denying the existence of human free will: "Everything we say and every change of position that we effect fall *outside* the sphere of any possible free will." In doing so, he also takes the stance (consistent with his denial of free will) of denying moral responsibility. According to Russell, we cannot possibly be held responsible for any of our actions.

We will later see just how sharply Tolkien's views contrast with this, but first we should make it clear that Russell is not an anomaly. The famous behavioral psychologist B. F. Skinner wrote in *Beyond Freedom and Dignity*:

What is being abolished is autonomous man—the inner man, the homunculus man, the possessing demon, the man defended by the literatures of freedom and dignity.

His abolition has long been overdue. Autonomous man is a device used to explain what we cannot explain in any other way. He has been constructed from our ignorance, and as our understanding increases, the very stuff of which he is composed vanishes. . . . To man qua man we readily say good riddance. Only by dispossessing him can we turn to the real causes of

2. Bertrand Russell, "Has Religion Made Useful Contributions to Civilization?" published in *Why I Am Not A Christian* (New York: Simon and Schuster, 1967), pp. 37–39.

16

human behavior. Only then can we turn from the inferred to the observed, from the miraculous to the natural, from the inaccessible to the manipulable.[4]

Skinner here takes the extra step of not only denying free will—the notion of an "autonomous man"—but of criticizing the *literatures* of freedom and dignity that suggest the existence of free will. In fact, he explicitly attacks the literature of Tolkien's good friend C. S. Lewis. Any heroic literature that depends upon a human's responsibility for his or her actions falls under this attack as a literature of freedom and dignity. Tolkien's writing would certainly fit the category so disdained by Skinner. Tolkien would most certainly have disagreed with comments such as this one by Skinner, or an earlier one from the same book: "Personal exception from a complete determinism is revoked as scientific analysis progresses, particularly in accounting for the behavior of the individual."[5]

These are just two of dozens of influential writers and thinkers whom we could quote, and while Bertrand Russell is no longer as widely read today, B. F. Skinner continues to be a staple in college and university curricula. While working on this book, I stumbled on an article in the *Boston Globe* quoting Chris Frith, a neuroscientist at University College, London. His thoughts illustrate the prevalence of this materialist thinking: "I think in the next few years we will have quite a good understanding of the brain mechanisms that underlie our feeling of being in control of our actions."[6] In other words, the notion of having free will, of "being in control" is an illusion that science is supposedly on the verge of eliminating. In short, if one thinks in terms of an overall worldview and not just of philology, then Shippey was greatly understating the situation when he wrote, "Tolkien's answers . . . are wildly at odds with those given even by many of his contemporaries" (Sh, p. ix).

4. B. F. Skinner, *Beyond Freedom and Dignity*, cited in Francis Schaeffer, *Back to Freedom and Dignity*, vol. 1 of *The Complete Works of Francis Schaeffer* (New York: Knopf, 1971), p. 374.
5. Ibid., p. 21.
6. *Boston Globe*, 15 October 2002, sec. C, p. 3.

This book explores many of these issues. It begins with the question of how Tolkien portrays war and battle. At the surface, this addresses the phantom criticism that his writings glorify war, but more important, it sets the stage for the coming chapters in which we listen together to the Wise of Middle-earth and hear what they have to say about war, and then explore the contrast between moral victory and military victory, seeing how the former was much more important to Tolkien than the latter. In the middle chapters, we then delve into the central theme of this book, which I also claim to be a central theme in all of Tolkien's writing: the reality of human free will and the moral responsibility that goes with it. It is the "doom of choice," as Aragorn calls it when questioned by Éomer. In light of this, we look at the result of our moral choices, or more specifically at what results in each of us because of our moral choices. What becomes of Boromir? Of Théoden and Denethor? Why is Gollum's fate important, and how did Bilbo escape the same fate? In the final chapters, I return to the question of war and put much of the rest of this book, and thereby much of Tolkien's writing, into the context and perspective given to us by the *Ainulindalë,* the opening part of Tolkien's book *The Silmarillion.* It is in these chapters, perhaps, that I take the greatest risk in dealing with certain philosophical and even spiritual issues; that is, I tread on some sacred ground on which Tolkien himself was cautious of treading—cautious not because it was unimportant to his beliefs, but because it was so *vitally* important.

Underlying this whole discussion is Tolkien's belief that the reality of the universe involves both spiritual and physical planes: both the seen and unseen dimensions. Tolkien was challenging his readers to look beyond the temporal values of the moment to see the eternal values where the spiritual and physical planes come together: at eternity.

1

Epic Battles

"The world is changed," begins the mesmerizing voice of Cate Blanchett's Galadriel. "I feel it in the water. I feel it in the earth. I smell it in the air." Within moments, we witness Sauron himself, standing beside the great fires of Mount Doom, holding aloft the Ruling Ring. Galadriel's narration continues. "And into the Ring he poured his cruelty and his malice." Soon a vast army of snarling Orcs comes sweeping down off the slopes of the mountain, like a wave breaking over the forces of the Last Alliance of Elves and Men led by Elrond, Elendil, and Isildur. The cinematic score grows. We see Elrond's hair ruffle in the wind as his flawless Elven archers release a massive volley of arrows. The first wave of Orcs falls. Then the swords of this Last Alliance, glittering gold and silver, come swinging around in glorious unison, slicing through Orcs like scythes flashing through wheat. The king of Gondor lifts his polished sword high in victory. Only then do we hear Galadriel's fateful words: "Victory was near, but the power of the Ring could not be undone." Sauron himself appears. At a single swing of his terrible mace, hundreds fall.

So begins Peter Jackson's recent film version of J. R. R. Tolkien's masterpiece *The Fellowship of the Ring*. It is a powerful work of cinema: an evocative and graphic scene that immediately draws the viewer into the world of Middle-earth, and especially into the epic scope of Sauron's evil that must be confronted in *The Lord of The Rings*. The same could be said about the film version of *The Two Towers*, which is dominated by the long scenes of the Battle of Helm's Deep. As the music rumbles to its intense crescendo, we see the Orc siege ladders swing upward against the wall; in slow motion, we witness the wall explode and send giant stones hurtling down on friend and foe alike; we watch Legolas glide down the stone steps on an abandoned shield, shooting arrow after arrow almost faster than the eye can follow; and we are stunned by the sight of Saruman's armies, "bred for a single purpose: to destroy the world of Man." It is nothing short of an intensely stunning visual display of modern filmmaking.

These are also scenes that may lend credence to an old criticism that Tolkien's works glorify war and violence. I first heard this criticism several years ago when I was teaching a course on *The Silmarillion* and *The Lord of the Rings*. It came from a colleague who was describing why she had ceased to appreciate J. R. R. Tolkien and had—as she put it—"grown out of" his writing. Having been a fan and student of Tolkien's works for several years, I was a little taken aback to hear this; it had never before struck me that his writing glorified war. Hearing this comment from a respected colleague, however, I began to wonder. After all, battles do hold a significant place in the tales of Middle-earth. *The Hobbit* culminates in the Battle of the Five Armies, in which many fortunes and futures are made (or lost), while the entire trilogy of *The Lord of the Rings* focuses on a single war, moving (or so it seems) from one battle to another: Weathertop, Moria, Amon Hen, Helm's Deep, etc. The same can be said for *The Silmarillion*, in which the battles are given lofty Elvish names, such as Dagor Agloreb, Dagor Bragollach, Dagor-nuin-Giliath, and Nirnaeth Arneodiad. Just the cinematic trailer to Jackson's film version of *The Two Towers*, with the violent battle scenes depicted there, might be enough to convince somebody to take that criticism seriously. The officially licensed video games with violent depictions of Orcs spilling gore (and having their gore spilled) were inevitable.

As I reflected back on Tolkien's own work, however, that particular criticism of his writing did not hold any lasting grip. Indeed, the more I considered it, the more absurdly false I realized it was. In hindsight, my initial response of being "taken aback" by my colleague's comments probably came not from any validity inherent in the criticism, but rather from a personal desire to be respected, which required that I hold views that were deemed "respectable." I don't think one can read Tolkien seriously and be left with the impression that he glorifies either violence or war. In fact, I wondered what serious critic could even *write* such a thing. The answer, as I discovered, was "nobody" or at least "nearly nobody." Several searches of the literature uncovered not a single critic who was willing, in print, to support the assertion that Tolkien glorified war. As I started writing this book, I discovered, as T. A. Shippey wrote, that "very few of Tolkien's critics . . . have been prepared to put their dislike into an organized shape which can be debated" (Sh, p. xxxiii).

Nonetheless, that particular criticism lives on and may well grow with the releases of each part of the film trilogy (or cross-marketed video games). In light of the vivid battle scenes in Jackson's films, it is instructive to explore just how Tolkien does portray war and battles and violence. How does he describe battle scenes? What images does he use? What narrative devices? What voices? Beginning an exploration here actually leads to a deeper understanding of what really is important in *The Lord of the Rings*. After all, as mentioned earlier, battles do play an important part in all of Tolkien's Middle-earth narratives. It is thus reasonable to assume that he must have something to say either with respect to war or in the context of war. And, indeed, he does. Many very important things: about free will, and moral responsibility, and the very meaning of life.

The Battle of Five Armies

As the first major battle in both *The Hobbit* and *The Lord of the Rings,* the Battle of Five Armies is an appropriate place to begin our exploration of Tolkien and war. From the perspective of Middle-earth's history (if not also from the perspective of the narrative), it is the second most important event in *The Hobbit,* second only to Bilbo's finding of the Ring. What can we learn from Tolkien's presentation of this event? Does this battle read like a description of a video game screen? Or like something altogether different?

As the battle approaches—in a chapter appropriately titled "The Clouds Burst"—the pace of the narrative increases toward its climax. Finally we read, "So began the battle that none had expected; and it was called the Battle of Five Armies, and it was very terrible" (TH, p. 237). Except that the battle did not begin quite yet, or at least the narrative account of the battle did not begin. Four and a half more paragraphs ensue that give an overview of the situation leading up to the battle from an omniscient narrative voice. This overview describes the historical setting for the battle, the geography of the battle site, and, most important, the work of Gandalf in bringing together the Elves, Men, and Dwarves who give up their enmity toward one another and unite to fight a common enemy. One thing we do get from this opening line, however, is the first adjective Tolkien uses to describe battle: *terrible.*

Then comes the first actual description of fighting: "A few brave men were strung before them to make a feint of resistance, and many there fell before the rest drew back and fled to either side" (TH, p. 238). At this point the battle begins in earnest, and as it does, *The Hobbit* takes an interesting turn in its narrative voice; Tolkien temporarily abandons the omniscient view and begins to describe the battle from the very limited viewpoint of Bilbo, the Hobbit:

> It was a terrible battle. The most dreadful of all Bilbo's experiences, and the one which at the time he hated most—which is to say it was the one he was most proud of, and most fond of recalling long afterwards, although he was quite unimportant in it. (TH, p. 238)

Again we see the same word, *terrible,* as the descriptive adjective for battle. Definitions of *terrible* include "very unpleasant or harrowing" and "unwell or extremely unhappy," in contrast, for example, to the word *glorious,* which means "beautiful in a way that inspires wonder or joy." One cannot help but see in this depiction something of Tolkien's own World War I experience, fighting in battle in 1916 as an infantryman. He viewed the war from the trenches, unable ever to see the big picture or to understand how his actions fit into the broader perspective of the war as a whole, or even into that particular battle. Tolkien lost two of his closest friends and then himself got trench fever (Ca). But the main point I wish to make is that this approach—the switch from an omniscient overview to Bilbo's perspective—personalizes the battle while adding distance to it. That is, the focus of Tolkien's narrative at this point, rather than being on the details of the fighting, shifts to the feelings of one individual involved. In this case, moreover, the individual is one who is "quite unimportant" from a military or strategic viewpoint, who doesn't really understand what is happening, and who in fact is invisible to the rest of the combatants. This helps connect the battle with the individual reader, who would likely feel much the same in a battle of that scope, while adding a certain spatial distance to the narrative, as of one watching the events from afar. Tolkien adds even more distance to the battle—this time a temporal distance—by describing it in the way that this unimportant character Bilbo remembers it "long afterward," rather than the way he views it at the moment. A conclusion one might draw is that Tolkien is more concerned with those involved in the battle than with the battle itself. (We will return to this point later.)

The battle continues from there, but it is described in broad brushstrokes, once more from a high and distant perspective, with hours flashing past in just a few sentences. We get this in such simple statements as, "Day drew on" (TH, p. 239). As for description of the fighting itself—swords whacking off body parts, spears plunging into enemies, or any of the sort of visual detail we might expect in a modern video game—there is almost none. In over twenty paragraphs that narrate the battle, there are only a handful of descriptions that might be called graphic: "The rocks were stained black with goblin blood" (TH, p. 238).

"Many of their own wolves were turning on them and rending the dead and the wounded" (TH, p. 239). "Thorin wielded his axe with mighty strokes" (TH, p. 239). "Once again the goblins were stricken in the valley; and they were piled in heaps till Dale was dark and hideous with their corpses" (TH, p. 240). Note that even these descriptions are broad and general—only the third of these four mentions a specific person—leaving it to the reader's imagination to fill in the detail. And it is not likely to be pleasant detail. It is a gruesome and very negative picture of war: bloodstained rocks, betrayal, and dead bodies.

That's about all we are given for detailed graphic description of the violence of the fighting. Then the narrative returns again to Bilbo.

> On all this Bilbo looked with misery. . . .
> "Misery me!" [thought Bilbo.] "I have heard songs of many battles, and I have always understood that defeat may be glorious. It seems very uncomfortable, not to say distressing. I wish I was well out of it." (TH, p. 240)

As we know, of course, the battle does not end in defeat for Bilbo, but in victory. Tolkien, however, altogether avoids describing the victory, because his narrator is knocked unconscious before the battle ends: "'The Eagles!' cried Bilbo once more, but at that moment a stone hurtling from above smote heavily on his helm, and he fell with a crash and knew no more" (TH, p. 241). This is rather significant. If one were to glorify war at all, then victory is the ideal moment to do so. Yet Tolkien doesn't even let us experience victory. It is not until well later, after the battle is over and victory won, that Bilbo awakens:

> When Bilbo came to himself, he was literally by himself. He was lying on the flat stones of Ravenhill, and no one was near. A cloudless day, but cold, was broad above him. He was shaking, and as chilled as stone, but his head burned with fire. . . .
> "Victory after all, I suppose!" he said, feeling his aching head. "Well, it seems a very gloomy business." (TH, p. 242)

Between these two passages, Tolkien is quite explicit. Battle is glorious neither in defeat (contrary to what Bilbo had always thought) nor in victory. Rather, it is miserable, "uncomfortable," "distressing," and overall "a very gloomy business." Indeed, it would be difficult to look at the scene to which Bilbo awoke and call it victory. Many good Elves, Men, and Dwarves lie dead, and many others mortally wounded. In short, there is little glory in it—not in Tolkien's narrative.

The Black Gate and the Skirmish with Southrons

If we move from *The Hobbit* to *The Lord of the Rings*, the three biggest battles are (in chronological order): the Battle of Helm's Deep, the Siege of Minas Tirith (also called the Siege of Gondor), and the battle in front of the Black Gate at the end of book 5. We will start with the last of these and move backward, as the final battle is probably the most important—not important from a military standpoint, as there is no particular objective for the Captains of the West, but important as a diversion to draw Sauron's attention away from Mount Doom. Furthermore, the final battle involves the greatest forces, including names "that are worth more than a thousand mail-clad knights apiece" (ROTK, p. 158).

Interestingly enough, Tolkien describes the battle in front of the Black Gate in a way so closely parallel to the Battle of Five Armies in *The Hobbit* that I can only imagine the parallel is intentional. Both are the final major battles in their respective books, both involve several different armies coming together to fight a common foe, both involve a single Hobbit (as an unimportant character), and both end with the unexpected coming of the Eagles presaging an unlooked-for hope and victory. Both battles also involved Gandalf as a critical agent in bringing the allied forces together to fight the common enemy.

The battle in front of the Black Gate begins with the armies of Mordor sweeping down upon Aragorn's army as Sauron springs his trap. Four paragraphs describe Aragorn's quick ordering of his troops as the enemy rushes toward them from all sides. Then, as with the Battle of Five Armies in *The Hobbit*, the narrative suddenly switches from a distant omniscient view to the perspective of the unimportant Hobbit—which in this case is Pippin:

> Pippin had bowed crushed with horror when he heard Gandalf reject the terms and doom Frodo to the torment of the Tower; but he had mastered himself, and now he stood beside Beregond in the front rank of Gondor with Imrahil's men. For it seemed best to him to die soon and leave the bitter story of his life, since all was in ruin.
>
> "I wish Merry was here," he heard himself saying, and quick thoughts raced through his mind, even as he watched the enemy come charging to the assault. . . .
>
> He drew his sword and looked at it, and the intertwining shapes of red and gold; and the flowing characters of Númenor glinted like fire upon the blade. "This was made for just such an hour," he thought. "If only I could smite that foul Messenger with it, then almost I should draw level with Old Merry. Well I'll smite some of the beastly brood before the end. I wish I could see cool sunlight and green grass again!"
>
> Then even as he thought these things the first assault crashed into them. . . .
>
> "So it ends as I guessed it would," his thought said, even as it fluttered away; and it laughed a little within him ere it fled, almost gay it seemed to be casting off at last all doubt and care and fear. (ROTK, pp. 168–69)

As noted, this narrative switch in perspectives comes the moment the battle begins. At this point, the focus turns to the thoughts and feelings of the *character* rather than the graphic details of the *battle*. The words used to describe Pippin's thoughts on this battle are similar to those used of Bilbo's perspective on the earlier battle: horror, doom, bitterness, and ruin. There are, however, two contrasts between the scenes. First, though this battle is dramatically more significant to the peoples of Middle-earth than that at the end of *The Hobbit*—and involves considerably larger and more powerful armies—it is described with far fewer words. Once the preliminary bargaining and diplomacy are over, and Gandalf has rejected the terms of Sauron's emissary, barely over one page (eight paragraphs) is given to the actual description of this important battle, all of which comes from Pippin's perspective. Then Pippin (like Bilbo) is knocked unconscious.

A second difference is that the reader gets somewhat *more* of the Hobbit's thoughts and feelings *at the moment* (rather than *retrospectively*), which is surprising since there is *less* overall narrative devoted to this battle than is devoted to the Battle of Five Armies. In particular, not only is the narrator concerned with Pippin's role and position as the battle begins, but he tells us just what is going through the Hobbit's mind during those first few moments. Certainly some of his thoughts are directed toward the present instant: the horrors he is about to face and what he hopes to accomplish against his foes. But much of his thought is turned toward things having little to do with battle: first toward his friend Merry, and then toward "cool sunlight and green grass." These are the things—friends, sunlight, grass—that are really important in the tale; this, and not war and battles, is the stuff of life: the stuff that counts. And thus this, even in the midst of a battle scene, is what Tolkien's narrative brings us back to.

These are not the only two instances where Tolkien uses a Hobbit to give us a perspective on the wars of Men. Nowhere is that Hobbitish view more stark than the view we get from Sam of the small skirmish fought between Faramir's men and the Southron forces passing through Ithilien.

> It was Sam's first view of a battle of Men against Men, and he did not like it much. He was glad that he could not see the dead face. He wondered what the man's name was and where he came from; and if he was really evil of heart, or what lies or threats had led him on the long march from his home; and if he would not really rather have stayed there in peace. (TT, p. 269)

Here Tolkien not only personalizes those on the "our side," as we might call the Free Peoples of Middle-earth, but he personalizes one of the enemy soldiers. He has a name, a heart, and a history. He may be evil, or he may not be. He may, Sam realizes, even have a desire for peace; he may be as much a victim of Sauron's threats and lies as the folk of Gondor. Even the long march he followed to this battle is one that took him from a home, much as Sam himself had arrived at that same spot on a long march taking him away from his own home. In short, the fallen figure has a face, and Tolkien lets us know he has a face even though we cannot see it. It is a dead face that Sam is glad he cannot see, and that comment alone strengthens the sense of the humanity of this foe: a humanity he shares with Sam, and with the soldiers of Faramir who killed him. One cannot construe this as a glorious image of war.

The Rohirrim and the Anglo-Saxons

Working backward through the story, we turn next to the Siege of Minas Tirith: the longest and most involved of the battles in this war. It would take considerable time to examine that entire battle, as it spans more than four chapters of *The Return of the King*. Instead we will explore only the fight between Éowyn and the Nazgûl on the Pelennor Fields. However, one observation first needs to be made of the battle as a whole. Though the siege and battle last for many days (and many chapters), none of the narration takes place out on the battlefield until the very end of the battle and the coming of the Rohirrim. What little of the battle that Tolkien does give the reader is described from the perspective of those up on the walls—Pippin and Beregond—looking out at the distant battleground and trying to guess what is happening. In other words, there is little description of the warfare. Rather, the real narrative action takes place within the city and focuses on how the characters respond to the siege: what they feel; what they think; what they say. Indeed, the battle Tolkien describes in most detail is the battle against despair—a battle we will explore in a later chapter—and especially the ability of Gandalf and the Prince of Dol Amroth to bring hope to those who have lost it.

When the narrative finally switches from the spectators within the walls of Minas Tirith to the actual fighting taking place outside the walls, the one scene Tolkien chooses to emphasize is the battle between Éowyn and the Nazgûl, and the subsequent death of King Théoden: a microcosm, but an important one, within "The Battle of the Pelennor Fields" (ROTK, book 5, chapter 6). This fight is described with a very different narrative voice than the previous two battles I have commented on:

> But lo! Suddenly in the midst of the glory of the king his golden shield was dimmed. The new morning was blotted from the sky. Dark fell about him. Horses reared and screamed. Men cast from the saddle and lay groveling on the ground.
>
> "To me! To me!" cried Théoden. "Up Eorlingas! Fear no darkness!" But Snowmane wild with terror stood up on high, fighting with the air, and then with a great scream he crashed upon his side: a black dart had pierced him. The king fell beneath him.
>
> A great shadow descended like a falling cloud. And behold! It was a winged creature: if bird, then greater than all other birds, and it was naked, and neither quill nor feather did it bear, and its vast pinions were as webs of hide between horned fingers; and it stank. . . . Upon it sat a shape, black-mantled, huge and threatening. A crown of steel he bore, but between rim and robe naught was there to see, save only a deadly gleam of eyes: the Lord of the Nazgûl. To the air he had returned, summoning his stead ere the darkness failed, and now he was come again, bringing ruin, turning hope to despair, and victory to death. A great black mace he wielded.
>
> But Théoden was not utterly forsaken. The knights of his house lay slain about him, or else mastered by the madness of their steeds were borne far away. Yet one stood there still: Dernhelm the young, faithful beyond fear; and he wept, for he had loved his lord as a father. . . .
>
> And so he died, and knew not that Éowyn lay near him. And those who stood by wept, crying: "Théoden King! Théoden King!" (ROTK, pp. 115, 119)

In this battle, after Théoden is struck down, Éowyn (initially in the guise of Dernhelm) faces the Lord of the Nazgûl in combat. And with the aid of Merry, she defeats him—though in the process both she and Merry are wounded mortally (as it seems). As mentioned, it is a scene very different from the majority of Tolkien's battles. Unlike many other battles, in which the reader is given very little graphic description of the fighting, this battle is described in great detail: the "swift stroke" of Éowyn's "steel-blade"; the fall of the Nazgûl-Lord's mace; each word spoken between the combatants; even to the shivering of shield and breaking of bone. Why the difference? Why the sudden level of detail?

One thing to be considered here is that Éowyn is not facing a foe of flesh and bones. The Nazgûl whom she destroys is not a mortal being—it is not a physical enemy—but a spiritual foe: a wraith. Thus, though the battle between the two takes place in the physical world with physical weapons, Tolkien may be giving us a glimpse of the deeper nature of reality. There is both a physical plane and a spiritual plane: both a physical part of reality and a spiritual part of reality. Since the eye cannot see the spiritual plane, Tolkien visualizes it in the physical realm. We might well conclude that since the only foe we see close up on the Pelennor Fields is a wraith, the real enemy that must be faced in Middle-earth is a spiritual enemy. No battle against a physical foe is depicted with such detail.

There are also at least two other important reasons for the particular narrative voice and style of description that Tolkien uses in this scene, neither of which have the purpose of glorifying war—or the *effect* of glorifying war when read in their context. The first reason lies in understanding who Théoden and Éowyn are, and more generally who the Rohirrim are. Tolkien models the Rohirrim—the people of Rohan—directly after the Anglo-Saxon people, although he does so with one ironic little twist: that the real Anglo-Saxons inhabiting England were not, by any stretch of the imagination, lovers of horses. The language of Rohan is Old English (Anglo-Saxon). The word *Riddermark*, for example, comes from *Ridenna-mearc* (ROTK, Index, p. 435); *ridan* is Old English for "to ride," *ridda* for "rider," and *mearc* for "border" or "marches"; hence, *Ridenna-mearc* for "riders of the border." *Meduseld* means "mead hall." Likewise, names of many people in Rohan are often just Anglo-Saxon words. *Théoden* is simply Old English for "prince" or "lord."

The poetry of Rohan takes the exact same verse form in meter and alliteration as that of Old English poetry. (Those familiar with Old English poetry should consider the poem sung by Éomer after Théoden's death: "Mourn not overmuch! Mighty was the fallen" [ROTK, p. 119].)

Even the speech patterns of the Rohirrim are modeled after Old English heroic verse. Consider the "welcome" given to Gandalf, Aragorn, Gimli, and Legolas by the guards at the gates of Edoras (the palace of King Théoden):

"None are welcome here in days of war but our own folk, and those that come from Mundburg in the land of Gondor. Who are you that come heedless over the plain thus strangely clad, riding horses like to our own horses? Long have we kept guard here, and we have watched you from afar. Never have we seen other riders so strange, nor any horse more proud than is one of these that bear you. He is one of the Mearas, unless our eyes are cheated by some spell. Say, are you not a wizard, some spy from Saruman, or phantoms of his craft? Speak now and be swift!" (TT, p. 113)

This speech is borrowed almost directly from the welcome given to Beowulf and his warriors by the beach-guards when they arrive at Heorot to visit Hrothgar in the Old English poem *Beowulf*. The Dane's coastguard speak thus:

"What are you, bearers of armor, dressed in mail-coats, who thus have come bringing a tall ship over the sea-road, over the water to this place? Lo, for a long time I have been guard of the coast, held watch by the sea so that no foe with a force of ships might work harm on the Danes' land: never have shield-bearers more openly undertaken to come ashore here; nor did you know for sure of a word of leave from our warriors, consent from my kinsmen. I have never seen a mightier warrior on earth than is one of you, a man in battle-dress. That is no retainer made to seem good by his weapons—unless his appearance belies him, his unequalled form. Now I must learn your lineage before you go any farther from here, spies on the Danes' land. Now you far-

dwellers, sea-voyagers, hear what I think: you must straightway
say where you have come from." (B, lines 237–57, p. 5)

Nobody deeply familiar with *Beowulf* could miss the simi-
larities: "Who/what are you that come . . . over the plain/sea-
road"; "Long have we kept guard here . . ."; "I have never seen a
horse/warrior more proud/mightier than is one of you"; "some
spy from Saruman/spies in the Dane's land"; "Speak now and
be swift." About the only significant difference is that in the
former case the arriving party has come by horse, and in the
latter case by ship.

So why is this connection important? What does it matter that the Rohirrim are Tolkien's Anglo-Saxons who found
their way into Middle-earth? Part of the answer is simply the
narrative richness imparted in the tale. If the Rohirrim have
Anglo-Saxon names and Anglo-Saxon speech patterns, and
sing the poetry of Old English heroic verse, then in a scene
that focuses on the death of their great king, it makes sense for
the narrative voice—in addition to the voices of the characters
themselves—to complete the richness by using the idiom of Old
English heroic verse. That is what Tolkien has done. (Remember that he was himself a scholar of Anglo-Saxon language
and literature, and thus this was not only appropriate for the
richness of the setting, but also easy and natural for him as
a writer.) So we consider this scene. It begins with a phrase
similar to that at the start of *Beowulf:* "Lo!" or "But, Lo!" It
continues in a manner very consistent with Old English narrative style, namely, that really important actions are described
three times with three slightly different images. *(Shield was
dimmed. Morning was blotted. Dark fell.)*

But the language and literature of the Anglo-Saxons (and
thus of the Rohirrim) comes out of an early-Germanic culture,
in which war was glorified. Or, if not war, then at least the
warrior—whether in *death* or in *victory.* A chieftain became a
chieftain because of his prowess in battle, and when he died
he was buried with his weapons and with those of his van-
quished opponents. The great heroes at the start of *Beowulf*
are praised for their military victories and brave deeds, and

especially for conquering other peoples and making them pay
tribute. In short, we are seeing this scene alternately through
the eyes of the Rohirrim (Théoden, Éowyn, and later Éomer)
and Merry. When seen through the eyes of the Rohirrim, we
do get a glimpse of this glorification of the life and death of a
warrior that would have characterized the society of Rohan.
"I go to my fathers," Théoden says. "And even in their mighty
company I shall not now be ashamed" (ROTK, pp. 117–18).

Merry, however, provides us another perspective on this
battle—much as Bilbo, Pippin, and Sam had done for the three
battles already discussed. Or, rather, Tolkien—while giving us the
narrative richness of Anglo-Saxon verse—provides us through
Merry another perspective that is less glorious. Indeed one might
say that the Hobbits, when present at a battle, bring realism to
our understanding of war. So war, as seen through their eyes,
is as close as we can come in the book to war as seen through
the author's eyes. Even in a society that glorifies the warrior,
such as that of the Rohirrim, Tolkien uses the Hobbits to give
us a clearer picture of what war is really about—to de-glorify
it when others have glorified it. At the Pelennor Fields, when
seen through Merry's eyes, there is no glory but only sorrow,
dread, and blind, sick horror (ROTK, p. 115). And it is through
Merry's eyes, not those of the Rohirrim, that the narrator gives
us our final glimpse of this battle: Théoden is dead, Éowyn
unconscious, and Éomer gone. The outcome is not glory, but
death, and tears, and sorrow.

So Fair, So Desperate

Without diminishing the importance of the narrative richness of Tolkien's depiction of the people of Rohan, I believe
there is a second and more significant reason that this scene is
described as it is, and why Tolkien's narrative gives it a certain
glory. We must look at each of the three characters involved:
Théoden, Merry, and Éowyn. Consider, first, King Théoden.
Just days before this battle begins, he is "a man so bent with
age that he seemed almost a dwarf" (TT, p. 116). If he were

bent with age because his body really is old and decrepit, then the reader would have no reason to be dismayed. But Théoden is only *deceived* into thinking himself too old and frail to do anything. In reality, there is still considerable strength left in his bones and muscles. As the visitors to his hall notice, "his eyes still burned with a bright light," and "bent though he was, he was still tall" (TT, pp. 116–17). What has happened to him? The most obvious thing is that he has listened to the lies of Saruman, spoken through his supposed counselor Gríma son of Gálmód (whom all save Théoden have aptly named "the Wormtongue") that "those who truly love him would spare his failing years" (TT, p. 124). Thus he has come to believe himself old and frail, and his people weak, and has been convinced that his only hope is to withdraw into a defensive cocoon and let the world's problems pass over him and his country. Gandalf later tells him, "And ever Wormtongue's whispering was in your ears, poisoning your thought, chilling your heart, weakening your limbs, while others watched and could do nothing, for your will was in his keeping" (TT, p. 126). And because of that deception—that falling under the spell of Saruman—Théoden is unwilling to fight in the battle against Sauron or to lend the aid of his people to the desperate need of his neighbors in Gondor.

We must also note that in addition to the illness brought about by this deceit, there is yet a subtler decline of the nobility of the House of Eorl, one that perhaps has gone back many generations. Théoden himself later describes this condition:

> "Long have we tended our beasts and our fields, built our houses, wrought our tools, or ridden away to help in the wars of Minas Tirith. And that we called the life of Men, the way of the world. We cared little for what lay beyond the borders of our land. Songs we have that tell of these things, but we are forgetting them, teaching them only to children, as a careless custom."
> (TT, p. 155)

In short, the kings of Rohan have ceased to believe in the wisdom of the old stories passed on from generation to generation;

they have forgotten how broad and wonderful and mysterious is the wide world around them. This fall is evident in the dark tales and words they have of Galadriel, calling her a "sorceress" and "net-weaver"—as Gimli says, speaking evil of "that which is fair beyond the reach" of their thoughts. It is equally evident in the fact that they no longer have any knowledge of, belief in, or concern for the Ents of Fangorn Forest, which is on the very border of Rohan.

When Gandalf comes to the Golden Hall, however, a healing begins for both of these ills. The deceit of Saruman, being the more recent, is the more quickly and easily cured. Breaking this spell—in part by silencing Wormtongue—Gandalf helps Théoden see that there is still strength in his bones, still strength in his people, and still hope if they can "stand unconquered a little while" (TT, p. 121).

> "It is not so dark here," said Théoden.
>
> "No," said Gandalf. "Nor does age lie so heavily on your shoulders as some would have you think. Cast aside your prop!"
>
> From the king's hand the black staff fell clattering on the stones. He drew himself up, slowly, as a man that is stiff from long bending over some dull toil. Now tall and straight he stood, and his eyes were blue as he looked into the opening sky.

In a very real sense, Théoden has been healed; Gandalf has set him free from the chains of deceit that bound him to inaction. As the imagery suggests, he moves from darkness to light; he has been blind and now he sees.

With this healing accomplished, Théoden's eyes are also opened to the decline that has come with the loss of the old wisdom and the shrinking of his world. A few days later, Gandalf—aided by the appearance of the Ents—spurs this process, reopening Théoden's eyes:

> "Is it so long since you listened to tales by the fireside? There are children in your land who, out of the twisted threads of story, could pick the answer to your question. You have seen Ents, O King, Ents out of Fangorn Forest, which in your tongue

you call the Entwood. Did you think that the name was given only in idle fancy? Nay, Théoden, it is otherwise: to them you are but the passing tale; all the years from Eorl the Young to Théoden the Old are of little count to them; and all the deeds of your house but a small matter. . . . You should be glad, Théoden King. . . . For not only the little life of Men is now endangered, but the life also of those things which you have deemed the matter of legend. You are not without allies, even if you know them not." (TT, p. 155)

What happens here, fundamentally, is that Gandalf restores Théoden's perspective (his sight). When the world of the House of Eorl had grown too small, then it is only natural that the kings of Rohan had considered themselves larger and more important than they really were. They had become selfish, forgetting that their own needs and problems were but a small part of Middle-earth, in both time and space. As the contact with the Ents reminds Théoden, however, their lives are but a small matter in the broad sweep of time, and their kingdom is just one of many kingdoms in danger from Sauron. Yet in realizing this, Théoden also realizes that he is not alone; he has allies even if he knows them not. And this gives him both the motivation to begin to fight for a bigger cause and the hope that this larger battle may be won.

And so the real glory of the scene at the Battle of Pelennor Fields is not the glory of a physical battle, whether victory or defeat, but the glory of those who choose to use whatever strength they have in them to resist evil. "You may say this to Théoden son of Thengel:" said Aragorn, "open war lies before him, with Sauron or against him" (TT, p. 36). If Théoden does not choose to fight against Sauron, he will be serving him. He must choose. And he does. Thus, though he falls slain in the physical battle, he is victorious in the moral battle to *choose* well.

The stories of Merry and Éowyn are also important in understanding this scene. Merry is the easier of the two to understand. In addition to providing the Hobbitish perspective we explored earlier, there is something personal about his individual story that is worth exploring. Merry is terrified of battle in general and terrified of the Black Rider in particular. He has no love whatsoever of war. He is a Hobbit, and although he is (or is to become) more adventurous and more noble than most of the other folk of the Shire, he is not one to long for battle or to see it as glorious. For Meriadoc Brandybuck, the victory comes in overcoming his fear in order to come to the rescue of Éowyn, even if it means doing so in the most *in*glorious fashion of crawling along on his belly and stabbing the Nazgûl from behind: "She should not die, so fair, so desperate! At least she should not die alone, unaided." And the glory of the scene is also his love for a king who had become like a father: "'King's man! King's man!' his heart cried within him. 'You must stay by him. As a father you shall be to me, you said.'" The glory is the awakening of the "slow-kindled courage of his race" (ROTK, p. 116). It is his sheer choice to move and act, despite the terror that would have paralyzed him. It is his will not to give in to terror and despair. That this choice is made in the context of a battle, and involves a sword, is not the critical aspect of the heroism (or glory), for we see the same glory in each step taken by Sam and Frodo across the plains of Mordor. Indeed, the battle itself is very inglorious.

By contrast, Éowyn's character is far more complex. We do see in this scene a certain glory in the love that she holds for her uncle: she is "faithful beyond fear," loving Théoden "as a father." And as with Merry, we see a glory in her courage, "so fair, so desperate." But Tolkien is working something else in her character. Like her uncle Théoden, Éowyn also needs to find healing, but it is a different type of healing. While her uncle is so afraid of death that he has become shameful, she is so afraid of shame that she seeks death. As Gandalf later describes to Éomer, Éowyn's brother:

> "She, born in the body of a maid, had a spirit and courage at least the match of yours. Yet she was doomed to wait upon an old man, whom she loved as a father, and watch him falling into a mean dishonoured dotage; and her part seemed to her more ignoble than that of the staff he leaned on." (ROTK, p. 143)

And so, in her despair, seeing nothing left in life, Éowyn seeks glory in death, and in particular, glory through death *in battle* (an Anglo-Saxon ideal). But unlike Théoden, whose healing has already come and who is willing to die, and who finds death though he does not *seek* it, Éowyn is denied the very death she seeks. In sparing her from death, Tolkien gives his reader the opportunity to see the healing she later finds. It is by the author's grace that Éowyn does not die but is able to learn that the type of glory she sought earlier is not the answer.

To understand that healing, we must understand the illness. Éowyn's illness is twofold. The first part is observed by both Aragorn and Éomer: she loves Aragorn, but he does not return her love. "Few other griefs amid the ill chances of this world have more bitterness and shame for a man's heart than to behold the love of a lady so fair and brave that cannot be returned" (ROTK, p. 143). The second part of her illness is described by Gandalf: she suffers the shame of watching the king she loved as a father falling into "mean dishonoured dotage; and her part seemed to her more ignoble than that of the staff he leaned on." And yet the two illnesses are really one. As Aragorn observes, she doesn't so much love him as "only a shadow and a thought: a hope of glory and great deeds, and lands far from the fields of Rohan." That is, her "illness"—if *illness* is even the right word—is a desire for glory. In other words, if what we earlier observed about the Rohirrim and their Anglo-Saxon love of the warrior's glory is true, then Éowyn is simply the manifestation of her people's weakness—exaggerated to an extreme by the taunting of Wormtongue, perhaps, but still true to the character of her people. And so, while her bravery and loyalty embody the best traits of the Rohirrim, her longing for glory in battle—which Tolkien illustrates so vividly in that battle scene—is their weakness. In this we see the skill of Tolkien as a writer, in this subtle presentation of both the strengths and weakness of a "real" character in a "real" world.

Éowyn's physical healing, from the wound inflicted by the Nazgûl, comes at the hands of Aragorn. Her spiritual healing, however, is administered by the steward Faramir in the Houses of Healing at Minas Tirith.

"I wished to be loved by another," she answered. "But I desire no man's pity."

"That I know," he said. "You desired to have the love of the Lord Aragorn. Because he was high and puissant, and you wished to have renown and glory and to be lifted far above the mean things that crawl on the earth. And as a great captain may to a young soldier he seemed to you admirable. For so he is, a lord among men, the greatest that now is. But when he gave you only understanding and pity, then you desired to have nothing, unless a brave death in battle. Look at me, Éowyn!"

And Éowyn looked at Faramir long and steadily; and Faramir said: "Do not scorn pity that is the gift of a gentle heart, Éowyn! But I do not offer you my pity. For you are a lady high and valiant and have yourself won renown that shall not be forgotten; and you are a lady beautiful, I deem, beyond even the words of the Elven-tongue to tell. And I love you. Once I pitied your sorrow. But now, were you sorrowless, without fear or any lack, were you the blissful Queen of Gondor, still I would love you. Éowyn, do you not love me?"

Then the heart of Éowyn changed, or else at least she understood it. And suddenly her winter passed, and the sun shone on her. (ROTK, pp. 242–43)

The healing seems instant here, but it really takes place over several days. It is only completed at this moment, as we see through Éowyn's response: "I will be a shieldmaiden no longer, nor vie with the great Riders, nor take joy only in the songs of slaying. I will be a healer, and love all things that grow and are not barren" (ROTK, p. 243). Éowyn is willing to give up her pursuit of glory, especially the glory of the warrior: the glory of "slaying," the glory of the "shieldmaiden" and the "great Riders." And so, through the Rohirrim in general and through the battle of Éowyn with the Nazgûl in particular, Tolkien gives us a view of a culture that really does glorify war and battle, and the life of a warrior. But through Éowyn's illness he also shows us what such pursuits and values ultimately lead to, while through her healing he also shows us the good that results when such pursuits are renounced.

Hope and Healing

One other note is in order regarding Éowyn. In her story, one might be tempted to see a male chauvinist attitude: that a woman's healing comes by finding the love of a man, giving up the world at large, and settling down to the supposedly more feminine pursuits of home and kitchen. Several chapters could be written on Éowyn alone, but this would represent quite a divergence from the main subject of this book. I will limit myself to a few brief comments. Tolkien's professional world as an Oxford professor was unquestionably a male world, and certainly there is something of a male romantic image in the way he portrays Éowyn's healing as coming through the love of a man. But to simplify it further would miss most of what we can learn from this scene. Among other things, it is remarkable that Tolkien gives voice to this very concern. That is, he gives voice to Éowyn as a woman living in a man's world.

> "All your words are but to say: you are a woman, and your part is in the house. But when the men have died in battle and honour, you have leave to be burned in the house, for the men will need it no more. But I am of the House of Eorl and not a serving-woman. I can ride and wield blade, and I do not fear either pain or death." (ROTK, p. 58)

If Tolkien thought that Éowyn's argument here—made in response to Aragorn when he reminds her of her duty to her people—is fundamentally flawed, he could have put a reply to this argument into Aragorn's mouth, for surely Aragorn understands duty and responsibility. Instead, Aragorn shows only sympathy and understanding, asking her what it is that she does fear.

Probably the most important evidence against the claim of chauvinism in this particular instance lies in the fact that Faramir, a man, is as much opposed to battle as Éowyn becomes. (Faramir's views on war are explored in this book's next chapter.) In particular not only does Tolkien's female character commit herself to "be a healer" and to "love all things that grow and are not barren," but Faramir himself is committed to the same. "Let us cross the River," he says, "and in happier days let us dwell in fair Ithilien and there make a garden. All things will grow with joy there" (ROTK, p. 243). In fact, the great desire of Sam and Frodo, and even of Merry and Pippin, is to give up their swords, return to the Shire, and take up peaceful pursuits such as gardening. In short, Tolkien does not portray it as solely a womanly virtue to abandon the glories of the battlefield, and turn instead to the house and garden and the pursuit of peace, but as a manly virtue as well.

The "Contest" at Helm's Deep

We end this chapter with a look at the Battle of Helm's Deep. Though it involves considerably smaller armies than either the Siege of Minas Tirith or the battle in front of the Black Gate, and though it lasts only one night, an entire chapter is devoted to this battle, and it seems to take on an importance even beyond that. (I am not surprised that this one chapter dominates Peter Jackson's film version of *The Two Towers*.) This battle is somewhat different than the others we have explored. Rather than being viewed with the spatial and temporal distance we have observed in the narrative descriptions of other battles, Helm's Deep is described *in the present*, by characters who are *physically present*. Of greater significance, it is the one important battle at which there is no Hobbit!

Some might argue that the evidence of Tolkien's glorification of war may be found in this battle, in the contest between Legolas and Gimli as to who would kill the most Orcs. That such a sport is made of war and killing is certainly disturbing. Why, then, does Tolkien include it? Before seeking to answer this, we must make two important observations. Though the battle is described in a very concrete present, with some description of the actual hand-to-hand fighting—in particular, of some of the bold sorties made by Aragorn and Éomer—as with the battles previously discussed, there is little graphic description of violence. The greater part of the narrative is devoted to dialogue among the defenders during moments of respite, and especially to the current state of their hope or despair, while we get only occasional glimpses of the defenses at some particular strategic moment.

More specifically, with respect to the contest, even though the narrator recounts some of the dialogue wherein Gimli and Legolas boast to each other of their current scores, we witness very few of the actual tallies. We are with Gimli for numbers one, two, and twenty-one (of forty-two), and that is all. And little picture do we get even of these three: "An axe swung and swept back. Two Orcs fell headless. The rest fled" (TT p. 139). As for Legolas, we see only number thirty-nine (of forty-one), and that from a distance. "The foremost fell with Legolas' last arrow in his throat, but the rest sprang over him" (TT p. 143). In other words, the "contest" receives little attention, and is not the central subject in the narrator's recounting of the battle. Indeed, it's remarkable that Legolas and Gimli together fell eighty-three Orcs during the battle, and yet only four times is any explicit description given.

It is also important to note that it is Gimli who initiates the contest, when he boasts of his first two slain Orcs. And Gimli, though he is noble for a Dwarf and grows to be wiser than most others of his race, is yet a Dwarf and not the symbol of wisdom in Tolkien's tales. That is, he represents the values of his people, and not the values of the author. (In the next chapter, we will look into the question of which characters are presented by the author as wise.)

With this in mind, we look at what Tolkien does accomplish in the chapter "Helm's Deep" and why he would include not only the battle itself, but also the subplot of the contest between Gimli and Legolas. Indeed, there are a number of reasons we can see in the text, none of which are for the glorification of killing. It is here at the Battle of Helm's Deep that Aragorn keeps the word he gave to Éomer when the two first met.

"When your quest is achieved," [spoke Éomer,] "or is proved vain, return with the horses over the Entwade to Meduseld, the high house in Edoras where Théoden now sits. Thus you shall prove to him that I have not misjudged. In this I place myself, and maybe my very life, in the keeping of your good faith. Do not fail."

"I will not," said Aragorn. (TT, p. 41)

In giving his aid to Aragorn, Éomer places his life in Aragorn's hands. Aragorn repays that trust and more; he also honors Éomer's plea for help: "Return with what speed you may, and let our swords hereafter shine together!" This is why it is important not only that they meet again, but that they draw swords together. Aragorn is meeting the real need of the people of Rohan, which is for military aid against the threat of Saruman. Furthermore, he is doing so at great personal risk, not only to his own life but also to all his dreams and plans. Certainly such self-sacrificial giving on Aragorn's part is worthy of glory. Indeed, it is in Rohan that Aragorn's great nobility begins to show visibly, when he first meets Éomer ("Gimli and Legolas looked at their companion in amazement, for they had not seen him in this mood before . . . in his living face they caught a brief vision of the power and majesty of the kings of stone" [TT, p. 36]). It is seen again at the battle ("So great a power and royalty was revealed in Aragorn, as he stood there alone above the ruined gates before the host of his enemies, that many of the wild men paused" [TT, p. 145]). And as the future king of Gondor risks his life for the people of Rohan, he earns the allegiance of Rohan's future king.

Yet it is more than mere allegiance. A deep bond of friendship is forged between the two at Helm's Deep. In fact, three friendships are either forged or solidified at the battle. The second is that of Gimli and Éomer, for Gimli also risks his life, several times in the battle, to help the people of Rohan. When he saves the life of Éomer—interestingly enough, by tallying his first two Orc-heads—and Éomer thanks him for it, we should recall the harsh words spoken between the two at their first meeting, and how close they came to deadly blows. Though only a little more is said of their friendship as the book continues, we may assume that there is something significant to it. It is Gimli, and not Aragorn or Legolas, who is at Éomer's side when the battle is over, and when the War of the Ring is finally over, the

Dwarf returns to Rohan and makes his permanent home at the Glittering Caves of Aglarond, as Éomer's neighbor.

It is also here in the context of war that we really see the blossoming of the friendship between Gimli the Dwarf and Legolas the Elf and the real care they have for each other. This, too, is greatly significant, considering not only the ancient animosity between their races but also the tension between the two individuals at the start of the Quest. Even after they had passed through Moria, there was enough tension between the two that Legolas grumbled, "A plague on Dwarves and their stiff necks!" (FOTR, p. 362). By the time the Battle of Helm's Deep is over, however, it seems that Legolas's greatest concern is the well-being of his friend Gimli. He is certainly more concerned for Gimli than for their contest: "I do not grudge you the game, so glad am I to see you on your legs!" (TT, p. 148). It is shortly after the battle that the two make their famous agreement, epitomizing a friendship between Elf and Dwarf that may be unique in the entire history of Middle-earth: Gimli will visit Fangorn with Legolas if Legolas will return with Gimli to Aglarond.

The point here is that one may glorify the friendship that is born in the context of war, and see the goodness in that friendship, without glorifying the violence out of which that good came. Many friendships have been born in times of hardship, and there is no greater hardship than the type of battle that is fought upon Helm's Deep that night—or the type of battle in which Tolkien himself fought, was wounded, and lost most of his own close friends. Put another way, it is said that there is no greater love than to lay down your life for a friend, and it is in war that the opportunity to do so is most apparent.

In a similar vein, we must also realize what a great burden such an evil night is upon those involved, even the strongest-willed among them. It is a night that even Aragorn describes as "a night as long as years" (TT, p. 142). This burden can probably be fully understood only by those who have suffered it themselves. Such a contest as Gimli and Legolas have, however grim it may be, acts to lighten the heavy load and may even be necessary to the survival of those forced to endure war as soldiers. That such a contest is required of Legolas and Gimli serves to show the horror of war, not glory.

War, and the Individual vs. Fellowship

In looking at what Tolkien's writing does *not* do in its depiction of war—it does not glorify war or violence—we have also seen some positive things that Tolkien does accomplish. We have begun to see, in the battle of Éowyn and the Nazgûl, that something is happening at the unseen or spiritual level that is as significant as what goes on in the seen physical world. We have also seen that the individuals involved are more important in the great battles of Middle-earth than is the military outcome. Tolkien reveals to his readers what the participants of battle think and feel; what they value. We see that green grass and friendship are far more valuable than glory. In focusing on the individual character rather than on the physical details of the battle, Tolkien places value on the individual life, whether that of a Hobbit, or a Man, or even one of Sauron's slaves.

This is not to say, however, that Tolkien was an "individualist"—not in the way that word might be understood in the late twentieth or early twenty-first century. Though, as we have seen, the value of life is more important than the military outcome of a battle, this does not mean that the individual is more important than society. It is rather to the contrary. Time and again through the books, the main characters subjugate their own desires for the good of the community to which they belong. When the Elves of Lothlórien single out Gimli the Dwarf to be blindfolded before entering their kingdom, Aragorn insists that the entire Fellowship, including himself, be blindfolded; the unity of the Fellowship as a whole is more important than Aragorn's (or any other member's) own individual pride and comfort. Aragorn, when he chooses to pursue the Orcs in hopes of rescuing the two Hobbits at the start of *The Two Towers*, is putting aside the longing of his own heart to go to Minas Tirith. Their contest at Helm's Deep aside, we get the strong impression that Gimli's welfare is more important to Legolas than his own welfare. And that can often be said of all the members of the Fellowship. Even Boromir, at the end of *The Fellowship of the Ring*, gives up his own pursuit of glory in an attempt to save Merry and Pippin. Gandalf, though he may have been the most important foe of Sauron, sacrifices his life to save the others. By contrast, in the few instances that we are given a close-up view of the Orcs, we see the exact opposite: the individual Orcs—Uglúk, Grishnákh, Shagrat, Gorbag—usually put themselves and their own goals above the good of the community. Or, looking at the relationship between the individual and community from a different perspective, when Gandalf goes to Rohan and rescues Théoden, he does not simply restore an individual king but an entire kingdom. Likewise, when he comes to Minas Tirith, he does not merely bring help to Denethor and Faramir, but brings hope to all those atop the walls of Minas Tirith who are fighting the battle.

In fact, this observation is consistent with the other observations we have made so far, and it ought to be seen as central to the conclusion of the chapter. If the individual, as an individual, really *is* the most important thing, then pursuit of personal glory in battle would make sense. But pursuit of glory in war is not what Tolkien espouses. Galadriel does not tell the members of the Company that hope remains as long as each individual is strong and brave, but rather that "hope remains while *all the Company* is true" (FOTR, p. 372, emphasis mine). In other words, their commitment to one another and to community is more important than their individual strength. The nine who set out on the Quest from Rivendell, in contrast to the Nazgûl, are not *nine individuals* but *one Fellowship*. The choice of title of the first book of the trilogy ought to tell us something about Tolkien's view of community!

2

The Wise of Middle-Earth

Wisdom, simply defined, is the ability to make good decisions and judgments. It is the ability to discern between various choices of action. A part of wisdom may come from knowledge—usually the knowledge that comes with experience—and yet it is distinct from knowledge. One can have considerable knowledge and yet leave the path of wisdom, as both Saruman and Denethor do. Or one can have little worldly knowledge and yet be proven wise, as some may argue is the case with many of the important Hobbits in Tolkien's tales. In the previous chapter, I explored several battle scenes from *The Hobbit* and *The Lord of the Rings*, seeking to illustrate important aspects of how Tolkien portrayed war in Middle-earth. Another way we might understand war in Tolkien's writing is to examine the words and actions of those characters whom he portrays as wise. For if a particular character speaks and acts in a particular way, and the author presents that character as being wise, we may safely assume that this character's words and actions are a representation of what that author views as wisdom.

So who are the Wise of Middle-earth, and what did Tolkien say through them about war? The goal here, remember, is to understand J. R. R. Tolkien's writing. It is not to look for those characters whose thoughts are most like our own—that is, those whom we might think of as wise were we to meet them in our own world—but to look at those whom Tolkien portrays as wise in *The Lord of the Rings*. Fortunately, the author gives us plenty of clues as to which of his characters are to be viewed as wise. Sometimes he communicates this very directly, as in *The Silmarillion* where we read: "And the house of Elrond was a refuge for the weary and the oppressed, and a treasury of good counsel and *wise* lore. . . . and because he knew in his *wisdom* that one should come . . ." (TS, p. 369, emphasis mine). In other places, wisdom is communicated more indirectly—though still in a way that should make it clear to the reader that we are to understand a particular character as wise (or, conversely, as foolish).

Indeed, I think there is very little doubt about whom Tolkien leads the reader to understand as being wise in his writing. Before looking at the text to see who these characters are, I illustrate this last point from personal example. I have given numerous talks on Tolkien's writing at colleges and universities around the country, and have often asked my audiences to identify whom they consider to be the "Wise of Middle-earth." The answers are consistent and uniform. Gandalf is always at the top of the list, with Aragorn a close second. Faramir is usually near the top of the list also (though his brother, Boromir, is not.) Those who have watched only the films and have not read the books might not mention Elrond or Galadriel as being among the Wise—in part because both were portrayed in a somewhat more sinister fashion in the film version than in Tolkien's book—but readers of the *books* will almost always list these two Elven Powers as well. Treebeard, Glorfindel, and Tom Bombadil are also likely to be named a little farther down the list. (Neither Bill Ferny nor Ted Sandyman have ever been named.) Even Frodo, though not wise in quite the same way as Gandalf, must also be listed as possessing a certain type of wisdom; indeed, by the end of *The Lord of the Rings*, he very much echoes Gandalf's wisdom.

It is important to note that these answers by no means come from homogeneous audiences. People from all different backgrounds—readers whose worldviews, religions, nationalities, and backgrounds diverge widely from each other's, from mine, and from Tolkien's—will still identify the same list of characters as wise *within the context of Tolkien's writing*. Why? Because Tolkien has used the authority of his narrative voice to make it clear. A few examples illustrate how Tolkien communicated the wisdom of those characters, especially Gandalf.

The Wisdom of Gandalf

In a personal letter written in 1954, Tolkien describes the nature of Gandalf in particular and of the wizards in general. His description gives insight into Gandalf's wisdom:

> There are naturally no precise modern terms to say what he was. I wd. venture to say that he was an *incarnate* "angel." . . . That is, with the other *Istari*, wizards, "those who know," an emissary from the Lords of the West, sent to Middle-earth, as the great crisis of Sauron loomed on the horizon. By "incarnate" I mean they were embodied in physical bodies capable of pain, and weariness, and of afflicting the spirit with physical fear, and of being "killed," though supported by the angelic spirit they might endure long, and only show slowly the wearing of care and labour.
>
> Why they should take such form is bound up with the "mythology" of the "angelic" Powers of the world of this fable. At this point in the fabulous history the purpose was precisely to limit and hinder their exhibition of "power" on the physical plane, and so that they should do what they were primarily sent for: train, advise, instruct, arouse the hearts and minds of those threatened by Sauron to a resistance with their own strengths; and not just to do the job for them. (Letters, p. 202)

In other words, Gandalf is sent to Middle-earth to provide *wisdom*, and not to provide "power on the physical plane" or what one might call "military might." In fact, his natural "angelic" powers were intentionally limited to hinder their exhibition.

Thus, the purpose of the Istari is not so much to *do* or to *act*, but rather to *know*.[1] Put another way, Gandalf was sent for reasons having to do with the spiritual plane rather than the physical plane. He was sent for training, advising, instructing, arousing. And this, as mentioned in the previous chapter, is precisely what we see Gandalf doing throughout the book. He rouses first Théoden, and later, in the Siege of Gondor, he walks the walls of Minas Tirith, along with the Prince of Dol Amroth, encouraging the hearts of the defenders so that they do not lose strength and hope. As for his function of instructing and training, what is that other than passing wisdom on to others?

Readers of the trilogy and viewers of the film, however, may not have had the opportunity to consult Tolkien's personal correspondence (published or unpublished), and so it is fair to ask what evidence is provided in the story itself of the wisdom of these characters. What are the specific hints that lead readers to the universal acknowledgment of the wisdom of Gandalf, Aragorn, Faramir, Elrond, etc.? The first and simplest evidence, of course, is when Tolkien tells us outright. This is the case when Elrond is introduced in *The Hobbit*: "He was as noble and as fair in face as an elf-lord, as strong as a warrior, *as wise as a wizard*, as venerable as a king of dwarves, and as kind as summer" (TH, p. 51, emphasis mine). In this, we learn not only of Elrond's wisdom but indirectly of Gandalf's as well (since Gandalf is a wizard).

Through the eyes—or rather the intuitive sixth sense—of Pippin, we also see how much greater Gandalf's wisdom is than that of the steward Denethor:

> Denethor looked indeed much more like a great wizard than Gandalf did, more kingly, beautiful, and powerful; and older.

1. Of course Gandalf does *do* and *act*. He doesn't merely sit around *knowing*. The point, however, is that much of his *doing* has to do with either the *gathering* of knowledge—for example tracking Gollum around Middle-earth in order to discover what he can about the Ring—or with the *passing on* of knowledge: arousing the *minds* of those threatened by Sauron. The rest of his doing focuses on arousing the *hearts* of those threatened by Sauron. This is a role we shall consider in later chapters when we deal with stewardship and hope.

Yet by a sense other than sight Pippin perceived that Gandalf had the greater power and the deeper wisdom, and a majesty that was veiled. (ROTK, p. 29)

This veiled majesty is likely a reference to the "angelic" nature that Tolkien intended for Gandalf. Yet it is probably even deeper than that, for Saruman is also one of the Istari and shares that same nature, and yet is fallen from that majesty, while Gandalf's majesty has increased since his return from death. In any case, Gandalf's wisdom—whether angelic or not—is the greater and deeper, and though it is coupled with considerable knowledge, it goes beyond knowledge. It is Gandalf who first recognizes Bilbo's ring as the One Ring, even though the ring-lore of Saruman is much greater.

Even without such occasional direct references to his wisdom, we see Gandalf's wisdom in the respect given him by those around him. In "The Last Debate," Aragorn charges the other captains: "Let none now reject the counsels of Gandalf. . . . But for him all would long ago have been lost." Likewise, Galadriel—the eldest and noblest of the Elves still remaining in Middle-earth—thinks so highly of Gandalf's counsel that she argued for him to be the head of the White Council, which she herself summoned (FOTR, p. 372). When Celeborn questions Gandalf's wisdom after his fall in Moria, Galadriel defends the wizard:

> "And if it were possible, one would say that at the last Gandalf fell from wisdom into folly, going needlessly into the net of Moria," [said Celeborn].
> "He would be rash indeed that said that thing," said Galadriel gravely. "Needless were none of the deeds of Gandalf in life." (FOTR, p. 369)

It is interesting to note that even Celeborn, when questioning the Company's decision to enter Moria, acknowledges Gandalf's long record of wisdom and finds it nearly (though not quite) impossible to question it. And Galadriel chides her own husband as "rash indeed," when he does question it. Her reply, in many ways, is the ultimate testimony to Gandalf's wisdom: None of his deeds were vain or meaningless.

Galadriel's statement leads to a broader point, which is that we may judge the wisdom of many types of choices by the fruit that they bear. (I speak here of *strategic* choices, rather than *moral* choices. As I will later discuss, there is a moral good in being willing to do what is right even when the outcome is in doubt.) Thus Gandalf's wisdom may also be seen, for example, in his insistence on allowing the young Hobbits Merry and Pippin to join the Fellowship. Without them, the Ents might never be roused, nor the Nazgûl-Lord slain by Éowyn, nor Faramir rescued from the pyre. Foremost, therefore, we see Gandalf's wisdom in the final outcome of the War of the Ring itself. In "The Council of Elrond" and later, in "The Last Debate," the gathered leaders choose to follow Gandalf's strategies—initially sending a small group into Mordor to destroy the Ring, and later sending a large army to the Black Gate to distract Sauron—even though, at the time, those strategies seem foolish and desperate to many:

> "Despair, or folly?" said Gandalf. "It is not despair, for despair is only for those who see the end beyond all doubt. We do not. It is wisdom to recognize necessity, when all other courses have been weighed, though as folly it may appear to those who cling to false hope. Well, let folly be our cloak, a veil before the eyes of the Enemy!" (FOTR, p. 282)

Looking only at Gandalf's advice, and not at the outcome, we might not be in a position to judge *his* wisdom save by our *own* preconceived notion of what is wise. If we don't read to the end of the book, we could join the voice of the Elf Erestor (to whom Gandalf is responding): "That is the path of despair. Of folly I would say, if the long wisdom of Elrond did not forbid me." Denethor, also, called Gandalf's plan little more than "a fool's hope" (ROTK, p. 87). Even Gandalf, at the "last debate" (ROTK, book 5, chapter 9), leaves open the question of whether his strategy is "wisdom or folly" (ROTK, p. 156). But the outcome of the trilogy leaves no doubt. It is Gandalf's strategy that eventually results in the victory. As we read in "Of the Rings of Power and the Third Age," the fourth part of *The Silmarillion*, "Now all these things were achieved for the most part by the counsel and vigilance of Mithrandir, and in the last few days he was revealed as a lord of great reverence, and clad in white he rode into battle" (TS, p. 378). And Treebeard tells Gandalf toward the end of the trilogy, "You have proved mightiest, and all your labours have gone well" (ROTK, p. 257). He might equally have said, "You have proved wisest."

Military Might and True Hope

So, accepting Gandalf as one of the Wise, what does he say with respect to war, and battle, and arms? And what of Frodo, whom Gandalf trained? Or Faramir, whose father blamed him for being the pupil of Gandalf? What words does Tolkien put in the mouths of the Wise?

When speaking to Denethor about his own role in Middle-earth, Gandalf says:

> "I will say this: the rule of no realm is mine, neither of Gondor nor any other, great or small. But all worthy things that are in peril as the world now stands, those are my care. And for my part, I shall not wholly fail of my task, though Gondor should perish, if anything passes through this night that can still grow fair or bear fruit and flower again in days to come." (ROTK, pp. 30–31)

This is not a comment made explicitly about battle, and yet we can gain insight from these words. They are spoken in the context of a conversation about the war, and several of Gandalf's deepest values are revealed. Assuming that Gandalf speaks truthfully—a safe assumption, given how important words are to him—we see first that the wizard is not interested in rule, or authority, or command. We learn also that he has a "care," or "task." More to the point of this discussion, it also appears that battle itself is not what most concerns him: certainly not any glory associated with battle. Indeed, it is rare that Gandalf ever takes a direct physical role in battle. He is not present at the Battle of Helm's Deep; he appears only at the end of the battle, when he leads into the fray Erkenbrand and his host of a thousand foot soldiers (changed in the film to Éomer and his host of a thousand mounted Rohirrim). Even then, we don't witness Gandalf fight, but are left with the impression that his primary task was to bring Erkenbrand to Theoden's aid. Nor is Gandalf present on the Pelennor Fields when that battle is won, though earlier in the siege he does use his might to rescue Faramir on more than one occasion. In particular, though Gandalf lends his wisdom to the Battle of Minas Tirith, works tirelessly to bring hope to those fighting, and at a few rare times uses his power, the success of his task is not dependent on military victory.

Later, in "The Last Debate," Gandalf tells the gathered captains: "Victory cannot be achieved by arms, whether you sit here to endure siege after siege, or march out to be overwhelmed beyond the River" (ROTK, p. 154). That is a very telling statement. Certainly Gandalf hopes for victory in the war against Sauron, and he works hard to accomplish it. Yet he does not see physical victory of armies involved in a battle as the key to overall victory in the war. This could be viewed simply from a strategic viewpoint: that the destruction of the Ring is the key to victory, and everything else is ultimately insignificant. Certainly this is true. Yet Gandalf's comment could—and, I believe, should—also be understood at a much deeper level.

There comes a point in *The Silmarillion* when Ulmo, one of the greatest and wisest immortal Powers of Middle-earth, sends a very similar message to Turgon, Elven king of the hidden realm of Gondolin: "Love not too well the work of thy hands and the devices of thy heart; and remember that the true hope of the Noldor lieth in the West, and cometh from the Sea" (TS, p. 297). For all of the hidden might of Gondolin—it is the last of the great Elven kingdoms of the First Age to fall—its hope ultimately could not rest in its own strength. Morgoth, the enemy, to whom Sauron is merely a vassal, is too powerful for any Elven lord. For Turgon, as for the Captains of the West, victory cannot be achieved by arms.

Gandalf, whose sword was forged in Gondolin years earlier for those very wars, understands this. When trust is placed in human strength, then the glorification of the warrior is very natural. But Gandalf and Ulmo warn against trusting in strength in arms. Unlike the World Wars of the twentieth century of our world, for example, where the outcome was dependent on military might and military strategy, *The Lord of the Rings* was crafted by Tolkien in such a way that the outcome is *not* ultimately dependent on such things. For all of the glory given to those who lost or risked their lives in battle at the Field of Cormallen, the highest honor is given to Frodo and Sam, who do not fight in any physical battle at all.

Even His Slaves

One other reason Gandalf might eschew the glorification of war is the great value he places on life. One of the most significant dialogues in all of *The Lord of the Rings* takes place near the beginning of the first book, when Gandalf is explaining to Frodo some of the history of the Ring. When Frodo laments that Bilbo, the Elves, and Gandalf all chose to let Gollum live, Gandalf replies, "Many that live deserve death. And some that die deserve life. Can you give it to them? Then do not be too eager to deal out death in judgement. For even the very wise cannot see all ends" (FOTR, p. 69). With all of their editing of hundreds of pages of writing down to a few hours of screenplay, the screenwriters for Peter Jackson's film version of *The Fellowship of the Ring* left this speech almost completely intact, word for word (though they moved the dialogue out of Bag End and into Moria). It is a significant comment, and it gets at the heart of why Tolkien does not glorify war. People die in war. War is won by killing the enemy. And lives, even enemy lives, have value. "And for me," Gandalf says, "I pity even [Sauron's] slaves" (ROTK, p. 87).

Gandalf's ability to teach and train others in this kind of wisdom is seen clearly at the end of *The Return of the King* when the four Hobbits return to the Shire to find it ravaged by Saruman. As Frodo, Sam, Merry, and Pippin prepare to reenter the Shire after many months away—not yet aware of what has happened to their home—to their dismay, Gandalf leaves them. As the wizard goes his way, his parting words are:

> "I am not coming to the Shire. You must settle its affairs your-selves; that is what you have been trained for. Do you not yet understand? My time is over: it is no longer my task to set things to rights, nor to help folk to do so. And as for you, my dear friends, you will need no help. You are grown up now." (ROTK, p. 275)

Gandalf is correct about the Hobbits not needing his help. His wisdom is proven once again, as we see just how much the Hobbits have learned! Consider that it is Frodo, near the beginning of the story, who laments the fact that nobody killed Gollum. Contrast this with the Frodo at the end of *The Lord of the Rings*.

> "Fight?" said Frodo. "Well I suppose it may come to that. But remember: there is to be no slaying of hobbits, not even if they have gone over to the other side. Really gone over, I mean; not just obeying ruffians' orders because they are frightened. No hobbit has ever killed another on purpose in the Shire, and it is not to begin now. And nobody is to be killed at all, if it can be helped. Keep your tempers and hold your hands to the last possible moment!" (ROTK, p. 285)

Frodo's voice here is the voice of mercy. It is the voice that val-ues life: not only friendly Hobbit life, but the life of the enemy, the Hobbit that has "really gone over" or the evil "ruffian" men. It is an echo of the voice of Gandalf, who pities even Sauron's slaves. Frodo's voice is also the voice of restraint. As we read later, "Frodo had been in the battle, but he had not drawn sword, and his chief part had been to prevent the hobbits in their wrath at their losses, from slaying those of their enemies who threw down their weapons" (ROTK, pp. 295–96). He does not urge the Hobbits to seek glory in battle as they regain the land that has been taken from them, but rather his urging is that they refrain as much as possible from fighting: to "hold [their] hands to the last possible moment." This is the wisdom of Tolkien's Wise, and it is not a wisdom that glorifies violence.

The greatest test of Frodo's new wisdom and mercy is given him when he returns to the doorsteps of Bag End and finds his beloved home in shambles and his neighborhood in ruins. For he then comes face to face with the one who is most responsible for the evil: Saruman. Unlike some of the Hobbits or Men, who have been acting in either fear or petty greed, Saruman has acted in unmitigated spite, with a desire to destroy. Yet still, Frodo shows not only mercy, but uncommon wisdom of the type that Tolkien espouses: "It is useless to meet revenge with revenge: it will heal nothing," he says, as he commands the Hobbits to spare Saruman's life (ROTK, p. 298). Even when Saruman draws a knife and seeks (vainly) to kill him, Frodo's mercy prevails. "Do not kill him even now," he tells the others. "For he has not hurt me. And in any case I do not wish him to be slain in this evil mood" (ROTK, p. 299). Frodo not only hopes for Saruman's cure and is wise enough to know that he does not have authority to judge another person, but he is also wise enough to realize that the very "mood" of such attempts at vengeance is "evil." It would harm the avengers as much as the one taken vengeance upon. Oddly enough, it is Saruman's words to Frodo that capture the situation: "You have grown very much. You are wise, and cruel." Even Saruman must acknowledge Frodo's wisdom, though sadly in the wizard's fallen state—a state that could well be described as a pitiable self-hatred—he sees Frodo's mercy as cruelty.

Faramir

Though there are many other voices of wisdom within Tolkien's story, the only other one I will explore in this chapter is that of Faramir, son of Denethor. From our first meeting with

Faramir, we catch in his speech a glimpse of his wisdom—or at least his desire for such: "Even so, I spare a brief time, in order to judge justly in hard matter" (TT, p. 273).

Faramir is interesting for several reasons. For one, he is one of the few characters—along with Elrond and Gandalf—who make any allusion to a Divine Authority.

> Before they ate, Faramir and all his men turned and faced west in a moment of silence. Faramir signed to Frodo and Sam that they should do likewise.
> "So we always do," he said, as they sat down: "we look towards Númenor that was, and beyond to Elvenhome that is, and to that which is beyond Elvenhome and will ever be." (TT, pp. 284–85)

Even if one has not read *The Silmarillion*, and thus does not recognize "that which is beyond Elvenhome and will ever be" as Eru Ilúvatar, the Creator, it is still hard *not* to understand this action as a sort of prayer. Whatever the reader thinks of prayer, in Tolkien's world it is a mark of humility and wisdom to acknowledge one's dependence on something beyond oneself—as Gandalf and Elrond often do—and such an acknowledgment is at the heart of prayer.

A second interesting aspect of Faramir's character is that he is portrayed as "pupil" of the wizard Gandalf (though, in fact, the two had met on only a few occasions). Denethor chides Faramir:

> "Your bearing is lowly in my presence, yet it is long now since you turned from your own way at my counsel. See, you have spoken skilfully, as ever; but I, have I not seen your eye fixed on Mithrandir, seeking whether you said well or too much? He has long had your heart in his keeping." (ROTK, p. 85)

And a little while later he adds more bluntly, "Boromir was loyal to me and no wizard's pupil" (ROTK, p. 86). As Denethor recognizes, with some jealousy, Faramir looks more to the wizard for wisdom and guidance than he does to his own father.

Given what we have already seen of Gandalf's wisdom, we must assume that for Faramir it is a sign of his own wisdom to fix his eyes on the wizard, whatever his father might say. Indeed, we see much of Gandalf in Denethor's younger son; the fact that Faramir could learn so much wisdom from the wizard in only two meetings is remarkable, and shows that he really is among the Wise of Middle-earth.

A third thing to note about Faramir's character is the contrast between him and his brother, Boromir, and even between him and his father, Denethor. For example, though "prayer" is an important custom to Faramir and his men, we see no hint of Boromir or Denethor adhering to this custom. Whereas Faramir has a very good understanding of his father and brother—of their strengths as well as their weaknesses—and he can appreciate them for who they are, there is little indication that Denethor has much understanding of his younger son. In describing Denethor to Pippin, Gandalf makes reference to this difference between the sons:

> "[Denethor] is not as other men of this time, Pippin, and whatever
> be his descent from father to son, by some chance the blood
> of Westernesse runs nearly true in him; as it does in his other
> son, Faramir, and yet did not in Boromir whom he loved best."
> (ROTK, p. 31)

That Faramir is more like Denethor than is Boromir makes it more interesting that Denethor would love Boromir better. As we later learn, however, Faramir is like Denethor only with respect to having inherited more truly the blood of Númenor and the possibility of real nobility; we also learn that this nobility fails in Denethor, who becomes like "the heathen kings, under the domination of the Dark Lord" (ROTK, p. 129), while it does not fail in Faramir. Anyway, this tension within the family makes for some of the most powerful and moving dialogue within *The Lord of the Rings*—and one of the most tragic subplots. But the point for the reader, with respect to this chapter, is that Faramir is portrayed by Tolkien as the wiser of the two brothers, and thus his voice is the one we should look to more for the values Tolkien is putting forth in his work.

One of the first glimpses we get of war through Faramir's eyes is his comment to Frodo: "I do not slay man or beast needlessly, and not gladly even when it is needed" (TT, p. 273). In other words, Faramir takes no pleasure and finds no glory in war. A short time later, he shares this view more explicitly:

> "War must be, while we defend our lives against a destroyer who would devour all; but I do not love the bright sword for its sharpness, nor the arrow for its swiftness, nor the warrior for his glory. I love only that which they defend: the city of the Men of Númenor; and I would have her loved for her memory, her ancientry, her beauty, and her present wisdom. Not feared, save as men may fear the dignity of a man, old and wise." (TT, p. 280)

As we later see, Faramir is a very valiant warrior. He is not only strong, but brave as well: the first in attack and the last to retreat. Yet he takes no pride in this. He loves his city and his country and is willing to die to defend the lives of his people "against a destroyer who would destroy all," but he sees no glory in the work of the warrior. For all his valor and might in battle, he would rather wield the hoe of a gardener than the sharp sword or swift arrow of the soldier. This may be seen most clearly in Faramir's view of the state of Gondor: "We . . . can scarce claim any longer the title High. . . . We now love war and valour as things good in themselves, both a sport and an end; and . . . we esteem a warrior . . . above men of other crafts" (TT, p. 287). Faramir sees the love of war, the practice of war as a sport, and the esteeming of the warrior not as signs of the current glory of Gondor, but rather as signs of its fall. It would be hard to imagine a much clearer statement from a valiant warrior such as Faramir that war is not to be glorified.

Now consider Boromir's character in contrast to the wisdom portrayed in Faramir. It would be an injustice to say that Boromir kills gladly or needlessly, and yet he does see war and battle as opportunities for personal glory and, in particular, the chief place where glory is to be earned. Our first glimpse of Denethor's elder son is at the Council of Elrond. In pleading with the Council to use the Ring against Sauron, Boromir says: "Valour needs first strength, and then a weapon. Let the Ring be your weapon, if it has such power as you say. Take it and go forth to victory!" (FOTR, p. 281). His speech, though not explicitly in opposition to the words of Faramir, is nonetheless filled with talk of strength, weapons, power, and victory. We see the folly of Boromir's desire reach its fullest expression when he seeks to take the Ring from Frodo.

> "It is a gift, I say; a gift to the foes of Mordor. It is mad not to use it, to use the power of the Enemy against him. The fearless, the ruthless, these alone will achieve victory. What could not a warrior do in this hour, a great leader? What could not Aragorn do? Or if he refuses, why not Boromir? The Ring would give me power of Command. How I would drive the hosts of Mordor, and all men would flock to my banner!"
>
> Boromir strode up and down, speaking ever more loudly. Almost he seemed to have forgotten Frodo, while his talk dwelt on walls and weapons, and the mustering of men; and he drew plans for great alliances and glorious victories to be. (FOTR, p. 414)

For Boromir, what matters is military victory. If one needs to be ruthless to achieve it, then one should be ruthless. He equates being a "great leader" with being a warrior. As the last line tells us, he does see glory in victory. Indeed, he sees a glory in the battle itself: the power of command, the driving of the hosts of Mordor, the flocking of men to his banner. In short, he seems to thrive on the promise of war and all that comes with it, from the "great alliances" to the "glorious victories." He is, without doubt, the lesser of the two brothers as Tolkien portrays them.

Now we may excuse Boromir in this last instance, and say merely that he is under the spell of the Ring at this time and might not otherwise have spoken in such a way. Yet these words do reveal his character. Faramir loves his brother, Boromir, and in many ways respects him, but he also understands his weaknesses. "If [*Isildur's Bane*] were a thing that gave advantage in battle," Faramir says, "I can well believe that Boromir, the proud and fearless, often rash, ever anxious for the victory of Minas Tirith (and his own glory therein), might desire such a thing and be allured by it" (TT, p. 280). And if through the outcome of all of Gandalf's efforts, Tolkien offers the final judgment of the wizard's wisdom, then through the outcome of Boromir's action—his own death and the breaking of the Fellowship—we are offered the judgment of the worldview that glorifies war.

Of Film and Fiction

If Pippin's comment to Frodo that "short cuts make long delays" (FOTR, p. 97) is true, then detours make even longer ones. Nonetheless, this chapter concludes with a little detour. It has to do with Peter Jackson's film adaptation of the trilogy. If you attended a lecture on Tolkien before the fall of 2001, you could assume that a vast majority of the audience had read *The Hobbit* and that a considerable portion had also read *The Lord of the Rings*. There were usually even one or two who had read *The Silmarillion*. With the release of the films, things have changed. The interest in Tolkien has increased even further, and now it may be found among many persons who have never read any of his books. As a result, a talk on Tolkien after December 2001 might draw a much larger audience, but a smaller *percentage* of that audience will actually have read the books. This is not a complaint. In many ways, the films did an admirable job of representing Tolkien's work. Even where there were changes in the film version of the story—the absence of Tom Bombadil, the enhancement of Arwen's role, the loss of the sixteen-year gap between Bilbo's birthday party and the start of Frodo's quest, etc.—most of the new or changed scenes and dialogues remain true to the nature of Tolkien's characters.

It was several months after seeing the first film when I realized how well it captures some important aspects of the books.

I was at a lecture on Tolkien, given by the author of a relatively recent book. Not long into the lecture, I began to feel that there were several important dimensions of Tolkien's work that the speaker/author—although he certainly knew plenty of facts about Tolkien—either did not understand or was blatantly ignoring. Among other things, he seemed to have missed out on the spiritual and moral sides of Tolkien's writing. During the discussion time after the lecture, I asked a question about Gandalf's role, and the speaker's response confirmed my feeling. Not wanting to enter a debate, I simply fell silent and endured several subsequent questions and answers. Then a voice piped up from the back of the room with one more observation and question that caught my attention. By his own admission, this audience member had not read any of the books; he had only seen the first film of the trilogy. And yet he also sensed that there was a profound spiritual side to *The Lord of the Rings* that had been dismissed or ignored in the talk and ensuing question period. In other words, just from viewing Peter Jackson's film, he seemed already to have gained an understanding of certain fundamental ideas in Tolkien's writing that the speaker had missed. This was a tremendous testament to Peter Jackson's work.

Nonetheless, despite the superb and careful job done in the film to stay true to the books, there are significant differences between the two. At least two such ways in which they diverged are important to consider in the context of this chapter and the last. One is the different slant given to the characters of Elrond and Galadriel. In Tolkien's writing, both of these great Elven Powers are presented as very noble. Elrond, as we saw earlier, is described in *The Hobbit* as being "as noble and as fair in face as an elf-lord, as strong as a warrior, as wise as a wizard, as venerable as a king of dwarves, and as kind as summer." A few paragraphs later we learn that he "grieved to remember the ruin of the town of Dale and its merry bells" (TH, p. 52). Earlier I emphasized the wisdom, but we must also notice that he is "as kind as summer"; he appreciates not only timeless Elvish things, but even the merriness of the world of Men and Dwarves. In the trilogy he is similarly described: "The face of Elrond was ageless, neither old nor young, though in it was written the memory of many things both glad and sorrowful. . . . Venerable he seemed as a king crowned with many winters, and yet hale as a tried warrior in the fulness of his strength" (FOTR, p. 239). He frequently smiles and laughs, especially around the Hobbits. One of the first actions the reader sees Elrond perform in *The Fellowship of the Ring* (the book) is gently waking Bilbo in the Hall of Fire so that he can be reunited with Frodo. Elrond is also famous as a healer. It is he who cures Frodo, and—in another image of gentleness—tends him for days when he is brought in (FOTR, p. 233). It must also be noted that even as early as the Council, it is Elrond's plan to aid not only the Company that sets out from Rivendell but also Gondor and the world of Men. "You have done well to come," he tells Boromir. "You do not stand alone. You will learn that your trouble is but part of the trouble of all the western world" (FOTR, p. 255). He sends out a "fair number" of Elven scouts in advance of the Company, and even considers sending some from his own household as part of the Fellowship of the Ring (FOTR, pp. 285, 289).

As much, or more, could be said of Galadriel. One of the most profound moments of racial healing I have read in fiction comes when Gimli and Galadriel meet, and the centuries-old animosity between Dwarf and Elf is broken down by Galadriel's love and understanding:

> She looked upon Gimli, who sat glowering and sad, and she smiled. And the Dwarf, hearing the names given in his own ancient tongue, looked up and met her eyes; and it seemed to him that looked suddenly into the heart of an enemy and saw there love and understanding. (FOTR, p. 371)

The words spoken here by Galadriel are identical to those spoken earlier by Gimli himself in the chapter "The Ring Goes South": "Dark is the water of Kheled-zâram, and cold are the springs of Kibil-nâla." Thus she shows not only her knowledge and understanding of his ways and mind, but her love and compassion as well. As Aragorn says of her, "There is in her and in this land no evil, unless a man bring it hither himself. Then let him beware!" (FOTR, p. 373).

Unfortunately, the film representation of these two is considerably different from that of the books. The Elrond portrayed by Hugo Weaving is darker and more sinister than Tolkien's Elrond and lacks some of his grace, nobility, and compassion. This is not a criticism of the film, per se, or of Weaving's acting; it is the interpretive part of filmmaking and may well have been a conscious choice on the part of the director. Yet we must be aware not to interpret Tolkien's characters by what we see in the film. The film Elrond is disdainful toward Men in a way that Tolkien's Elrond is not. He tells his daughter, Arwen, that there is no hope in general for the world of Men, and no hope for Aragorn that he will return. In doing so, he is demonstrating either a lack of foresight or of honesty. Weaving's Elrond also uses guilt to manipulate Aragorn into convincing Arwen she should leave Middle-earth. He is almost heartless in wanting, from the start, to put onto Frodo the burden of taking the Ring to Mordor, while the more compassionate Gandalf resists. Indeed, the film's Elrond shows no sympathy to the Hobbits' fear or weakness, or to their desire to go home, despite Gandalf's concern for them. This is not at all the case in the books. Rather, when Frodo volunteers to be the Ringbearer, Elrond affirms the choice but adds with great sympathy: "But it is a heavy burden. So heavy that none could lay it on another. I do not lay it on you" (FOTR, p. 284). Whereas Elrond's own two sons, Elladan and Elrohir, play active roles in Tolkien's account of the war, it is only very late in Jackson's *The Two Towers* that Elrond changes his mind and decides to send his help to Théoden and Aragorn.

Likewise, the film version of Galadriel portrayed by Cate Blanchett plays up on the legends of her being a dark sorceress and, as with Elrond, emphasizes her power more than her grace or gentleness, which are so vividly communicated in Tolkien's writing. In short, though we get glimpses of their noble character, the overall images we get of Elrond and Galadriel in the films are not predominantly ones of kindness, love, or understanding—the words used by Tolkien to describe them—but images that are harsh and almost sinister. The upshot of this is that if we have seen only the films and have not read the books, we might miss the weight Tolkien gives to their words; we might not name them among the most wise of Middle-earth, though they certainly belong to that group.

The second contrast between the books and films is not so much a flaw in the films as simply a difference between the two media. In his essay "On Fairy-Stories," Tolkien comments briefly on some of the differences between literature and drama; the reader is referred to that work for Tolkien's treatment (see FS, pp. 140–42, the section titled "Fantasy"). Film is a visual medium. I am not a film critic, and so I will say little to this point, but I do mention it because it relates to the first chapter. As a visual medium, film's portrayal of battles is, by definition, more graphic. *The Fellowship of the Rings* film opens with a startlingly violent depiction of the battle in which Isildur cuts the Ruling Ring from the hand of Sauron. The Battle of Helm's Deep in the second film is equally dark and violent (and considerably longer). Even the "battle" between Gandalf and Saruman, when Gandalf first goes to Isengard for advice and is locked atop Orthanc, is made by the film version into a very physical (and visual) duel of staffs and wizardry (more at home in *Harry Potter* than in *The Lord of the Rings*). I leave to the scholars of film the deeper discussion of whether the film versions glorify violence, and I make only the point that one must not judge Tolkien's writing by the interpretation of it in a very different medium.

3

Military Victory or Moral Victory?

For Boromir, son of Denethor, what really matters—as we saw in the previous chapter—is military victory. He sees glory in war and in all that goes along with it in the life of the warrior. However, the picture painted by J. R. R. Tolkien, through his narrative and through the voices of the Wise of Middle-earth, is much different than that modeled by Boromir. This raises a question. If it is not the military outcome of a battle that matters most, then what does? Much of the rest of this book deals with that question, the consideration of which leads to some interesting observations. Our first observation is that in Tolkien's writing, moral victory is more important than military victory. We see this in several ways. We see it in the way that Gollum is treated. We see it in the costs that the main foes of Sauron are, and are not, willing to pay for victory—and in the moral choices that are made in the context of the war. Ultimately, we see it in many of the responses to the temptation of the Ring.

Victory, at What Cost?

It is interesting to note the mercy and compassion with which Gollum is treated by many of the foes of Mordor, including, at one time or another, Gandalf, Aragorn, Faramir, King Thranduil and the Wood-elves, Frodo, and even Sam. In Tolkien's writing, mercy is a mark of wisdom. Though it has become clear to most of those mentioned that Gollum has done great evil, and is still capable of doing much more evil, they still show him mercy on many occasions. When he is finally caught by Aragorn, and Gandalf questions him and learns his story—both the evil he has done and the revenge he still plots—he is sent to the Wood-elves, who keep him in prison but treat him "with such kindness as they can find in their wise hearts" (FOTR, p. 69). That he should receive such kindness is not at all obvious, given his past acts, and it bothers more than a few people. It is not only Frodo who wonders why Gollum is not put to death. "He is a small thing, you say, this Gollum?" asks Boromir at the Council. "Small, but great in mischief. What became of him? To what doom did you put him?" (FOTR, p. 268). Even Glóin the Dwarf, who has been a prisoner of the Elves himself (as told in *The Hobbit*), notes with bitterness, "You were less tender to me" (FOTR, p. 268).

Yet Gollum is shown mercy and compassion, and even "over-kindliness" (FOTR, p. 268). Why? One reason is Gandalf's foresight that Gollum will play a later role, presumably for good, "a part . . . that neither he nor Sauron have foreseen" (FOTR, p. 269). But most of the others at Elrond's Council, even among the Wise, don't seem to share that foresight. Aragorn comments, "His malice is great and gives him a strength hardly to be believed in one so lean and withered. He could work much mischief still, if he were free." When he finds out that Gollum has escaped, Aragorn continues, "That is ill news indeed. We shall all rue it bitterly, I fear" (FOTR, p. 268). When Sam finally has a chance to kill him on Mount Doom, he sees that act not only as "just," but also as "the only safe thing to do." And yet he refrains from hurting him. "Deep in his heart there was something that restrained him" (ROTK, p. 221).

So the question remains: Why are the foes of Mordor willing to pay such a price—or at least to take such a risk—in order to help Gollum? The answer is that certain moral victories are more important to Tolkien's most noble characters than are military victories. To put it another way, we simply restate the question as an observation: To the foes of Sauron, moral decisions such as treating a prisoner well hold greater value than does military victory. Showing mercy is the right thing to do. It is right for many reasons. Some of the acts of mercy come from a real concern for helping Gollum find his "cure." (The nature of that cure, and the significance of it, we shall come back to.) But whether Gollum is cured or not, showing him mercy is right. Showing mercy is not only a means to an end; mercy is an end in itself.

In *The Hobbit*, Tolkien has Bilbo face a difficult decision at the end of his interaction with Gollum, shortly after the famous riddle game. Bilbo is trying to escape from Gollum's tunnels, and Gollum is guarding the only way out:

> Bilbo almost stopped breathing, and went stiff himself. He was desperate. He must get away, out of this horrible darkness, while he had any strength left. He must fight. He must stab the foul thing, put its eyes out, kill it. It meant to kill him. No, not a fair fight. He was invisible now. Gollum had no sword. Gollum had not actually threatened to kill him, or tried to yet. And he was miserable, alone, lost. A sudden understanding, a pity mixed with horror, welled up in Bilbo's heart: a glimpse of endless unmarked days without light or hope of betterment, hard stone, cold fish, sneaking and whispering. All these thoughts passed in a flash of a second. He trembled. And then quite suddenly in another flash, as if lifted by a new strength and resolve, he leaped. (TH, pp. 79–80)

Though the confrontation is not a military battle, it is similar to a battle in that there are two opponents, and the likely outcome is the death of one or the other of them, with the spoils going to the victor. It is an unfair battle, however, because Bilbo has acquired the Ring and is now invisible. Furthermore, Bilbo has a sword, while Gollum is unarmed. Thus, Bilbo has a choice between what appears to be an easy escape route, namely, stabbing Gollum in an unfair fight, and the more difficult path of showing mercy to the creature and trying to get past him without killing him. The obvious (and justifiable) choice is to fight Gollum in the unfair battle. But Bilbo, in a debate that "passed in a flash of a second," chooses instead the values of fairness and pity, even though by that course he takes upon himself a much greater risk of defeat.

The Hobbits' treatment of the ruffians in the Shire at the end of *The Return of the King* is much the same. Some rightly perceive that the Men are dangerous and will harm and kill the Hobbits if given the chance. It would seem advantageous, from a strategic standpoint, to attack them first and ask questions later—especially given what the Hobbits have already suffered at their hands. But Frodo, as we saw earlier, forbids killing them.

There is an old question, often asked: "What are we willing to fight for?" Every war ever fought raises that question. In *The Lord of the Rings,* we see that the Free Peoples of Middle-earth are willing to fight Sauron in order to protect their own lives and freedom. When the four Hobbits return to the Shire, they find that their people are willing to fight the ruffians—and even to die doing so—in order to regain their freedom. But in a sense, Tolkien has also turned this question around. As much as the question is "For what causes are we are willing to fight (and seek victory)?" an equally important question is "For what values we are willing to suffer defeat?"

The issue of what moral choices are made by Tolkien's heroes in the context of battle—what values these people are willing to suffer defeat in order to preserve—is illustrated in many ways besides the treatment of Gollum. Aragorn's decision at Parth Galen to pursue the captured Hobbits Merry and Pippin, rather than to head straight to Gondor, can be seen in this light. There were three choices before Aragorn at the time: pursuing Frodo and Sam to the east, traveling south to Minas Tirith to follow his own heart in hopes of bringing aid to Gondor and taking up his throne, or going west in an effort to rescue the two young Hobbits. Of these three choices, the first two are far more advantageous from a strategic viewpoint, at least according to the light of knowledge Aragorn has at the time. "Boromir has laid it on me to go to Minas Tirith, and my heart desires it," says Aragorn to himself, "but where are the Ring and the Bearer? How shall I find them and save the Quest from disaster?" (TT, p. 16). These are the strategic questions. In the war against Sauron, two young Hobbits would seem to have little importance, while the Quest of the Ringbearer and the military might of Minas Tirith are of great import. Yet Aragorn chooses the third of these options:

> "I will follow the Orcs," he said at last. "I would have guided Frodo to Mordor and gone with him to the end; but if I seek him now in the wilderness, I must abandon the captives to torment and death. My heart speaks clearly at last: the fate of the Bearer is in my hands no longer. The Company has played its part. Yet we that remain cannot forsake our companions while we have strength left." (TT, p. 21)

Aragorn's choice, ultimately, is not made for strategic and military reasons, but for what might be called "moral" reasons. He cannot abandon Merry and Pippin to "torment and death"; it would be wrong to forsake them. Even in the midst of the war, it is the clear speaking of Aragorn's heart to which he listens. The moral good is more important than the military good. To understand this is one of the highest marks of wisdom in Tolkien's writing.

Aragorn is not alone in how he chooses, nor in what he values most. His choices are echoed by many, if not all, of those whom Tolkien provides as the heroes of his work. Once again, Faramir gives us two of the best examples. Early in the conversation after Frodo and Faramir have first met, Frodo realizes that the son of Denethor has been testing him. He feels deceived and suggests that he has been lied to. Faramir responds: "I would not snare even an Orc with falsehood" (TT, p. 272). This is a telling statement (and what we see of Faramir through the remainder of the story would suggest that he is speaking the truth about himself). For this Captain of Minas

Tirith, and heir to the Stewardship of Gondor, the value of truth is so important that he would not lie even to an enemy—not even to win a battle. The moral victory of speaking the truth is more important than any military victory that might be won through lies and deceit.

We see a similar principle when Faramir weighs the moral good of Frodo's keeping his promise to Gollum to have him as a guide, against the physical harm that might result from that promise should Gollum choose to betray him and guide him into evil (which, in fact, he does).

> "You would not ask me to break faith with him?" [asked Frodo].
>
> "No," said Faramir. "But my heart would. For it seems less evil to counsel another man to break troth than to do so oneself, especially if one sees a friend bound unwitting to his own harm. But no—if he will go with you, you must now endure him." (TT, p. 301)

Faramir wisely sees the danger ahead for Frodo: that Gollum is not trustworthy and, thus, that Frodo is bound "to his own harm." He rightly predicts the evil that Gollum will seek to do against Frodo and Sam, though he does not know that it will take the form of Shelob's Lair. Yet Faramir also acknowledges that it is a moral evil to knowingly break one's word: to break a promise, or "break faith," or "break troth." Moreover, he recognizes that it is an evil even to "counsel another man to break troth"—though *perhaps* a lesser evil than to actually break troth oneself. And so, when he realizes that Frodo has made a promise to Gollum, both he and Frodo agree that they must stick to the moral good of keeping that promise, even though it brings about a great physical danger. No, he tells Frodo, he will not counsel him to break faith. In his moral integrity, he will not tell another to do what he himself would not do: to abandon the moral good for the sake of personal safety.

Faramir's integrity and high moral values come even more to the forefront when he returns to Minas Tirith and faces his father, Denethor. When Denethor realizes that his son has had a chance to obtain the Ring of Power, and that he has let it go, he is furious. He chastises his son, telling him that his "gentleness may be repaid with death." To which Faramir replies, "So be it" (ROTK, p. 86). The simplicity of this response is wonderfully powerful. There is nothing else that needs to be said. Faramir understands clearly the choices his father has laid before them. Again, he would choose the moral victory of being gentle, even if it means his own death.

Denethor, by contrast, is of a different mind than his younger son. For the Steward of Gondor, to be "lordly and generous as a king of old, gracious, gentle" is fine for times of peace, but all of those things must be sacrificed in time of war, in "desperate hours," for the sake of military victory. He goes so far as wishing, in Faramir's presence, that Faramir were the one who died and not Boromir. "[Boromir] would have remembered his father's need, and would not have squandered what fortune gave. He would have brought me a mighty gift. . . . Would that this thing had come to me!" (ROTK, p. 86). In Denethor's defense, we must acknowledge, at least on the surface, his claim that he would not have used the Ring. "To use this thing is perilous," he agrees. Unless, of course, the defeat of Gondor were at stake. "Not used, I say, *unless* at the uttermost end of need, but set beyond all grasp, save by a victory so final that what then befell would not trouble us, being dead" (ROTK, p. 87, emphasis mine). The problem is that even as he speaks these words, Denethor is already there; in his mind, the *uttermost end of need* has already arrived. He is willing to betray moral virtue for the sake of victory—or, rather, for the sake of avoiding defeat. (We should note here that this is not an abstract choice that appears only in literature. How often has my own country been willing to support ruthless, oppressive dictators as long as they are military allies?) Unlike Denethor, Faramir is not willing to sacrifice moral good for military victory. Neither is Gandalf. The tale, of course, ultimately vindicates Faramir and Gandalf and their wisdom.

The Temptation of the Ring: Gandalf and Elrond

That moral victory is more important than military victory for Tolkien's most heroic characters should be understood as one of the chief issues (and also one of the most interesting to explore for its own sake) related to their refusal to use the One Ring. Indeed, we could draw the conclusion that moral victory is the more important victory merely from the way that the wisest and noblest of Middle-earth—Gandalf, Elrond, Galadriel, Aragorn, and Faramir—are all given the opportunity to possess the Ring for themselves, and all refuse despite their dire need for strength in the fight against Sauron. Their temptations are key scenes in Tolkien's writing (as well as in the film version) and are worth exploring one at a time.

We begin with the temptation of Gandalf. In fact, Gandalf is faced with this temptation several times, at different parts of the story. The film version, for example, gives us a memorable shot of the Ring falling to the floor of Bilbo's house when Bilbo departs the Shire after his birthday party. And Gandalf, watching it fall, is unwilling even to touch it long enough to set it on the mantel or return it to the envelope. He leaves it lying where it is on the floor, for he knows how great the temptation would be to keep it and use it, if once he touched it. Later, Frodo explicitly offers the Ring to Gandalf. This time, Tolkien gives us the wizard's reply:

> "Will you not take the Ring?" [pleads Frodo].
> "No!" cried Gandalf, springing to his feet. "With that power I should have power too great and terrible. And over me the Ring would gain a power still greater and more deadly." His eyes flashed and his face was lit as by a fire within. "Do not tempt me! For I do not wish to become like the Dark Lord himself. Yet the way of the Ring to my heart is by pity, pity for weakness and the desire of strength to do good. . . . I shall have such need of [strength]. Great perils lie before me." (FOTR, pp. 70–71)

The first thing we note is how adamant Gandalf's response is. We see it in the wizard's body: his springing to his feet, the flashing of his eyes, and the light on his face. That his words garner two exclamation points from Tolkien is worth something too. He explicitly labels the offer as a "temptation," a word suggesting both that the Ring is something he desires and that it is something he ought not to take.

Elrond, with similar obstinacy, also refuses the ring—not only for himself but for all those gathered at the Council: "Alas, no. We cannot use the Ruling Ring. . . . I fear to take the Ring to hide it. I will not take the Ring to wield it" (FOTR, p. 281). Much has been made of these passages and others like them, where the refusal is not just for one individual, but for all involved. For Elrond, it is not merely that "I" cannot use the Ruling Ring, but that "we" cannot use it. Why does he refuse that power for everybody else? One idea is that Tolkien viewed all power as essentially corrupting. Certainly, Saruman and Denethor appear to have been corrupted by their own power. And yet Gandalf, Elrond, and Galadriel are three of the most powerful figures in Middle-earth—bearers of the three Elven-rings of power, in fact—and none of these three are corrupted. "But do not think that only by singing amid the trees, nor even by the slender arrows of elven-bows," Galadriel tells Frodo, "is this land of Lothlórien maintained and defended against its Enemy" (FOTR, p. 380). That Galadriel wields such power and yet remains uncorrupted—"There is in her and in this land no evil, unless a man bring it hither himself," Aragorn says of her—is evidence that Tolkien did not hold the view that all power is fundamentally corrupting. Even with Saruman and Denethor, who are both powerful and who both fall, a stronger case could be made that their ultimate downfall is caused not by their power but by a loss of hope. That loss itself is caused by the deceit of Sauron at work through the palantíri (the Seeing Stones), which are being controlled by Sauron and thus reveal only what Sauron wants them to reveal.

Whatever we may say about power in general, however, there is no doubt that the One Ring will eventually corrupt any bearer. Throughout the story, Tolkien shows its influence not only on Sméagol, but on Isildur, Bilbo, and Frodo as well. Even some like Boromir, who never actually bear the Ring but only come near to it, feel its corrupting influence. The only two bearers who are ever able freely to give it up are Bilbo and Sam, but Sam bears it only a short time, while Bilbo gives it up only after a very long and difficult struggle. Nonetheless, we have to ask whether this corrupting influence is inherent in *any* sort of power, or whether it has to do with the specific nature of the power of the One Ring. We will return to that specific power later in this book. Meanwhile, we need to consider why the Ring is tempting, and how adamant are the refusals of that temptation. What the Ring would have meant to the foes of Mordor is "strength," and particularly "strength to do good" (or so it would seem.) Indeed, even Elrond sees it as a real possibility that "one of the Wise should with this Ring overthrow the Lord of Mordor" (FOTR, p. 281). Gandalf, as the chief agent in the war against Sauron, has need of power for the many perils he faces.

Yet both Gandalf and Elrond refuse. Gandalf guesses, more clearly than any of the others, that using the Ring could actually bring military victory for the foes of Mordor: victory, that is, in the sense of defeating Sauron's armies and overthrowing his power. "War is upon us and all our friends," he tells Aragorn, Gimli, and Legolas shortly after their reunion, "a war in which only the use of the Ring could give us surety of victory" (TT, p. 103). And later he tells the gathered captains, in "The Last Debate," that Sauron "is now in great doubt. For if we have found this thing, there are some among us with strength enough to wield it" (ROTK, p. 155). On the other side, Gandalf also knows that without using the Ring they have only a fool's hope of defeating Sauron's might. He also tells the Captains of the West: "This war then is without final hope, as Denethor perceived. Victory cannot be achieved by arms, whether you sit here to endure siege after siege, or march out to be overwhelmed beyond the River" (ROTK, p. 154). And a little later he adds, "We have not the Ring. . . . Without it we cannot by force defeat his force" (ROTK, p. 156). So strong is this understanding that when Gandalf first returns after his fall in Khazad-dûm, he briefly doubts the wisdom of his own choice, and wonders about going after the Ring:

He rose and gazed out eastward, shading his eyes, as if he saw things far away that none of them could see. Then he shook his head. "No," he said in a soft voice, "it has gone beyond our reach. Of that at least let us be glad. We can no longer be tempted to use the Ring. We must go down to face a peril near despair, yet that deadly peril is removed." (TT, pp. 103–4)

In short, then, the situation is plain. Use of the Ring, by the right one of Sauron's enemies, would give a sure military victory. Refusal of the Ring leaves them no hope at all of military victory—a defeating of his force by their own force—and only a fool's hope in the overall war: a "peril near despair." They choose the fool's hope. And this choice is central to the entire trilogy. It is one of the choices that characterize the great among Tolkien's characters. They choose the moral victory—the moral good of refusing the corruption of the Ring—over the military victory that would come from using the Ring.

The Temptation of the Ring: Galadriel and Faramir

The temptations of Faramir and Galadriel are also important. The former stands in stark contrast to the failure of Boromir under similar circumstances, while the latter is one of the more vividly portrayed scenes in *The Fellowship of the Ring*, both book and film.

Faramir is given his opportunity to possess the Ring when Frodo and Sam stumble into his hands in Ithilien. Though Frodo says nothing about what he carries, Faramir knows enough of the lore, and has enough of the wisdom and power of the true blood of Númenor, that he is able to guess much that Frodo does not reveal. Though he knows not the form of Isildur's Bane—that it is a ring—he knows both that Frodo carries it and that it possesses great power. Unlike Gandalf and Galadriel, Faramir is not offered the Ring, and yet it is certainly in his power to take it. In contrast to his brother, however, he does not attempt to do so. In a statement similar to his earlier comment that he would not snare even an Orc with falsehood, he says of the Ring:

> "I would not take this thing, if it lay by the highway. Not were Minas Tirith falling in ruin and I alone could save her so, using the weapon of the Dark Lord for her good and my glory. No, I do not wish for such triumphs." (TT, p. 280)

Faramir is *explicit* in stating what I earlier suggested was *implicit* in the refusals of Gandalf and Elrond: he would rather suffer total military defeat than do the evil that would need to be done to win the war by the use of the Ring. In fact, he would sacrifice not only his own life but also his land, rather than give in to such moral evil. Given the choice between doing good and having Minas Tirith fall into ruin, or doing evil but winning a triumph on the battlefield, he would choose the ruin. These are not idle words, but ones proven by deeds. Faramir does what his brother could not do: he lets the Ring depart with the Ringbearer. Gentleness may be repaid with death? So be it.

Galadriel's temptation is perhaps the most telling of any of them. For one thing, her temptation is given the most attention and time in the narrative, and the most vivid imagery. Yet there is another factor at work as well. With the others, the moral good of refusing the Ring brings a *risk* of defeat but not a *sure* defeat; for Gandalf and Elrond there is still hope of victory over Sauron—though not by force of arms—when they choose to send the Ring to Mordor. Galadriel, however, knows with certainty that if she does not take the One Ring for herself, then whether the Quest of the Ringbearer succeeds and Sauron is overthrown or not, she will suffer a defeat. She speaks of this to Frodo:

> "Do you not see now wherefore your coming is to us as the footstep of Doom? For if you fail, then we are laid bare to the Enemy. Yet if you succeed, then our power is diminished, and Lothlórien will fade, and the tides of Time will sweep it away. We must depart into the West, or dwindle to a rustic folk of dell and cave, slowly to forget and to be forgotten." (FOTR, p. 380)

As Tolkien explains in the book, Galadriel is the bearer of one of the three great Elven-rings of power: Nenya, the Ring of Adamant. Like the other Elven-rings, it was forged for "understanding, making, and healing, to preserve all things unstained" (FOTR, p. 282). It is by the power of that ring that Lothlórien itself is preserved unstained. Unfortunately, though the Elven-rings were never corrupted by Sauron, their power is caught up in the power of the One Ring. Sauron forged the One Ring for the very purpose of ruling the others, and Galadriel understands that if the One Ring is destroyed, then the Three will fall also, and all that was made by their power will fade.

In fact, Elrond also guesses at this, though he seems less certain than Galadriel:

> "Some hope that the Three Rings, which Sauron never touched, would then become free, and their rulers might heal the hurts of the world that he has wrought. But maybe when the One has gone, the Three will fail, and many fair things will fade and be forgotten. That is my belief." (FOTR, p. 282)

Saruman also knows this, and when the fall of the Three comes to pass at the end of the book, he gloats over Galadriel. "I did not spend long study on these matters for naught. You have doomed yourselves, and you know it. And it will afford me some comfort as I wander to think that you pulled down your own house when you destroyed mine" (ROTK, pp. 261–62). It is not idly that Galadriel says of herself and her husband, Celeborn, "Together through ages of the world we have fought the long defeat" (FOTR, p. 372).

Into this situation steps Frodo. Seeing Galadriel as "wise and fearless and fair" (FOTR, p. 380), he offers her the Ring. Her response to this temptation is tremendously vulnerable and sincere, and more thoroughly explored than that of either Gandalf or Elrond. In Galadriel's articulation of her thoughts to Frodo, Tolkien gives the reader great insight into just what the temptation is about at many levels:

"I do not deny that my heart has greatly desired to ask what you offer. For many long years I pondered what I might do, should the Great Ring come into my hands, and behold! it was brought within my grasp. . . .

"And now at last it comes. You will give me the Ring freely! In place of the Dark Lord you will set up a Queen. And I shall not be dark, but beautiful and terrible as the Morning and the Night! Fair as the Sea and the Sun and the Snow upon the Mountain! Dreadful as the Storm and the Lightning! Stronger than the foundations of the earth. All shall love me and despair!" (FOTR, p. 381)

As we consider Galadriel's temptation, we must do so in light of what we have previously seen: that if the Ringbearer even *attempts* the Quest, then whether he succeeds *or* fails it will mark the end of Lothlórien. Thus his coming to Lothlórien truly is, as she said, the coming of "the footstep of Doom." What the Ring offers to Galadriel is a way out of this doom: a third alternative to having Frodo either fail or succeed. To preserve that land and those works, she would need both to keep the Ring from Sauron and also to keep it from being destroyed. It is an alternative she has long pondered, and even greatly desired, as she admits to Frodo. It is a twofold temptation. Part of her desire for power is, as with Gandalf, the desire to defeat Sauron. It is the desire to do good and to prevent evil. As Sam puts it, she would "make some folk pay for their dirty work" (FOTR, p. 382). Yet unlike with Gandalf, there is the added dimension of her great desire to take the Ring simply to save her kingdom and all she has worked for from an otherwise sure demise.

Yet with all of this, Galadriel still refuses the temptation. Her refusal is as beautiful and profound as it is simple:

"The love of the Elves for their land and their works is deeper than the deeps of the Sea, and their regret is undying and cannot ever wholly be assuaged. Yet they will cast all away rather than submit to Sauron: for they know him now. . . . Yet I could wish, were it of any avail, that the One Ring had never been wrought, or had remained for ever lost." (FOTR, p. 380)

Galadriel might wish the One Ring had never been made or was still lost, but such wishes are of no avail. To preserve Lothlórien, she would need to take the Ring for herself. And yet taking the Ring for herself, she knows, would be a great moral evil. And thus, though using (or at least preserving) the power of the Ring is her one hope to preserve what she has created in Lothlórien, she will accept defeat rather than do what she knows would be evil. So it is that Galadriel's answer to this temptation is the same as that of the other great Powers:

> She let her hand fall, and the light faded, and suddenly she laughed again, and lo! she was shrunken: a slender elf-woman, clad in simple white, whose gentle voice was soft and sad. "I pass the test. I will diminish, and go into the West, and remain Galadriel." (FOTR, p. 381)

In these last two passages, Galadriel summarizes the point of this chapter: that moral victory is the most important victory; that it is better to suffer a military defeat and a loss of everything than to suffer a moral defeat; better to "cast all away rather than submit to Sauron."

Human Freedom and Creativity

That the Wise of Middle-earth freely choose to refuse the temptation of the Ring is undeniably important in *The Lord of the Rings*, but by no means is that the only important choice. The fact that Tolkien emphasizes so many choices is significant. There is a prominent place given in Tolkien's works to choice and freedom (Human, Dwarvish, Elvish, and Hobbitish) and to the cousin of freedom, creativity. Before exploring this aspect of Tolkien's works more deeply, it is important to remember the prevailing worldviews of materialism and determinism that I mentioned in the introduction. They state that the material universe is all that exists, and that humans are simply complex machines, all of whose actions—along with the entire workings of the universe—are already determined by the laws of science. Bertrand Russell encapsulates the idea as follows:

> Man is a part of nature, not something contrasted with nature. His thoughts and his bodily movements follow the same laws that describe the motions of stars and atoms. . . .
>
> The total number of facts of geography required to determine the world's history is probably finite; theoretically they could

all be written down in a big book to be kept at Somerset House with a calculating machine attached, which, by turning the handle, would enable the inquirer to find out the facts at other times than those recorded.[1]

In the introduction, I gave some other sample quotes from mathematician/philosopher Bertrand Russell, as well as some from behavioral psychologist B. F. Skinner and neuroscientist Chris Frith, which reflect the same ideas. Indeed, I could have quoted from any several hundred other noted scientists and philosophers of the twentieth and early twenty-first century to illustrate my point. The doctrine preached today is that of determinism: Free will is an illusion, and "it is quite clear that nobody believes in it in practice," claims Russell.[2]

J. R. R. Tolkien, of course, did indeed believe in free will and the reality of human choice in practice as well as in theory. What we will see is just how sharply his view of human freedom, as expressed in his Middle-earth writings, differs from this prevailing materialist view. Indeed, it is difficult to overlook the extent to which his writings stress the reality of choice—of what Skinner calls the "autonomous man" and what Russell refers to as "the doctrine of free will," and what both argue vehemently against. This reality runs through *The Hobbit* and *The Lord of the Rings* from top to bottom. It is in its very fabric. It is what makes this writing "heroic literature." As obvious as this may be, it is also still worth exploring, not only because of the "answers" we find but because of the new questions that the insights raise.

The Reality of Choice

We could begin our exploration of the reality of free will and the importance of choice in Tolkien's writing with the

1. Bertrand Russell, "What I Believe," published in *Why I Am Not A Christian*, pp. 48–49.
2. Bertrand Russell, "Has Religion Made Useful Contributions to Civilization?" published in *Why I Am Not A Christian*, p. 39.

obvious: passages that explicitly describe and even emphasize the choices being made. I mentioned earlier that one of my favorite scenes in *The Lord of the Rings* is the first meeting between Gimli and Galadriel, during which the Elven queen breaks down the centuries-old enmity between Elf and Dwarf. Gimli looks into her eyes and sees a friend where once he saw an enemy. So incredible is this reconciliation and healing of wounds that afterward Gimli is ever ready to go to blows against anybody who speaks ill of the Lady of the Wood. If it weren't so noble, it would be almost comic when at their parting the stammering Dwarf asks—to the murmuring and astonishment of all present—for a single strand of the Lady's hair rather than for any other gift. Likewise, Gimli's bravado would be ridiculous were it not so moving when Tolkien has him stand up to Éomer and 104 of his mounted Rohirrim over a perceived insult given to Galadriel. Gimli is ready to face certain death to defend the honor of this great Elven queen.

In fact, what emerges is a love—though not of a romantic kind—of Gimli for Galadriel, and for the "light and joy" he finds in her kingdom. When he leaves Lothlórien, he is dismayed at the loss. "I have taken my worst wound in this parting, even if I were to go this night straight to the Dark Lord," he bemoans. "Alas for Gimli son of Glóin." The response of Legolas gets at the heart of this chapter:

> "Alas for us all! And for all that walk in the world in these afterdays. For such is the way of it: to find and lose, as it seems to those whose boat is on the running stream. But I count you blessed, Gimli son of Glóin: for your loss you suffer *of your own free will,* and you might have *chosen* otherwise." (FOTR, p. 395, emphasis mine)

Legolas speaks directly of the Dwarf's "own free will" and then goes on to further emphasize the reality of that free will by saying that Gimli "might have chosen otherwise." Being free and able to choose between different courses of action is the very essence of what it means not to be determined. We also get a taste of what heroism means: The hero is the one who makes the brave choice, even when it brings about his own suffering. For that, Legolas counts Gimli blessed.

Tolkien gives us a similar comment at a very critical moment toward the end of *The Fellowship of the Ring*. In order to escape Boromir, Frodo puts on the Ring and climbs to the top of Amon Hen. There Sauron becomes aware of him, and the Eye begins to seek him out, only narrowly being drawn away at the last moment by some other power—which we later learn is Gandalf. It is as Frodo sits "perfectly balanced" between the "piercing points" of these two powers that "suddenly he was aware of himself again. Frodo, neither the Voice nor the Eye: free to choose, and with one remaining instant in which to do so" (FOTR, p. 417). Here we see again the emphasis that Frodo is "free to choose." There is even more than that. It is not only that he is free to choose, but that the *essence* of his existence as Frodo—what he remembers when he becomes "aware of himself"—is this freedom to choose. He is neither the Voice nor the Eye; he is not *compelled* to do Good or to do Evil, but must choose on his own which he will do. And yet, under the strain of those powers, he almost forgets that. Or, put another way, he almost forgets himself. It is his awareness of himself that makes him aware of his freedom to choose. Why? Because the freedom to choose is fundamental to what it means to be a self.

It is also this "freedom to choose" that makes heroism possible, for it is the choices one makes that determine whether that one is a hero. This is what Elrond tells Frodo when Frodo accepts the Quest:

> "But it is a heavy burden. So heavy that none could lay it on another. I do not lay it on you. But if you take it freely, I will say that your choice is right; and though all the mighty elf-friends of old, Hador, and Húrin, and Túrin, and Beren himself were assembled together, your seat would be among them." (FOTR, p. 284)

As with Legolas's earlier remark to Gimli, we see again in Elrond's words the double emphasis on Frodo's free will: that his action is done "freely" and that it is a "choice." That it is a free choice is exactly what makes Frodo a hero, in fact—a hero whose seat belongs with the greatest heroes of Middle-earth. By contrast, the materialist worldview of Bertrand Russell, in which people are not responsible for their actions, does not allow for heroes. That is why Russell wrote that it is "absurd to put up a statue to" somebody who writes a poem or who does something that Tolkien might call "heroic." Tolkien's Middle-earth is full of metaphoric statues because it is a world where heroism is possible and where heroes exist: heroes like Hador, Húrin, Túrin, Beren, and (yes) Frodo. Tolkien's books are full of the *language* of heroism, which is to say, the language of choice. It is what Skinner would have called, derisively, a "literature of freedom."

We don't need to travel very long in Middle-earth before we see this. *The Hobbit* is more lighthearted and less deeply heroic than *The Lord of the Rings*. As Gandalf points out at the beginning of that story, "in this neighborhood heroes are scarce, or simply not to be found" (TH, p. 27). Nonetheless, we see the glimmering of heroic traits in Bilbo (and through him, the potential for heroism in all of us simple folk). Interestingly enough, it is not in seeking adventure or danger that Bilbo shows these traits—in fact, he has no desire for adventure or danger—but rather in being willing to do what he *ought* to do, even when it is uncomfortable. He calls it his "duty"—a word used quite frequently in the books to describe how Bilbo makes his choices. As the story progresses, this sense of heroic duty is developed further. We see it when Bilbo is willing to go back into the goblin caverns after the Dwarves, however miserable he feels about it, because he fears they have been left behind and that it is his duty to return for them. In that sense, the Dwarves—who are certainly more skilled in battle and more used to danger and adventure than the Hobbit—are shown to be much less heroic: they will not choose to do for Bilbo what he is willing to do for them.

Bilbo's greatest act of heroism, according to the narrator, comes when he is in the tunnel preparing to descend into Smaug's lair for the first time: "It was at this point that Bilbo stopped. Going on from there was the bravest thing he ever did. The tremendous things that happened afterwards were nothing compared to it. He fought the real battle in the tunnel alone" (TH, p. 184). What is this brave thing? It is not any of his battles: neither his attempted thievery from the trolls, nor his fight against the spiders in Mirkwood, nor his daring dialogue with Smaug, nor even his small role in the battle against the goblins at the end. It is, simply, the choice to go on: to put one foot in front of the other. This is precisely the sort of "battle" that is important in Tolkien's writing. It is much more important than any military battle. It is a battle that even servants must face—that is to say, a *choice* that even servants are given—as Sam learns when his master falls in Shelob's Lair. In a description closely akin to that of Bilbo in the lair of Smaug, we read that Sam "took a few steps: the heaviest and the most reluctant he had ever taken" (TT, p. 343). Indeed, the observation that this "bravest thing," the "real battle" as it is called, has nothing at all to do with military battle also says much to the subject of whether Tolkien glorifies violence.

The fundamental nature of this relationship between heroism and choice is captured wonderfully in the peculiar wisdom of Sam on the Stairs of Cirith Ungol:

> "But I suppose it's often that way. The brave things in the old tales and songs, Mr. Frodo: adventures, as I used to call them. I used to think that they were things the wonderful folk of the stories went out and looked for, because they wanted them, because they were exciting and life was a bit dull, a kind of a sport, as you might say. But that's not the way of it with the tales that really mattered, or the ones that stay in the mind. Folk seem to have been just landed in them, usually—their paths were laid that way, as you put it. But I expect they had lots of chances, like us, of turning back, only they didn't." (TT, p. 321)

It is not the big battles and exciting brave adventures that make the hero, but the decision to go on and not turn back. It is a decision that is made not just once, but continuously, even as the chances of turning back come at the hero continuously. It is also a decision that ordinary "folk" can make and that turns those ordinary folk into heroes when they do make them. Sam and Frodo themselves make this choice, akin in nature to the choice of Bilbo, but more difficult and more significant: the choice to keep going in Mordor and not to give up, to take one step after another across Udûn and up the side of Mount Doom, "every step of fifty miles" (ROTK, p. 210). Even when their steps turn to crawling, they go on: "'I'll crawl, Sam,' [Frodo] gasped. So foot by foot, like small grey insects, they crept up the slope" (ROTK, p. 219). Why is this heroic? Because they are free. They have the choice to give up or to go on. That they choose the latter is the essence of their heroism.

Aragorn and the Doom of Choice

How important is choice in Tolkien's writing? Choices form the bookends of *The Two Towers,* which ends with a chapter titled "The Choices of Master Samwise" and starts with a chapter that might well have been called "The Choices of Aragorn, Son of Arathorn." If there is one character in whom, and for whom, the importance and difficulty of choice is captured, it is Aragorn. When Éomer first meets Aragorn, he senses something deep and noble about this stranger to Rohan. "What doom do you bring out of the North?" he asks. "The doom of choice," answers Aragorn (TT, p. 36). In other words, when Aragorn answers, "The doom of choice," he is really answering, "freedom"; freedom is his fate, his destiny, his punishment. Though only four words long, that answer is truly one of those sentences that—like the proverbial picture—is worth a thousand words. Many different understandings are layered there. Even the word *doom* is loaded. In its Anglo-Saxon roots, it refers simply to a law. Yet it can also connote a judgment or sentence passed down, a destiny or fate laid upon one, or some terrible thing waiting to happen. It is also one of the root words of *freedom,* or "free-doom": the state in which one's doom, or destiny, is free for one to choose.

At one level, then, Tolkien is making a statement about all the race of Men: Choice is our doom. Not only are we free and *able* to choose, it is our destiny as beings of free will that we *must* make choices—and then live with the *consequences* of those choices! As Aragorn tells Frodo at Parth Galen:

> "I fear that the burden is laid upon you. . . . Your own way you alone can choose. In this matter I cannot advise you. I am not Gandalf, and though I have tried to bear his part, I do not know what design or hope he had for this hour, if indeed he had any. Most likely it seems that if he were here now the choice would still wait on you. Such is your fate." (FOTR, p. 412)

Here Tolkien's emphasis is on Frodo's choices. Twice Aragorn reminds Frodo of the reality and "burden" of choice: "You alone can choose," he tells him, and "the choice would still wait on you." Choice is Frodo's "fate"—a statement that is itself an ironic twist.

Yet Aragorn is also aware of his own choices, and of the "part" he himself has to "bear," especially in Gandalf's absence. Choice is the fate of all in Middle-earth; each *alone* can *choose* his or her *own way*. Though Frodo is already quite aware of his difficult choices, Tolkien puts this most intense statement of those choices into Aragorn's mouth, probably because Aragorn is so conscious of his own burden of choice. Thus, when Aragorn answers Éomer, he is, as has been pointed out, making a statement about all members of his race, but he is also answering this question in a painful and personal way. He is particularly aware of his own destiny, the many difficult choices he has had to make, and those he will soon have to make. Almost from the moment Gandalf falls and Aragorn takes over leadership of the Fellowship, he is plagued by the choice of where and how to lead the Fellowship. "Would that Gandalf were here!" he says, on the Great River. "How my heart yearns for Minas Anor and the walls of my own city! But whither now shall I go?" (FOTR, p. 409). Thus, as much as he would like to help Frodo, he seems relieved at Parth Galen that the final choice falls upon the Ringbearer, and not himself.

Indeed, Tolkien shows us an Aragorn who is nearly over-whelmed at times by the choices facing him, and who is filled with great human doubt about his ability to make them. On several different occasions, we hear him lament the choices he has made. On the opening page of *The Two Towers,* as the Fellowship is falling apart, he cries: "Alas! An ill fate is on me this day, and all that I do goes amiss" (TT, p. 15). And a short time later, capturing both his doubt about past decisions and his confusion about current ones, he continues:

> "Vain was Gandalf's trust in me. What shall I do now? Boromir has laid it on me to go to Minas Tirith, and my heart desires it; but where are the Ring and the Bearer? How shall I find them and save the Quest from disaster? . . .
> "Are we to abandon him? Must we not seek him first? An evil choice is now before us!" (TT, pp. 16–17)

The whole war against Sauron is a war to preserve freedom in Middle-earth. Yet we can see why Aragorn might refer to his own free-doom as a doom in the sense of punishment. He has three choices, and all of them come with the possibility of great loss. It is, truly, an "evil choice." Or, as Gimli comments, "Maybe there is no right choice" (TT, p. 18).

Despite Gimli's words, Aragorn does make a choice, though it comes after much painful deliberation. "I will follow the Orcs," he says, and "My heart speaks clearly at last" (TT, p. 21). And however hard that choice is, once it is made Aragorn sticks to it with determination (and several exclamation points). "'Come! We will go now. Leave all that can be spared behind! We will press on by day and dark! . . . With hope or without hope we will follow the trail of our enemies.' . . . On and on he led them, tireless and swift, *now that his mind was at last made up*" (TT, pp. 21–22, emphasis mine). As with many other choices throughout the books, Tolkien brings emphasis and clarity to the actual moment of decision, showing us just how real the choice itself is, and also how important the process of choosing is.

Even after Aragorn makes his choice to pursue Merry and Pippin, and guesses (albeit wrongly) that in making such a choice he may have removed himself from having any significant role in the remainder of the war—commenting "ours is but a small matter in the great deeds of this time"—he is still very conscious of his choices. "A vain pursuit from its beginning, maybe, which no choice of mine can mar or mend," he says, in deciding whether or not to risk taking a rest. "Well, I have chosen" (TT, p. 28).

There are many heroes in *The Lord of the Rings*, but among the race of Men, Aragorn represents the greatest. It is thus fitting that the burden of choice is shown to be greatest for him also. But freedom and wisdom do not imply moral infallibility for any created being in Middle-earth—not for the great or the small, neither for Aragorn nor for Sam, not even for wizards.

The Prophecies

Even Gandalf, at times, seems torn by the choices he must make. "Whence came the Hobbit's ring? What, if my fear was true, should be done with it? Those things I must decide" (FOTR, p. 264). Though he does not commit any obvious moral wrongdoing, he does make mistakes of choice. One such error of judgment is his early inaction with regard to the Ring. "I was at fault," he confesses. "I should have sought for the truth sooner" (FOTR, p. 264). Another is his decision, after hearing news from Radagast about the Nine being abroad, to go straight to Saruman rather than returning to the Shire. "Never did I make a greater mistake!" he confesses (FOTR, p. 271). The choice of which route the Fellowship should use in order to cross the mountains also burdens Gandalf, and it is the subject of debate and disagreement between him and Aragorn. Neither feels certain of the route, and both see evil and great danger in all paths. It is interesting, therefore, to note that Aragorn himself later defends the choices of Gandalf, whom he thinks dead at the time. "The counsel of Gandalf was not founded on foreknowledge of safety, for himself or for others," said Aragorn. "There are some things that it is better to begin than to refuse, even though the end may be dark" (TT, p. 43).

This comment brings us to a deeper subject, upon which Tolkien himself was hesitant to tread. Gandalf's plans were not founded on "foreknowledge of safety," and yet they were founded on some sort of knowledge beyond what was plainly visible. This brings us back to a point made in the introduction to this book. There is a strong sense in *The Lord of the Rings*, and even in *The Hobbit*, that the Wise of Middle-earth—especially Gandalf and Elrond—have a faith in a power higher than themselves and that this faith aids them in making the choices they need to make, no matter how difficult. To use my earlier terminology, there is both a seen and an unseen in Tolkien's Middle-earth: both a material plane and a spiritual plane. The spiritual plane, though less visible, is no less real to Tolkien. We see this in comments such as those of Gandalf to Frodo:

> "There was something else at work, beyond any design of the Ring-maker. I can put it no plainer than by saying that Bilbo was *meant* to find the Ring, and *not* by its maker. In which case you also were *meant* to have it. And that may be an encouraging thought." (FOTR, p. 65, emphasis Tolkien's)

The passive voice used twice for the verb *meant* implies an unmentioned and unseen subject of the verb. The subject is not the Ring's maker—that is, it is not Sauron—but rather a power higher than Sauron and thus able to overrule him. The words of Elrond spoken later to those gathered at the Council have similar implications:

> "That is the purpose for which you are called hither. Called, I say, though I have not called you to me, strangers from distant lands. You have come and are here met, in this very nick of time, by chance as it may seem. Yet it is not so. Believe rather that it is so ordered that we, who sit here, and none others, must now find counsel for the peril of the world." (FOTR, p. 254)

Again, there is a clear indication of some higher power at work: higher than that of Elrond. Indeed, it is a power capable of calling Men, Dwarves, and Elves from all over Middle-earth so that all arrive at Rivendell at just the right time. It is also a power with a purpose beyond chance, which has authority to give moral orders to the inhabitants of Middle-earth. For Gandalf it is this "encouraging thought" of a higher power at work, above and beyond any design of Sauron, that strengthens him to his task and to making difficult choices—choices that are not based on foreknowledge of his own safety and that appear to others as a fool's hope. To those who see only in the physical plane, the choices of Gandalf, who also sees in the spiritual plane, may seem foolish. The same could be said about Elrond's vision and his choices. However, the fact that those present were "called hither," though it should encourage them, does not remove their responsibility and duty to "find counsel for the peril of the world." In other words, the very thought of an Authority above our own free-doom enables rather than disables that free-doom. One cannot point to the Authority as an excuse to abdicate the responsibility of choosing.

Secondly, while it is clear that this higher Authority has a hand in shaping events—summoning, by dreams and other means, strangers from distant lands to come to Elrond's Council, and guiding the footsteps of Sméagol and Bilbo so that the Ring would one day fall into Frodo's hands—the presence, power, and plan of this Guiding Hand does not in any way remove the reality and significance of the free choices given to individuals in Middle-earth. As Gandalf says to Bilbo at the very end of *The Hobbit:* "Surely you don't disbelieve the prophecies, because you had a hand in bringing them about yourself?" (TH, p. 255). In the age-old theological debate between predestination and free will, Tolkien seems to come down solidly on the side of . . . both.

5

The Gift of Ilúvatar and the Power of the Ring

In the context of freedom and choice, we now return to the question of the Ring's nature. If Tolkien did not view *all* power as necessarily evil, then what is it about the *particular* power of the Ring that makes it fundamentally evil and corrupting? And why is it, in Tolkien's work, that moral victory and personal choices take on greater significance than do military victories? It has been speculated—perhaps because *The Lord of the Rings* was first published in the decade following World War II—that the story has allegorical significance pertaining to the war, and in particular that the Ring is a metaphor for the atomic bomb. Tolkien himself rejected all such ideas on numerous occasions, including in his "Foreword to the Second Edition." Fortunately, the first of those two questions is not difficult to answer and requires no such speculation. It is not only hinted at in many discussions of the Ring, but answered rather explicitly by Galadriel: the power of the One Ring is the power to dominate other wills.

Why that particular power is so evil is a more intriguing question and moves well beyond the old cliché that "power corrupts and absolute power corrupts absolutely." Tolkien's answer can be found, at least in part, in the significance he gives to human free will. Having seen how this reality and importance of choice is expressed throughout *The Lord of the Rings,* and even in *The Hobbit,* and understanding the nature of the One Ring as the power to dominate, we can begin to see why the Ring is so fundamentally evil that no good use of it is possible regardless of one's underlying motives.

The Domination of Wills

What is the particular power of the Ring that is so fundamentally evil? There are two ways we might go about answering this question. The first is by looking at the Ring itself: what is said about it (by the Wise) and what effect it has. The second approach is to look at the Ring's creator, Sauron, and to try to understand his power and purpose. We will take both approaches (and find that they lead to the same answer).

Galadriel goes a long way toward describing the nature of the One Ring in her dialogue with Frodo after his encounter with her mirror. She has already explained that Sauron is always searching for her, trying to discover her thoughts. If ever he recovers the One Ring, then her ring, Nenya, and all the works done by the power of that ring, will be laid bare to him. Frodo then wonders why he himself couldn't see her ring and read her thoughts, since he possesses (and has worn) the One.

> "I would ask one thing before we go," said Frodo, "a thing which I often meant to ask Gandalf in Rivendell. I am permitted to wear the One Ring: why cannot I see the others and know the thoughts of those that wear them?"
>
> "You have not tried," she said. "Only thrice have you set the Ring upon your finger since you knew what you possessed. Do not try! It would destroy you. Did not Gandalf tell you that the rings give power according to the measure of each possessor? Before you could use that power you would need to become far stronger, and to train your will to the domination of others." (FOTR, p. 381)

Before Frodo could use *that* power—that is, the power of the One Ring—he would need to train his will to domination, specifically to *the domination of others.* The essential power of the One Ring, it would seem from Galadriel's words, is thus the *power to dominate other wills.* We see this also in a comment Elrond makes about the three Elven-rings: "They were not made as weapons of war or conquest: that is not *their* power. Those who made them did not desire strength or *domination* or hoarded wealth, but understanding, making, and healing, to preserve all things unstained" (FOTR, p. 282, emphasis mine). Here, Elrond is contrasting the Three with the One. *Their* purpose, according to Elrond, is *not* conquest or domination. The implication, of course, is that the purpose of the One *is* conquest and domination. This, anyway, is what Saruman sees in the One when he tries to convince Gandalf to help him gain it: "Our time as at hand: the world of Men, which we must rule," he says. "But we must have power, power to order all things as we will, for that good which only the Wise can see" (FOTR, p. 273). Saruman wants to rule. This is the central issue in the temptation of the Ring to which he has succumbed. He wants power. It is not a power whose nature is to do good *for* others, but rather a power to impose (or order) his will *upon* others. Though he uses the word *good,* it is not a good that anybody else can see—that is, it is not a real good that would benefit anybody else—but one that only the Wise (by which he means himself) can see. In short, then, the power of the One Ring is the power to rule: the power to conquer, the power to command, the power to order, the power to enslave.

That is the simple answer, and it is consistent with the type of power we saw at work in the temptation of Boromir: "The Ring would give me power of Command," Boromir rightly understands. "All men would flock to my banner!" It is also consistent with what is engraved on the Ring itself: "One Ring to rule them all, One Ring to find them, One Ring to bring them all and in the darkness bind them." The One Ring is about ruling (exercising authority and domination over others) and about binding (forcing, compelling, enslaving). Sauron forged his Ring with the purpose of controlling the other rings and, through them, of controlling and enslaving other wills.

In a letter written late in 1951 to a potential publisher, Tolkien himself described the "primary symbolism of the Ring" as "the will to mere power, seeking to make itself objective by physical force and mechanism, and so also inevitably by lies" (Letters, p. 160). One might be tempted to understand the reference to "mere power" as implying that power itself is evil. In this context, however, the phrase "mere power" suggests rather _power for the sake of power_—that is, power for no other reason than to _be_ powerful and to _exercise_ power. It is the idea of power as an end, rather than a means. Contrast this type of mere power with the power of the three Elven ring-bearers, Gandalf, Elrond, and Galadriel, whose power always has some other end—that is, an end other than power itself—such as protecting the lives and freedom of others or preserving beauty and peace. ("The rule of no realm is mine," says Gandalf [ROTK, p. 30].) While Tolkien's comment about the symbolism of the One Ring does not explicitly mention domination, it does say that such power is gained through deceit and physical force—through manipulation, we might also say—which strongly suggests such domination. In any case, if we want to look outside _The Lord of the Rings_ itself toward Tolkien's letters, he gives a clearer picture of the power of the One Ring as well as the other great rings earlier in the same letter:

> The chief power (of all the rings alike) was the prevention or slowing of decay (i.e. "change" viewed as a regrettable thing), the preservation of what is desired or loved, or its semblance—this is more or less an Elvish motive. But also they enhanced the natural powers of a possessor—thus approaching "magic," a motive easily corruptible into evil, a lust for domination. (Letters, p. 152)

This last characteristic, a lust for domination, seems especially to be the trait of the One Ring, and of those that it most influenced: the Nine and the Seven, which we learn were _corrupted into evil_ by Sauron, while the Three were not. And in a personal letter (dated September 1963) Tolkien wrote, "It was part of the essential deceit of the Ring to fill minds with imaginations of supreme power" (Letters, p. 332). An exploration of the meaning of magic ("a motive easily corruptible into evil") in Tolkien's writing would itself be worthwhile, and might start with the words of Galadriel (this time to Sam): "For this is what your folk would call magic, I believe; though I do not understand clearly what they mean; and they seem also to use the same word of the deceits of the Enemy" (FOTR, p. 377). However, a full exploration of the meaning of magic and the power of deceit in Tolkien's writing would require at least another entire book! For now, the point worth noting is simply the connection, in Tolkien's own words, between the One Ring and domination, will, and power.

A second approach to understanding the nature of the One Ring is to explore Sauron's own power and purpose. Why? Because Sauron and the One Ring are inextricably tied together. It was Sauron's own power that he poured into the Ring when he forged it in secret. "Sauron would not have feared the Ring! It was his own and under his will," Tolkien wrote in the 1963 letter. As Elrond says at the Council, "It belongs to Sauron and was made by him alone, and is altogether evil" (FOTR, p. 281). Or as Gandalf tells Frodo, "He made that Ring himself, it is his, and he let a great part of his own former power pass into it, so that he could rule all the others" (FOTR, p. 61). And as Gandalf later tells the Captains of the West, "If it is destroyed, then he will fall; and his fall will be so low that none can foresee his arising ever again. For he will lose the best part of the strength that was native to him in the beginning" (ROTK, p. 155). This is why Elrond goes on to say, "If any of the Wise should with this Ring overthrow the Lord of Mordor, using his own arts, he would then set himself on Sauron's throne and yet another Dark Lord would appear." In other words, if anybody were to take up the Ring, they would not so much *overthrow* Sauron as they would *become* Sauron. Which is also why Galadriel tells Frodo that even the effort to wield the Ring himself would destroy him; it would destroy him by turning him into Sauron—or at least a smaller, weaker Sauron.

What is the power and nature of the Ring, then? It is the power and nature of Sauron himself, for that is what he poured into the Ring. So in order to understand the Ring's nature, we need only to understand Sauron's nature. This is not a difficult task. Tolkien gives illustrations of Sauron's power everywhere. It is the power to force others to his will. We see this in the sharp contrast between the *foes* of Mordor and the *forces* of Mordor. The former fight against Sauron of their own free will. The latter are little more than slaves, driven by fear. Aragorn, Gandalf, Faramir, and even Théoden are always at the forefront of their armies, leading by their own examples of courage. Saruman, Sauron, and, later, Denethor stay in their towers and rule from afar. "He uses others as his weapons," Denethor explains of Sauron. "So do all great lords, if they are wise, Master Halfling. Or why should I sit here in my tower and think, and watch, and wait, spending even my sons?" (ROTK, p. 92). We see it even in the different types of magic at work in Middle-earth. Tolkien wrote in his letters about the differences between Elven magic and the magic of Sauron, which are such entirely different things that two different words ought to be used. The Elves' magic "is Art, delivered from many of its human limitations: more effortless, more quick, more complete. . . . And its object is Art not Power, sub-creation not domination." While Sauron's magic "is always 'naturally' concerned with sheer Domination" (Letters, p. 146).

In other words, this second path to understanding the Ring—trying to understand Sauron himself—leads us to the same conclusion: the fundamental power of the Ring is the power of domination. It is the power to enslave: the power to rule over other wills. This explains why it is, as Gandalf says on several occasions, that the Ring can have only one master, not many: many people cannot simultaneously rule over each other.

At this point a brief aside is in order. In *Author of the Century*, T. A. Shippey raises the point that there are two possible understandings of the evil of the Ring; one he associates with a Boethian view of evil and the other with a Manichaean view (Sh, pp. 128ff.). In the Boethian view, evil is internal; the Ring has no innate power of its own to corrupt its bearer, but rather the bearer becomes corrupted by his or her own human sin and weakness, expressed as a greedy desire for the Ring. In a Manichaean understanding, evil is an outside force, and the Ring is actively at work (obeying the will of its master) to corrupt its bearer. Shippey defends the position that Tolkien is ambivalent in his presentation of the Ring's evil, and thus of evil in general, whether it is Boethian or Manichaean. Both aspects of evil seem to be at work at various times, along with a third force, which is simply that of addiction. "One can never tell for sure, in *The Lord of the Rings,* whether the danger of the Ring comes from inside, and is sinful, or from outside, and is merely hostile" (Sh, p. 142). In this chapter I have claimed that Tolkien associates a particular power and nature with the One Ring: the power to dominate other wills. If this understanding of Tolkien is correct, does that suggest that the debate sways one way or the other, toward the Boethian view or toward the Manichaean? The answer is no. With respect to whether the Ring's evil is internal or external, understanding that the power of the Ring is the power to dominate other wills offers an answer as ambivalent as the one Shippey claims Tolkien's is. The corruption associated with the Ring may come entirely from the internal desire of sinful Man to dominate other wills, or it may come from some external power at work through the Ring to corrupt the bearer into a desire to dominate. Or it may be both. As Shippey says, "Tolkien's double or ambiguous view of evil is not a flirtation with heresy at all, but expresses a truth about the nature of the universe" that can be found even in the Lord's Prayer.

The Flame Imperishable

If this is the nature of the One Ring—the domination of other wills—why is such a power naturally evil? Why could not Gandalf or Galadriel or Aragorn, or even Boromir or Faramir, put such a power to good use? To answer such a question, we return again to the importance, in Tolkien's writing, of free will. In doing so, we turn briefly to Tolkien's other masterpiece, *The Silmarillion.*

The Silmarillion, which recounts the story of the creation of Middle-earth and provides the historical richness that pervades and deepens so much of *The Hobbit* and *The Lord of the Rings,* was not published until four years after Tolkien's death. It was collected and edited (with considerable care and effort) by J. R. R. Tolkien's son Christopher, from numerous drafts and versions in existence. Because it was published posthumously, and because it was not clear in all instances what were the "final" (or authoritative) versions of various portions of the book, some readers discount the importance and legitimacy of *The Silmarillion* in understanding Tolkien's Middle-earth writing.

There can be no doubt, however, that J. R. R. Tolkien desired *The Silmarillion* to be published (in some form). He sought hard and frequently (though unsuccessfully) to get *The Silmarillion* published during his lifetime. In fact, his original goal was that *The Silmarillion* and *The Lord of the Rings* should be published together! One of the letters from which we quoted earlier in this chapter was actually some 10,000 words long, written to Milton Waldman of Collins publishing company, "with the intention of demonstrating that [the two works] were interdependent and indivisible" (Letters, p. 143). Tolkien had also earlier written a letter to Stanley Unwin (of the publishers Allen & Unwin, who had published *The Hobbit*), in which he had (in his own words) "made a strong point that the *Silmarillion* etc. and *The Lord of the Rings* went together as one long Saga of the Jewels and the Rings" (Letters, p. 139).

Unfortunately, Tolkien's efforts failed, and so we will never know exactly what final form *The Silmarillion* would have taken under his hands. (Indications are that even J. R. R. Tolkien himself would have had a difficult time deciding the exact final form, though a certain body of material was certainly part of his canon.) What we do know is that it was his life's work and his life's blood. It was not a piece added on to *The Hobbit* as an afterthought, but rather the other way around. More of the history of Tolkien's efforts at completing the mythology of Middle-earth (which has been given elsewhere) is not critical to this chapter other than to say that work on *The Silmarillion* began long before *The Hobbit* and *The Lord of the Rings*, and continued long after. As his son Christopher wrote in his foreword to the first edition, the "old legends ('old' now not only in their derivation from the remote First Age, but also in terms of my father's life) became the vehicle and depository of his profoundest reflections" (TS, p. xii).

It is in the *Ainulindalë*—the opening book of *The Silmarillion*, which recounts the Music of the Ainur and the creation of Middle-earth—that we are introduced to both the source and importance of free will in Tolkien's writing. Middle-earth was created by Eru, whose name means "the One" and who is also called Ilúvatar, "Father of All." But before Middle-earth was brought into being, Eru created first the Ainur, or "Holy Ones." These were the first beings, other than Eru Ilúvatar himself, to have wills and selves of their own. We read in the *Ainulindalë:*

> Then Ilúvatar said to them: "Of the theme that I have declared to you, I will now that ye make in harmony together a Great Music. And since I have kindled you with the Flame Imperishable, ye shall show forth your powers in adorning this theme, each with his own thoughts and devices, if he will." (TS, p. 3)

For those who have not (yet) read *The Silmarillion,* a little background is helpful. The Ainur are spiritual beings, most closely akin to angels in the biblical concept of Tolkien's Christian faith. When Eru creates Eä, the physical or material universe, and Arda, the earth itself, he gives the Ainur the opportunity to enter into this created order in order to assist Ilúvatar in creation. Many choose to do so, and those who make that choice have the ability to take incarnate forms like unto the stuff of Arda, and in the image of the coming Children of Ilúvatar (that of Elves in particular). Greatest among those who go to Arda are called the Valar, or the Powers of Arda. Manwë is their King, and Varda, also called Elbereth, is their queen. These Valar, and lesser spirits known as the Maiar, take up their residence in Valinor in the far West of Arda. Gandalf, in fact, is one of the Maiar, known originally as Olórin.

Of critical importance here is the idea of the "Flame Imperishable," with which Eru "kindled" the Ainur. What is this Flame Imperishable? It is closely associated with the gift of existence itself—that is, the gift of a *separate* existence, with a separate will, and an awareness of self, and the freedom to act.[1] Thus, each of the Ainur has "his own thoughts." Even more, Ilúvatar gives each the choice of whether or not even to participate in this Music of the Ainur. Each may do so, not under compulsion, but *"if he will."* That one of the Ainur, namely, Melkor, soon rebels against Eru, seeking to "increase the power and glory of the part assigned to himself," shows us quickly just how real this freedom is. Creation now has beings who, though dependent upon Eru for their existence, have wills of their own to choose and to act and even to rebel. (One cannot miss the echoes, in Tolkien's creation account, of Genesis 1–3 as well as of Milton's *Paradise Lost.*)

It is also important to realize that this Flame Imperishable is a gift—indeed, it is the great gift—given by Eru Ilúvatar to his created beings. It is this freedom that enables them to participate in Ilúvatar's Music and to themselves assist in sub-creating new beauty. In fact, so great a gift is it that none other than Eru Ilúvatar himself can give it. Not even Manwë can create beings having their own free will. Both Melkor and Aulë try, and both

---

1. In a personal conversation with Clyde Kilby, Tolkien suggested that the *Secret Fire,* a term used interchangeably with the *Flame Imperishable,* is meant to represent the Holy Spirit, the third person in the Trinity in the Christian understanding of God's divine nature. Rather than contradicting the assertion that the Flame Imperishable is associated with our free will, this strengthens the assertion. The Greek New Testament word for *spirit,* used in the title "Holy Spirit" (see Acts 2:4, for example) is *pneuma,* which comes from the word for "breath." But the Genesis 2:7 account of the creation of Man in the Septuagint—the Greek translation of the Old Testament—also uses the same word *pneuma* to describe the breath of life given to man as a free will being made in the image of God: "And the Lord God formed man of the slime of the earth: and breathed into his face the breath of life, and man became a living soul." The word *pneuma* may also be used to mean "life," "mind," or "reason," all concepts associated with free will. Even in ancient Hebrew, the same word used in Genesis 1:2 to refer to the *Spirit of God* is also used in Genesis 6:17 defining the *life of Man.* It is the life-giving Spirit of Genesis 6:3.

fail. As we read in the *Ainulindalë*, Melkor "had gone often alone into the void places seeking the Imperishable Flame; for desire grew hot within him to bring into Being things of his own. . . . yet he found not the Fire, for it is with Ilúvatar" (TS, p. 4). We later learn that this Flame Imperishable is also the gift given to Elves and Men (the Children of Ilúvatar): "For the Children of Ilúvatar were conceived by him alone. . . . Therefore when [the Ainur] beheld them, the more did they love them, being things other than themselves, strange and *free*" (TS, p. 7, emphasis mine). In other words, Elves and Men are also free will beings. This, then, is the source of their nature that we discussed in the context of *The Lord of the Rings*. This is the significance of the "doom of choice" that Aragorn has.

We see more of the significance and meaning of this great gift of freedom when it is bestowed upon the Dwarves also. It is the Vala Aulë who first creates the Dwarves (in form, at least). Aulë, however—though he has as a gift his own free will, which is exhibited in his choice to attempt such a thing on his own without the command of Ilúvatar—has neither the authority nor the power to complete his task and give these creatures their own independent being. That is, though Aulë creates the *form* and *features* of the Dwarves, he cannot give them free will. They are simply his puppets, moving when he thinks to move them and sitting idle when his thought is elsewhere. In repentance, therefore, he prepares to destroy his own creation. Ilúvatar, however, in his mercy, bestows upon the Dwarves the same gift of free will that he has designed for his other Children: Elves and Men.

> Then Aulë took up a great hammer to smite the Dwarves; and he wept. But Ilúvatar had compassion upon Aulë and his desire, because of his humility; and the Dwarves shrank from the hammer and were afraid, and they bowed down their heads and begged for mercy. And the voice of Ilúvatar said to Aulë: "Thy offer I accepted even as it was made. Dost thou not see that these things have now a life of their own, and speak with their own voices? Else they would not have flinched from thy blow, nor from any command of thy will." (TS, p. 41)

What it means for people to have this gift of freedom—their own free will—is that they can shrink even from the hand of their Creator. Ilúvatar's created beings can choose to participate in the Music in keeping with their part in the Theme of Ilúvatar, or they can choose to rebel and bring about discord. Referring back to our discussion of Aragorn, we saw that it is the *destiny* of free will beings that they *must* make choices, but we also see that this freedom, in Tolkien's writing, is a gift as well as a doom: a gift that even Melkor and Sauron envy.

The importance of the gift of freedom can be seen even in the relationship between the Children of Ilúvatar (especially the Elves) and the Valar:

> For Elves and Men are the Children of Ilúvatar. . . . For which reason the Valar are to these kindreds rather their elders and their chieftains than their masters; and if ever in their dealings with Elves and Men the Ainur have endeavored to force them when they would not be guided, seldom has this turned to good, howsoever good the intent. (TS, p. 37)

The Valar, though older and more powerful than Elves, Men, or Dwarves, are not given the right to take away this gift of freedom given to the Children. They are allowed to advise the Children, and to teach them, and to share wisdom with them, but any attempt made at *compelling* the Children to some course of action, no matter what the intention, leads to evil result. The clearest example of this in *The Silmarillion* is the summons the Valar issued to the Elves (who call themselves the *Quendi,* in their own tongue) that they should come to Valinor:

> Then again the Valar were gathered in council, and they were divided in debate. For some, and of those Ulmo was the chief, held that the Quendi should be left free to walk as they would in Middle-earth, and with their gifts of skill to order all the lands and heal their hurts. But the most part feared for the Quendi in the dangerous world amid the deceits of the starlit dusk; and they were filled moreover with the love of the beauty of the Elves and desired their fellowship. At the last, therefore, the Valar

summoned the Quendi to Valinor, there to be gathered at the knees of the Powers in the light of the Trees for ever; and Mandos broke his silence, saying: "So it is doomed." From this summons came many woes that afterwards befell. (TS, pp. 52–53)

The choice here is between being "left free," though in a "dangerous world," and being safe, but with a loss of freedom. Freedom is held the higher gift than safety! And the desire of the Valar, even if phrased in terms of "love" and "fellowship," still involves the Elves at their knees, which is a place of subservience. For this very reason, Ulmo, ever one of the wisest of the Valar, argues against such a summons, and Mandos foretells what doom will come of the Valar exercising authority over the Children. We see this same principle behind the refusal of the Wise of Middle-earth to wield the Ring. The power of the Ring is the power to compel other wills to one's own will. There is never a good use for such a power.

Now, much more could be said about this freedom, and about what it really means under the authority of Eru Ilúvatar, who promises that "no theme may be played that hath not its uttermost source" in him, nor can any "alter the music in [his] despite" (TS, p. 6). Again, there are strong biblical echoes, this time of passages such as Romans 8:28: "And we know that to them that love God all things work together unto good: to such as, according to his purpose, are called to be saints." The depth of this theology could (and has) been pondered for centuries. Indeed, we will return to this in the last chapters of this book. Meanwhile, just two more issues relating to the Imperishable Flame and human freedom must be explored before concluding this chapter.

The Firstborn and the Followers

The first issue pertains to the differences between Elves, or Quendi, who are the *Firstborn* Children of Ilúvatar, and Men, the *Followers* (called the Atani in the Elven tongue). Following is one of the longest passages cited in this book, but it is included because it lays much of the foundation for under-standing the races:

> For it is said that after the departure of the Valar there was silence, and for an age Ilúvatar sat alone in thought. Then he spoke and said: "Behold I love the Earth, which shall be a man-sion for the Quendi and the Atani! But the Quendi shall be the fairest of all earthly creatures, and they shall have and shall conceive and bring forth more beauty than all my Children; and they shall have the greater bliss in this world. But to the Atani I will give a new gift." Therefore he willed that the hearts of Men should seek beyond the world and should find no rest therein; but they should have a virtue to shape their life, amid the powers and chances of the world, beyond the Music of the Ainur, which is as fate to all things else. . . .
>
> But Ilúvatar knew that Men, being set amid the turmoils of the powers of the world, would stray often, and would not use their gifts in harmony; and he said: "These too in their time shall find that all that they do redounds at the end only to the glory of my work.". . .
>
> It is one with this gift of freedom that the children of Men dwell only a short space in the world alive, and are not bound to it, and depart soon whither the Elves know not. Whereas the Elves remain until the end of days, and their love of the Earth and all the world is more single and more poignant therefore, and as the years lengthen ever more sorrowful. For the Elves die not till the world dies, unless they are slain or waste in grief. . . . But the sons of Men die indeed, and leave the world; wherefore they are called the Guests, or the Strangers. Death is their fate, the gift of Ilúvatar, which as Time wears even the Powers shall envy. But Melkor has cast his shadow upon it, and confounded it with darkness, and brought forth evil out of good, and fear out of hope. Yet of old the Valar declared to the Elves in Valinor that Men shall join in the Second Music of the Ainur; whereas Ilúvatar has not revealed what he purposes for the Elves after the World's end, and Melkor has not discovered it. (TS, pp. 38–39)

Some things are clear in this passage, but many are less clear. What is clear is that Elves and Men are different. The obvious difference—one that could be understood even from a quick reading of *The Lord of the Rings* without the additional understanding to be gained from *The Silmarillion*—is that Elves are given immortality, whereas Men die of old age. Interestingly enough, it is also stated that both mortality and immortality, as well as freedom, are gifts. That is, they are all *meant* as good things; the ability of Men to "shape their life" is a "virtue," not a vice. As stated, Melkor seeks to turn Men (and Elves) away from Ilúvatar by making the gifts look bad or by making each envious of the gifts of the others, but the very fact that he must use deceit to make the gifts appear evil is a demonstration that they are, in fact, good. In any case, this reinforces the earlier observation that freedom is a good gift from Ilúvatar to his Children.

What is less clear, but is nonetheless hinted at, is that Men somehow have a greater or more meaningful freedom than do Elves. It is what Ilúvatar calls "a new gift." To the Elves, the Music of the Ainur is fate; no choices of Elves have the power to change what has already been foreseen (and foresung) in this Music. Men, by contrast, have the power to "shape their life" beyond the music. In fact, free will goes hand in hand with mortality. "It is one with the gift of freedom that the children of Men dwell only a short space in the world alive." This is similar, in some ways, to the story of Adam and Eve in Genesis 3, though there are also some important differences. It is when Adam and Eve disobey God—thus exerting their free will as separate beings and thereby discovering evil—that they are given mortality. The difference is that in Arda mortality is a gift (for Men), whereas in the Garden of Eden it was seen as a punishment for disobedience. With the Elves there is no such gift of mortality.

Does this mean the Elves do not have free will? How are Men more free? What does this "new gift" really mean? Tolkien does not spell out the answers to these questions—he was, after all, writing story and history and not theology or philosophy—and so one can only guess or infer the answers from other passages. What I think becomes clear from the rest of *The Silmarillion* is that the Elves do indeed have free will, even though all their choices will ultimately lead to the fulfillment of what has already been seen. If this were not the case, then the debate of the Ainur about whether to summon the Elves to Valinor or to leave them free to wander Middle-earth would be a meaningless debate. In particular, the Elves are responsible for their choices. We see this especially in the case of Fëanor, "mightiest in all parts of body and mind, in valour, in endurance, in beauty, in understanding, in skill, in strength and in subtlety alike, of all the Children of Ilúvatar," who finally rebels against the Valar and against Ilúvatar himself. When his rebellion and haughty words are made known to the Valar, Manwë weeps in sadness but then proclaims that some good will still be brought into the world through Fëanor's evil. To this statement Mandos, the judge of spirits, replies, "And yet [that evil of Fëanor will] remain evil" (TS, pp. 112–13). That Fëanor rebels at all shows that he, like Men, has freedom. That he and his evil will be judged shows not only that he is free, but that he is responsible for his freedom.

Free Will and Creativity

A second issue that relates to the Imperishable Flame and the gift of free will is the possibility of real creativity. Although puppet masters and computer programmers may be creative, neither puppets nor computer programs are. When Eru Ilúvatar gives the gift of freedom to the Ainur, the Quendi, and the Atani (as well as to the Dwarves), enabling them to have thoughts of their own and to act of their own initiative, he gives them the gift of creativity. The Ainur were to "adorn" the Theme of Ilúvatar. *Adorn* is a word that is full of artistic and creative connotations. Moreover, each is to do so with "his own thoughts and devices." And the Elves are to "conceive and bring forth more beauty" than all of Ilúvatar's Children.

There can be no doubt that creativity, and more specifically creative art, plays a very important role in Tolkien's writing. Throughout *The Silmarillion*, we are moved by story after story of one of the great of Middle-earth pouring thought and effort into some creative work of beauty. The whole history of the First Age of Middle-earth, told in *The Silmarillion*, revolves around two great creative acts. The first is that of Yavanna, the Vala who creates Telperion and Laurelin, the Two Trees of Valinor. The second is that of Fëanor, the Elf who creates the Silmarils, the living jewels in which dwells the mingled light of Telperion and Laurelin. So important are these two creative acts that it is written of the Two Trees, "Of all things which Yavanna made they have most renown, and about their fate all the tales of the Elder Days are woven" (TS, p. 33). The importance of Fëanor's jewels can likewise be understood from what is said about them, that they were "most renowned of all the works of the Elves" (TS, p. 72). We learn that "Varda hallowed the Silmarils, so that thereafter no mortal flesh, nor hands unclean, nor anything of evil will might touch them" (TS, p. 73). Indeed the book itself, *The Silmarillion*, gets its title from these three jewels. And these, though the most important in the history of the Elves, are merely two of many creative labors we read about in *The Silmarillion*. We could also speak of the White Ships of the Teleri Elves; of the Nauglamír, the great Necklace of the Dwarves; of Iluin and Ormal, the mighty lamps of the Valar; of the fountains of Gondolin; and so on. The great among Men, Dwarves, Elves, and Valar are often known by what they create. In other words, what we begin to see here and elsewhere is that creativity is a great and highly prized gift.

One of the most moving acts of creation is the making of Dwarves by Aulë, alluded to earlier. When J. R. R. Tolkien writes of Aulë picking up his great hammer to smite the Dwarves, one should picture Tolkien sitting beside the huge pile of papers comprising the manuscripts to his unfinished work and holding a lit match beside the pile. Both Aulë and Tolkien deeply loved their work, and both sought to give their work a life of its own. (By the Grace of Ilúvatar, Aulë succeeded beyond what he could have imagined. Those reading this book might agree that Tolkien succeeded, perhaps by the same grace.) And Tolkien, like Aulë, often doubted whether he had the power and authority to do what it was he was trying to do in his creative work. You can see this expressed in both his tale of Aulë and

Yavanna and in his very personal and deeply moving short fairy tale "Leaf by Niggle." In the same letter to Milton Waldman quoted earlier, Tolkien writes:

> Do not laugh! But once upon a time (my crest has long since fallen) I had a mind to make a body of more or less connected legend, ranging from the large and cosmogonic, to the level of romantic fairy-story—the larger founded on the lesser in contact with the earth, the lesser drawing splendour from the vast backcloths—which I could dedicate simply to: to England; to my country. . . . I would draw some of the great tales in full-ness, and leave many only placed in the scheme, and sketched. The cycles should be linked to a majestic whole, and yet leave scope for other minds and hands, wielding paint and music and drama. Absurd. (Letters, pp. 144–45)

So we picture Tolkien, his crest fallen, looking at his unpublished work, thinking it absurd, and lighting a match. "And he wept."

But we must also picture Tolkien defending what he had done, as Aulë does before Ilúvatar:

> Then Aulë answered: "I did not desire such lordship. I desired things other than I am, to love and to teach them, so that they too might perceive the beauty of Eä, which thou has caused to be. . . . And in my impatience I have fallen into folly. Yet the making of things is in my heart from my own making by thee; and the child of little understanding that makes a play of the deeds of his father may do so without thought of mockery, but because he is the son of his father." (TS, pp. 40–41)

In this one little speech by Aulë, Tolkien answers (with considerable profundity) one of the most important philosophical questions of history. Why are we creative? Or, put another way, where does our creativity come from? This is, of course, part and parcel of the question: From whence comes our free will? Bertrand Russell was forced to deny the existence of free will because his materialist worldview did not provide him any answer to where freedom *can* come from. In denying free will, he also has to deny the value of creativity, saying it is ridiculous to build a statue to somebody who writes a poem, since the writing of that poem is simply the effect of a cause for which he had no control. In other words, in writing a poem there is only an *illusion* of creativity. Now Russell was a hard-core philosophical materialist and thus doesn't necessarily represent the regular man or woman on the street, but even the soft-core *practical* materialist is faced with a similar dilemma: either denying free will and creativity and calling them mere illusions, or having to explain where they come from in a material universe.

Tolkien, by contrast, not only affirms both free will and creativity, but tells us from whence they came. Unlike a rock or mountain, Men (and also Elves and Dwarves and the Ainur) have from Ilúvatar the gift of the Imperishable Flame. Indeed, the first task of the Ainur after hearing the theme of Ilúvatar's music is to *create* music of their own. To broaden the answer from Ainur to Man, the making of things is in our hearts because of the way in which the Maker made us as making-creatures. We are children of a Father—Ilúvatar, the "Father of All"—who is a Creator. As his children, it is only natural that we also create. A message similar to that found in the story of Aulë and Yavanna can also be found in Tolkien's essay "On Fairy-Stories": "We make in our measure and in our derivative mode, because we are made: and not only made, but made in the image and likeness of a Maker" (FS, p. 145). Tolkien's powerful short story "Leaf by Niggle" has some equally wonderful meditations on the value of human art and creativity.

Now we can return to this question of why the Ring is so fundamentally evil. Its power, like the power of Sauron himself, is the power to dominate other wills. It is the power to take away freedom. Sauron is no different from his master, Melkor, in whose image both Sauron and the Ring take their shape. Of Melkor we read: "But he desired rather to subdue to his will both Elves and Men, envying the gifts with which Ilúvatar promised to endow them; and he wished himself to have subjects and servants, and to be called Lord, and to be a master over other wills" (TS, p. 8). The essence of the desire and power of the Ring is to master other wills: to have subjects and servants, to subdue—ultimately to replace the freedom of others. This is a fundamentally evil desire. Why? Because the gift of Ilúvatar—this gift of freedom, and the creativity that goes with it—is such a great gift. And this, finally, is our answer to the second question posed at the start of the chapter. If the greatest gift to Man is that of freedom, and with it the gift of creativity, then the greatest evil—the evil of Melkor, his servant Sauron, and Sauron's One Ring—is the taking away of that gift of freedom.

6

Moral Responsibility and Stewardship

We have raised several important issues. Free will is real. It is not only a gift, but a great gift, highly valued and given only by Eru Ilúvatar himself, and therefore not to be taken from another. This, in part, is why choice is so important in Tolkien's writing. It is also an answer to the question of why the One Ring is so inherently evil: its power is to dominate other wills and to remove their freedom.

There is, however, another part to the answer of why free will is so important in Tolkien's works. It relates to the notions of *objective morality* and *moral responsibility*. Objective morality—or what some people call "moral absolutes"—is a definition of good and evil that is real and true for every person (and every different culture), regardless of whether that person (or culture) happens to *believe* it to be true. In contrast to *subjective* morality, or moral relativism, objective morality is independent of the individual subject or subjects (whether it is a person, nation, culture, or era). Fëanor's evil deeds, for example, especially the tragic Kinslaying at Alqualondë, are going to be judged. But on what basis are they to be judged? Looking at the question another way, the discourse between Manwë and Mandos about Fëanor speaks of both good and evil: Manwë claims that Ilúvatar will bring some good out of the evil of Fëanor, and Mandos replies that the deeds themselves will yet remain evil. But the "good" and "evil" of which Manwë speaks are *moral categories* independent of any particular character, and this implies some *standard for judgment* that is likewise independent. What is the standard? Whatever it is, it is something outside of Fëanor. And, in fact, it is above even Manwë himself.

Before exploring the reality and importance of objective moral categories for judgment in Tolkien's works, it is important to identify the prevailing worldviews in our time and culture regarding morality—as we did with free will—so that we may see just how sharply the writings of Tolkien contrast with these prevailing views. We can begin with the denial of free will. Returning to our earlier analogy, we can note that a computer virus, no matter how inconvenient or destructive, is just an impersonal collection of computer code composed of bits (zeroes and ones) on a computer. A virus has no will of its own and cannot be considered evil or immoral. The *person* who *creates* a virus, by contrast, might well be considered evil, especially if the virus is designed with malicious intent. Put another way, if we have suffered the results of a malicious computer virus, we may seek to have the programmer of the virus punished (perhaps by a fine or by jail time), but we probably don't seek to punish the bits (zeroes and ones of computer code) that comprise the computer virus. Likewise, suppose that a person who commits a heinous crime is only acting as he or she is *programmed* to do, as the worldview of determinism states is the case. (For the sake of this discussion, it is irrelevant whether that programming comes by nature or nurture.) Then by no means can that *person* be evil; only the *programmer* of that person can be evil. In this case, however, the *programmer* is believed to be a blind impersonal force. In short, where there is no choice at all, there can be no moral (or immoral) choice. In a deterministic world, we may at worst consider another person's actions as inconvenient to us; we cannot call them "evil" or "immoral." Or, if we do, then we are really only calling "immoral" the universe itself:

the impersonal universe that programmed that person. In any case the word *immoral* has no meaning in this context. We are stuck saying, as Bertrand Russell writes: "When a man acts in ways that annoy us we wish to think him wicked, and we refuse to face the fact that his annoying behavior is a result of antecedent causes." The language of "good and "evil" (or "wickedness") has been replaced by that of convenience and annoyance. If we start with the presupposition of determinism and a denial of free will (which itself flows naturally from a materialistic worldview), then we can immediately conclude that there is no such thing as objective morality, and we are left with the popular position of moral relativism (or with no morality at all).

It must be pointed out that one need not believe in materialism in order to hold a view of moral relativism. One may be a theist, a deist, a polytheist, etc., and still hold to relativism. Also, there are many forms of moral relativism, including cultural forms, that claim that good and evil are defined by society and not the individual, and may be defined differently by different societies. The point is only that the prevailing credo of our time is this: Right and wrong are personal choices, like the type of ice cream we prefer. This view was already widely popular when Tolkien was thinking about a sequel to *The Hobbit*. Anthropologist Ruth Benedict, author of *Patterns of Culture* (1934), aptly expresses this relativistic worldview when she writes:

> It is a point that has been made more often in relation to ethics than in relation to psychiatry. We do not any longer make the mistake of deriving the morality of our locality and decade directly from the inevitable constitution of human nature. We do not elevate it to the dignity of a first principle. We recognize that morality differs in every society, and is a convenient term for socially approved habits. Mankind has always preferred to say "it is morally good," rather than "it is habitual," and the fact of this preference is matter enough for a critical science of ethics. But historically the two phrases are synonymous.[1]

1. Ruth Benedict, "Anthropology and the Abnormal," *Journal of General Psychology* 10, no. 2 (1934), pp. 59-80.

Benedict dismisses any notion that morality may be a first principle—that is, an objective reality from which other principles may be derived—and instead reduces moral virtue, or goodness, to mere habit. This view permeates modern thinking. The only remaining virtue that is still accepted as objective is that of tolerance; intolerance is the only thing we are free to be intolerant of. Whether or not one comes to the question of morality from a materialist determinist worldview, in the modern world objective morality is *out* and subjective morality is *in:* good and evil, if they exist as categories at all, are only personal or at best societal.

Tolkien, of course, does use the language of objective good and evil. This language is woven into the very fabric of his works, from start to finish. He rejects altogether the thinking behind Benedict's quote. Indeed, I think he must have had some suggestion of that form of relativism in mind when he wrote the dialogue between Gandalf and Saruman, when Saruman's treachery is first made known. Gandalf recounts this dialogue to the council:

> "I looked then and saw that his robes, which had seemed white, were not so, but were woven of all colours, and if he moved they shimmered and changed hue so that the eye was bewildered."
>
> "'I liked white better,' I said.
>
> "'White!' he sneered. 'It serves as a beginning. White cloth may be dyed. The white page can be overwritten; and the white light can be broken.'
>
> "'In which case it is no longer white,' said I. 'And he that breaks a thing to find out what it is has left the path of wisdom.'"
> (FOTR, p. 272)

Black and white have long been images of evil and good. Saruman rejects the very notion of white, saying that it is something that may be dyed, overwritten, broken. By doing so, he is denying—perhaps in an attempt to justify his actions—the existence of any higher moral law, or at least any higher law that applies to *him*. His preference for the imagery of multicolors over black and white is then a preference for relativism.

Gandalf's rebuttal probably gives us a good idea of what Tolkien thinks of this: such relativism is a departure from the path of wisdom. With the dialogue seen in this light, Saruman's fall may be seen as a fall away from objective morality into subjectivity, and may well represent Tolkien's view of the downfall of our whole society.

In any case, the existence of objective morals—definitions of good and evil that are true for everybody regardless of whether any person or culture believes them to be true—is central to *The Lord of the Rings* and *The Silmarillion*. Speaking of his encounter with Saruman and his subsequent captivity, Gandalf later comments: "There are many powers in the world, for *good* or for *evil*" (FOTR, p. 232, emphasis mine). Fëanor will be judged, and not by his own personal standards, or even by the standards of the Noldor. "Ye have spilled the blood of your kindred unrighteously and have stained the land of Aman," Mandos the Judge tells Fëanor. "For blood ye shall render blood" (TS, p. 99). This objective morality and basis for judgment is what we shall now explore.

Objective Morality and Judgment

We get glimpses of this objective morality even in *The Hobbit*. Start by considering the use of so many morality words: *evil, good, wicked, fair, unfair*, etc. "Evil things did not come into that valley," the narrator tells us of Elrond's domain of Rivendell, while of Wood-elves we are told, "Still Elves they were and remain, and that is Good People" (TH, pp. 51, 145). By contrast, the narrator also tells us that goblins "are cruel, wicked, and bad-hearted" (TH, p. 60). The casting of these moral judgments *by the narrator*, without any diminishing of their strength by qualification in some particular subjective or cultural or even situational context, suggests a moral authority that is above the characters within the story.

Tolkien also makes an important comment about Bilbo's understanding of morality at the end of his riddle-game with Gollum: "He knew, of course, that the riddle-game was sacred and of immense antiquity, and even wicked creatures were afraid to cheat when they played at it" (TH, p. 74). What Bilbo's thoughts convey is that the definitions of good and evil are known not only by those who are good, but even by those who are evil, or "wicked." "Wicked creatures" may choose to disobey the "sacred" moral laws, but even in their disobedience the law itself is not invalidated. Indeed, such is Gollum's knowledge of this moral law that when he breaks it—murdering his brother, thieving from his neighbors, not keeping his bargain with Bilbo—he makes excuses for why it is justifiable for him *in his particular circumstance* to do what he does, rather than just pretending that no such law exists. (The Ring was a gift, Bilbo's question wasn't fair, etc.) Tolkien felt the influence of moral law to be so powerful as to be understood even in an imaginary universe even by the wicked creatures.

In *The Lord of the Rings,* we see moral language and contrast between good and evil in many places. Shippey makes a point about the Orcs similar to the point made about Gollum in the previous paragraph. Drawing on the dialogue between Gorbag and Shagrat after they take Frodo prisoner, he writes that Gorbag "is convinced that it is wrong, and contemptible, to abandon your companions" (Sh, p. 132). Shippey goes on to conclude:

> Orcs here, and on other occasions, have a clear idea of what is admirable and what is contemptible behaviour, which is exactly the same as ours. They cannot revoke what [C. S.] Lewis calls "the Moral Law" and create a counter-morality based on evil, any more than they can revoke biology and live on poison. They are moral beings, who talk freely and repeatedly of what is "good," meaning by that more or less what we do. (Sh, p. 133)

Of course the Orcs rarely come close to living up to that moral law—there is no indication that they even make any effort—but this failure to put the law into *practice* by living good lives denies neither the existence of that objective law nor their knowledge of it.

Tolkien also shows us glimpses of this objective moral law in the internal debate between Sméagol's two sides (which is given such prominent importance in *The Two Towers*). The foundation for this debate is laid by Gandalf early on in *The Fellowship of the Ring:* "There was a little corner of his mind that was still his own, and light came through it, as through a chink in the dark. . . . But that, of course, would only make the evil part of him angrier in the end—unless it could be conquered" (FOTR, p. 64). The very fact that the two sides or "parts" of him are not merely different but *morally distinguishable,* with only one part being seen as "evil," gives insight into the moral nature of Middle-earth. The objective distinction between good and evil in Middle-earth is so clear and powerful that those among Tolkien's characters who are *morally attuned* may even sense it externally at times. "You have frightened me several times tonight," Frodo says to Aragorn shortly after they meet, "but never in the way that servants of the Enemy would, or so I imagine. I think one of his spies would—well, seem fairer and feel fouler, if you understand" (FOTR, p. 183). Aragorn later has the same experience when he first meets Gandalf after the wizard's return. "Aragorn felt a shudder run through him at the sound, a strange cold thrill; and yet it was not fear or terror that he felt: rather it was like the sudden bite of a keen air, or the slap of a cold rain that wakes an uneasy sleeper" (TT, p. 97). Evil has a feel to it, and it is different than the feel of good.

It is also a morality that is not situational. Consider the words of Faramir when he discovers what it is that Frodo is carrying:

> "We are truth-speakers, we men of Gondor. We boast seldom, and then perform, or die in the attempt. *Not if I found it on the highway would I take it* I said. Even if I were such a man as to desire this thing, and even though I knew not clearly what this thing was when I spoke, still I should take those words as a vow, and be held by them" (TT, p. 289).

We see that Faramir recognizes that it is wrong to break one's vow. Not even a situation in which breaking his vow were the only way for Faramir to save his country would turn the evil of breaking his vow into a good. Breaking a vow is an objective moral ill, independent of the situation. There are also echoes here of earlier words spoken by Faramir, that he would not slay even an Orc with a falsehood. Men of Gondor speak the truth, whatever the situation. Thus, the main conclusion of chapter 3, that moral victory is more important than military victory, is just one application of this broader principle: Morality is objective and does not change with the winds of the situation; the situation of military battle does not justify breaking moral law.

Tolkien gets even more specific in his articulation of objective morality. One of the most important passages among those that deal with the objective nature of morality is the dialogue between Éomer and Aragorn when the two first meet on the Plains of Rohan. We have already seen this passage in the context of free will and the "doom of choice." Let us explore it in more depth, continuing from the same place:

> "Tell me, lord," [Éomer] said, "what brings you here? . . . What doom do you bring out of the North?"
>
> "The doom of choice," said Aragorn. "You may say this to Théoden son of Thengel: open war lies before him, *with Sauron or against him.*" (TT, p. 36, emphasis mine)

Granted that there is not yet any explicit mention of good, evil, or morality in this passage. Yet Aragorn, in the context of a statement about "choice"—and in particular about the "doom" of those who must make choices—states that ultimately there are only two choices to be made in Middle-earth: to fight "with Sauron or against him." As Aragorn tells us, there is no neutral ground; for Théoden, the dividing barrier between black and white is a sharp line, with no gray territory. There are, of course, many different strategies and tactics the king might choose to use in the war, for one side or the other, but the definitions of the sides cannot be any clearer than Tolkien has painted them. This is, in fact, a very objective standard for making a choice. And Aragorn lays upon Éomer another equally clear choice: help the three hunters on their quest to find and free the captured Hobbits, or hinder them.

We don't, however, have to risk stretching Aragorn's words beyond what they were intended to mean in order to reveal the existence of an objective moral basis for judgment. Because of the paralysis of his king and uncle, Éomer has not yet been faced with the many difficult decisions Aragorn has had to make, and has not yet acquired the wisdom that comes with making those decisions. At a loss for whether or not to help Aragorn, he asks:

> "How shall a man judge what to do in such times?"
>
> "As he has ever judged," said Aragorn. "Good and ill have not changed since yesteryear; nor are they one thing among Elves and Dwarves and another among Men. It is a man's part to discern them, as much in the Golden Wood as in his own house." (TT, pp. 40–41)

Here is our straightforward proclamation of moral absolutes: "good and ill" are the same not only across cultures (of Dwarf, Man, Elf) but across times and eras as well, from yesteryear to today. The meaning of right and wrong does not, and has not, changed. "And this deed was unlawful," Mandos tells Fëanor, before pronouncing his judgment, "whether in Aman or not in Aman" (TS, p. 77).

Before exploring this objective morality, it is important to make one other explicit observation now, even though it may become implicitly clearer later. A moral law such as that we have described in Middle-earth is sometimes referred to as Natural Law: "The Rules," the Hobbits of the Shire sometimes call them. Now if by "Natural Law" we mean no more and no less than what we have said—namely a moral law that is not only universally in effect for all eras and all peoples, but also seems to be commonly known or felt even among those who disobey it—then "Natural Law" is the correct term. However if by "Natural Law" we mean a law whose source is nature itself, where nature is an impersonal object, then it is the wrong term. In Tolkien's Middle-earth, the Law has come down from

Ilúvatar through Manwë, and thus it bears the authority not just of nature, but of the *Creator* of nature. We see this in the words of the Vala Mandos when he reminds Fëanor both that Manwë is king over all Arda and that Mandos himself is the judge. Even the simple Hobbits, who never dwelt in Valinor with the Valar and have little contact with the Elves who did, have a vague understanding of this. "For they attributed to the king of old all their essential laws; and usually they kept the laws of free will, because they were The Rules (as they said), both ancient and just" (FOTR, p. 18). So it is that Gandalf can reply to Pippin, after Pippin tries to defend his looking into the palantír with the plea that he had no idea what he was doing: "Oh yes, you had. You knew you were behaving *wrongly* and foolishly; and you told yourself so, though you did not listen" (TT, p. 204, emphasis mine).

We should also note that even though Tolkien makes it clear that the distinction between good and evil is real and objective, when it comes to individuals—whether Elf, Dwarf, Man, or Hobbit—there are none who are either completely good or evil. Sauron alone might be considered completely evil, but even he was not so in the beginning, we are told. The ambiguity of good and evil doesn't lie in the Law itself, but in the moral state of those who follow (or disobey) the Law.

Moral Responsibility

Now we can begin to see even more deeply the significance of the gift of free will. Our choices mean more than which of two (or ten, or twenty) flavors of ice cream we will consume. There is good, and there is ill, and as Aragorn says, "it is a man's part to discern them, as much in the Golden Wood as in his own house." That there are moral absolutes upon which our choices may be *judged* is also to say that there are real—that is, moral—consequences to our actions, and where we have free will and moral consequences, we have *moral responsibility*. Aragorn and Éomer are free, and they must make choices; and because there is an objective definition of good and ill, Aragorn says, they have a moral responsibility—a "man's part"—to discover what that "good" is and to act accordingly.

Once again, though Tolkien gives these ideas a fuller expression in *The Lord of the Rings*, and a mythological (or theological) basis in *The Silmarillion,* we can see the notion of moral responsibility even in *The Hobbit.* For example, *The Hobbit* is full of references to *duty:* a word that refers to an obligation or responsibility of a moral or legal type. Time and again, we see Bilbo making moral choices about what he ought to do, usually in contrast to what he wants to do: "He had a horrible thought that the cakes might run short, and then he—as the host: he knew his duty and stuck to it however painful—he might have to go without" (TH, p. 16). Like many instances early in *The Hobbit,* the consequences of Bilbo's choice are not presented as especially significant at the moment; the issue at stake is only whether or not Bilbo or the Dwarves will get the last of the Hobbit's supply of cakes. Yet in basing even such small decisions on moral responsibility, Bilbo is training himself, so that when the more significant decisions are placed before him—whether or not he ought to risk going back into the goblins' caves to rescue the Dwarves—he is ready to perform his duty. This is just what we see: "He had just made up his mind that it was his duty, that he must turn back—and very miserable he felt about it—when he heard voices" (TH, p. 83). Though these two choices involve consequences of entirely different magnitudes, Tolkien uses a very similar voice in presenting them to the reader. In both cases the contrast is between doing what is comfortable and doing what is right, and Tolkien interrupts the sentence to let the reader know that the right thing is a "painful" or "miserable" choice. We also must note that in both cases there is no "legal" obligation on Bilbo to act in some particular way; in other words, the obligation implied by "duty" is a moral one.

This notion of duty is interesting. Some readers criticize Bilbo for acting only according to the dictates of duty, without having any warm feelings or heartfelt desire corresponding to his actions. According to this popular view, acting *only* in duty is somewhat less morally admirable: Bilbo should have *wanted* to do good rather than ill; he should have been *happy* to watch the Dwarves eat the rest of his cakes even if he went without. Some even go so far as to say that acting in duty only is hypocritical, in that our actions are not in unity with our real feelings and emotions. Whether or not the reader thinks this is the case, it is clear that Tolkien portrays a sense of duty as a virtue and makes it a mark of those characters in Middle-earth who are most heroic. (This illustrates again just how much Tolkien's worldview is in contrast with the prevailing way of thinking.) In another sense, however, a case could actually be made that Bilbo really does *want* to do his duty; that is, he wants to be comfortable *and* he wants to do his duty, but his *actions* show us that his desire to do his duty is greater than his desire to be comfortable. Again, whether one agrees with this understanding or not, the significant issue is that in this notion of duty Tolkien is emphasizing Bilbo's moral responsibility.

Moving from *The Hobbit* to *The Lord of the Rings,* Tolkien gives a more profound and explicit elucidation of this responsibility. In the important dialogue between Gandalf and Frodo in "The Shadow of the Past," near the start of *The Fellowship of the Ring,* Frodo laments that the burden of the Ring has fallen onto him:

> "I wish it need not have happened in my time," said Frodo.
> "So do I," said Gandalf. "And so do all who live to see such times. But that is not for them to decide. All we have to decide is what to do with the time that is given us." (FOTR, p. 60)

This, in a nutshell, is the summary of what moral responsibility means to every individual in Middle-earth. None can choose into what time they are born, nor can they choose what great events or great crises will come to pass in the time that is theirs. The times and their corresponding choices are beyond their control; they are given to them. They may be pleasant choices, such as those Bilbo faced throughout the majority of his long life, or they be painful choices, such as those faced by Frodo. In short, the characters in Tolkien's stories are not responsible for the actions and decisions of others. What they are responsible for—what they have to decide, as Aragorn says—is what to do with the choices given to them.

This is such an important concept that Tolkien repeats it on multiple occasions throughout his work. Gandalf lays out this moral responsibility to the Captains of the West in "The Last Debate," using the imagery of gardening:

> "Other evils there are that may come; for Sauron is himself but a servant or emissary. Yet it is not our part to master all the tides of the world, but to do what is in us for the succour of those years wherein we are set, uprooting the evil in the fields that we know, so that those who live after may have clean earth to till. What weather they shall have is not ours to rule." (ROTK, p. 155)

Again, the captains are not responsible for the decisions of others; they needn't master "all the tides of the world." Their responsibility—their "part"—is for how they act in *those years wherein they are set.* Each age (and even each person) will face a different set of evils: a different set of weeds in the gardens that they till. They needn't worry about the evils that others face in their own earth, and they needn't worry about the choices that others must make in the face of those evils; they are responsible only for the "evils in the fields that [they] know."

Gandalf gives even more insight in this speech when he speaks of doing "what is in us." The suggestion is that each person has been given certain strengths and abilities—a set of gifts, if you will—and each is responsible for how he or she uses that strength and those gifts. The implication is that more will be expected of those to whom more has been given: more of Denethor than of Pippin, more of Faramir than of one of his soldiers. This quote also explains another of the implications of decisions: the cleanliness of the earth of those who follow in days to come may well depend upon the choices made today.

A Word on Judgment

Before turning to the issue of stewardship, one important point needs to be made about objective morality and judgment. While Tolkien makes it clear that there is a real difference between "good and ill" and, furthermore, that it is a person's part to learn to discern, or judge, what that difference is and to act accordingly, the characters of his story are also warned strongly not to judge one another. That is, they can (and indeed must) judge between good and evil *actions*—and they themselves will be subject to the judgment of the Authority for how well they choose—but they are not given their own authority to judge other *people*. Frodo is told this lesson in a rather stern fashion by Gandalf when he suggests that Gollum ought to have been put to death for his crimes:

> "Do you mean to say that you, and the Elves, have let him live after all those horrible deeds [asks Frodo]? Now at any rate he is as bad as an Orc, and just an enemy. He deserves death."
> "Deserves it [Gandalf replies]! I daresay he does. Many that live deserve death. And some that die deserve life. Can you give it to them? Then do not be too eager to deal out death in judgement." (FOTR, p. 69)

Note that the command not to judge other people may be motivated by at least two different beliefs. It may be motivated by a belief that there is no objective morality by which actions may be judged. If all of our decisions come down at the end to mere personal preference, such as what flavor of ice cream we are going to eat, then it is ridiculous to judge another person for any particular decision he or she might make. Holding tolerance as the highest (and perhaps only) virtue makes perfect sense if morality is purely subjective; *of course* we must "tolerate" somebody choosing chocolate over vanilla. This understanding makes the command to not judge a very popular one in a society that has rejected moral absolutes, and whose only virtue is tolerance. It is therefore not surprising that in the entire long dialogue between Gandalf and Frodo, in which the wizard tells the Hobbit much of the history of the Ring—a dialogue from which many lines had to be cut for the sake of the screenplay—that this one line of Gandalf's would be especially chosen to *remain* (word for word) in the script of Peter Jackson's film (though it is moved to a different scene). It is a good line, and one true to Gandalf's character and to Tolkien himself.

It is clear, however, that the reason Tolkien gives for abstaining from "dealing out death in judgment" is not that there is no objective moral basis for judgment. As an infantryman in World War I, and later as a citizen of England in a war against Hitler's Nazi Germany, Tolkien confronted what he understood to be real evil in his world, and he understood that evil was something to be opposed. If nothing else, *The Lord of the Rings* forces the reader to confront real evil in Middle-earth. We see it not only in Mordor but in Isengard, in Bree, and later in the Shire itself. Tolerance *of evil* is *not* a virtue. A decision by one of the enemies of Sauron, such as Boromir, to make a personal choice to possess and use the Ring is no more to be tolerated than Sauron's enslavement of all Middle-earth. In short, it is as clear as day in Tolkien's writing that there are moral absolutes, and Gandalf's own words acknowledge such in that very quote: there are some who "deserve death." Thus Tolkien's *reason* for sparing judgment on others is *not* that there is no objective basis for such a judgment, or that people don't *deserve* to be judged. Rather, the reason for not judging—or, more specifically, for not dealing out *death* in judgment—is that none in Middle-earth has the authority to enact such justice. For one thing, no finite being in Middle-earth—not even Gandalf—has the wisdom to know fully who deserves life and who deserves death. And even lesser acts of judgment may often be beyond the wisdom of one person. In a comment Faramir makes to Gollum after the incident at the Forbidden Pool, we see something like this at work: "Nothing?" Faramir asks, when Gollum claims to have done nothing wrong. "Have you never done anything worthy of binding or of worse punishment? However, that is not for me to judge, happily" (TT, p. 298). First, Faramir is saying that there are moral crimes worthy of punishment, and second, he is guessing that Gollum has committed some of these. Yet Faramir is also confessing a lack of the knowledge and wisdom necessary to judge Gollum for anything beyond a very limited area in which he has been invested with authority to judge.

A second reason that nobody within Middle-earth can claim the ultimate authority of judgment—the sentencing to life or death—is that life, like free will, is so valuable a gift, given by Ilúvatar himself. It is too valuable for one person to take from another. Judgment must be served at times, as Mandos does with Fëanor. For a society to function, it must have laws and a means of enforcing those laws. However dealing out *death* in judgment is beyond mortal authority.

Third, and finally, none in Middle-earth have fully lived up to the moral law. In other words, everybody is deserving of some judgment, and so who can act as the judge? Tolkien spells this last point out in one of his letters, even as he affirms that there is an objective moral basis for judgment:

> Gollum was pitiable, but he ended in persistent wickedness, and the fact that this worked good was no credit to him. His marvellous courage and endurance, as great as Frodo and Sam's or greater, being devoted to evil was portentous, but not honourable. I am afraid, whatever our beliefs, we have to face the fact that there are persons who yield to temptation, reject their chances of nobility or salvation, and appear to be "damnable" . . . But we who are all "in the same boat" must not usurp the Judge. (Letters, p. 234)

Tolkien is explicitly saying that Gollum, though he might rightly be pitied, is nonetheless wicked and deserving of death. As with Fëanor, good is brought out of his wickedness, but also as with Fëanor, that is "no credit to him"; it does not change the fact that what he chose is evil. And here Tolkien is very explicit in holding views that are immensely unpopular today: "Whatever our beliefs, we have to face the fact that there are persons who yield to temptation . . . and appear to be 'damnable.'" This thread of thought, spelled out explicitly in this letter, runs implicitly through *The Lord of the Rings*. But we must also realize that "we who are all 'in the same boat' must not usurp the Judge."

The Steward of Middle-earth

And now we turn to the issue of stewardship, which is an important concept in *The Lord of the Rings*. It is important, in part, because the stakes are high. The greater the evil that must be confronted, the more wisdom is necessary to make good choices. The greater are the gifts that one is given—with freedom being the greatest of them all—the more wisdom is needed to use those gifts well. Stewardship refers to the responsibility one has for those things that have been placed under one's care. The word *steward* comes from the Old English *stigweard*, which itself is derived from two words: *stig* and *weard*. A stig is a hall, as in a mead hall or, later, an inn. *Weard* means "lord" or "keeper," and has a modern derivative in *warden*. Thus, a steward, or stigweard, is the keeper or warden of the mead hall. The word implies a certain set of responsibilities. The Anglo-Saxon stigweard was a host in charge of taking care of the guests of the hall. In *The Fellowship of the Ring*, Barliman Butterbur is something of a steward in this sense. He is the host of an inn, or mead hall of sorts (the Prancing Pony of Bree), and is responsible to his guests. This can be seen especially in his response after the attack of the Black Riders. "I'll do what I can," he tells the Hobbits, and he does. He buys a new pony for them (though he must pay three times its value for it), and he gives Merry another eighteen pence as compensation for his lost animals (FOTR, p. 191). In short, though he was not to blame for the losses, as the innkeeper (steward), he takes personal responsibility to make reparations to Mr. Frodo and company.

In its modern meaning, a steward is one who manages the possessions or affairs of another, oftentimes in the absence of that other. To be a steward of something implies both that you have a responsibility over that thing and that it belongs to another. A steward has authority, but it is an authority granted by and subject to some other higher authority. As Gandalf says to Denethor:

> "Well my lord Steward, it is your task to keep some kingdom still against that event [the return of the king], which few now look to see. In that task you shall have all the aid that you are pleased to ask for. But I will say this: the rule of no realm is mine, neither of Gondor nor any other, great or small. But all worthy things that are in peril as the world now stands, those are my care. And for my part, I shall not wholly fail of my task, though Gondor should perish, if anything passes through this night that can still grow fair or bear fruit and flower again in days to come. For I also am a steward. Did you not know?" (ROTK, pp. 30–31)

This is as close as Gandalf comes to identifying what his own role and purpose are in Middle-earth: he is a steward. Of what? Of "all worthy things." Of anything "that can still grow fair or bear fruit or flower." In short, he is the steward of Middle-earth itself, or of all that is good in Middle-earth. His responsibility—his "task," as he himself suggests—is to care for those things and to make good and wise choices concerning them. As the imagery suggests, he is like a gardener caring for a garden, helping it grow to maturity and to produce fruit. Thus, the essence of stewardship is really the essence of moral responsibility. But Gandalf's task is also to train others to good stewardship: first, to help the people of Middle-earth to realize that they *are* stewards, each one of them, and then to help them grow in the wisdom to be *good* stewards. This is at the heart of many of his speeches. In their freedom, the people of Middle-earth are responsible for what they do with *the time that is given them, or those years wherein they are set,* and also with the skills and abilities with which they have been endowed, or *what is in them.* They are stewards of these things—time, skills, freedom, abilities—as Gandalf himself is a steward. To be a steward, however, is to acknowledge the over-authority of another, just as Denethor as Steward of Gondor is (or ought to be) responsible to the king of Gondor if he should ever return: "to keep some kingdom still against that event."

Here is where there is a sharp contrast between Gandalf and Denethor, who holds the official role as Steward of Gondor and yet does not hold to the meaning of the word *steward*. For Denethor has begun to see himself more as lord (*weard*) than as steward (*stigweard*): "Yet the *Lord* of Gondor is not to be made the tool of other men's purposes," he says of himself to Gandalf. "And the *rule* of Gondor, my lord, is mine and no other man's, unless the king should come again" (ROTK, p. 30, emphasis mine). Although he gives lip service to the possibility that "the king should come again," he does not act as if that is even desirable. He is more concerned with his own rule and power. Indeed, when the king does return, Denethor will not even consider his claim to the throne. "With the left hand thou wouldst use me for a little while as a shield against Mordor," he says to Gandalf, "and with the right bring up this Ranger of the North to supplant me." He sees the Return of the King not as the hoped-for event for which he is to prepare, but as a threat to "supplant" his power. Ironically, it is in clinging to the title of Steward that he refuses to do the very thing a steward is called to do: to uphold the king's authority: "I will not step down to be the dotard chamberlain of an upstart. . . . I will not bow to such a one, last of a ragged house long bereft of lordship and dignity" (ROTK, p. 130). He will neither "bow" nor "step down."

Ultimately, under the pretence of stewardship, Denethor claims an authority that not even the wise kings of old had: to take his own life and the life of his son.

> "Authority is not given to you, Steward of Gondor, to order the hour of your death," answered Gandalf. "And only the heathen kings, under the domination of the Dark Power, did thus, slaying themselves in pride and despair, murdering their kin to ease their own death." (ROTK, p. 129)

It is interesting that Tolkien uses the word *heathen* to describe Denethor's behavior; a heathen is an "unbeliever," one who does not acknowledge God. If Tolkien really meant this word, then it implies that Denethor's real fault is deeper than his refusal to acknowledge the authority of a king; it is a refusal to acknowledge the higher Authority that is over even a king. Amandil, the grandfather of Isildur, in speaking of Ilúvatar says: "For there is but one loyalty from which no man can be absolved in heart for any cause" (TS, p. 340). In any case, a central point Gandalf is making is that there is an authority that a steward has and an authority that a steward does not have. The moral responsibility of those in Middle-earth is to be good stewards of their gifts—that is, of those things under the authority that has been given them—and not to usurp authority that is not theirs. Denethor eventually fails in both of these.

Gandalf, unlike Denethor, is the model of the ideal steward. He does not claim any lordship or authority over others. "The rule of no realm is mine," he says, and his actions validate that claim. Earlier I quoted a personal letter in which Tolkien himself describes who Gandalf is: "There are naturally no precise modern terms to say what he was. I wd. venture to say that he was an *incarnate* 'angel.'" We then explored the nature of Gandalf's wisdom in light of what Tolkien shared in this letter. This same passage also gives insight into Gandalf's role and nature as a steward: a role that is closely tied to his wisdom. In his letter, Tolkien leads into this description of Gandalf by explaining something about Gandalf's sacrifice at Khazad-dûm:

> Gandalf really "died," and was changed: for that seems to me the only real cheating, to represent anything that can be called "death" as making no difference. "I am G. the *White*, who has returned from death." Probably he should rather have said to Wormtongue: "I have not passed through death (*not* "fire and flood") to bandy crooked words with a serving-man." And so on. I might say much more, but it would only be in (perhaps tedious) elucidation of the "mythological" ideas in my mind. . . . G. is not, of course, a human being (Man or Hobbit). There are naturally no precise modern terms to say what he was. I wd. venture to say that he was an *incarnate* "angel." . . .

. . . At this point in the fabulous history the purpose was precisely to limit and hinder their exhibition of "power" on the physical plane, and so that they should do what they were primarily sent for: train, advise, instruct, arouse the hearts and minds of those threatened by Sauron to a resistance with their own strengths; and not just to do the job for them. . . .

[But] the crisis had become too grave and needed an enhancement of power. So Gandalf sacrificed himself, was accepted, and enhanced, and returned. (Letters, pp. 201–3)

This comment speaks to two different aspects of Gandalf's stewardship. We see that his own power is enhanced after his death and return. Some of the limitations on his exhibition of 'angelic' power have been removed, which is to say he is now more powerful on the physical plane. As a result, he is now responsible for the stewardship of an even greater gift, namely his *enhanced* power. We might say that Gandalf had proven to be a faithful steward with the gifts he had originally been given, and so he was given even greater responsibility. And he remains a good steward. He does not use his enhanced power to claim more rule or authority over others. Indeed, his relationship to those around him remains fundamentally the same as before his power was enhanced. He does not command, but as we saw before, he trains, advises, instructs. And, most especially, he arouses "the hearts and minds of those threatened by Sauron to a resistance with their own strengths." This is what he does with Théoden, first in Meduseld and later on the way to Isengard. As we mentioned earlier, it is also what he does on the walls of Minas Tirith. It is what he does with the Hobbits throughout the Quest, especially Frodo and Pippin. In other words, inasmuch as it is Gandalf's role to be a steward, it is also his role to train those around him to be stewards themselves. His goal is to see each person use his or her own time and abilities to fight against Mordor. He wants each person to understand the moral responsibility that comes with free will, and to choose well. This is why he does not do people's jobs for them. If he did others' jobs for them, so that they needn't use their own strength, then he would be removing their moral responsibility. It might make Gandalf's life simpler and accomplish his "military" goals more quickly if he were to exercise more power and do more, but his goal is not to make his own life simple. His ultimate aim is for the moral good of those around him, which is to say for their training in moral responsibility.

This returns us to the earlier conclusion that moral victory is more important than military victory, and to the importance of free will and choice. If there is no objective right and wrong, then one is free to win the military victory by whatever means is possible; power is what matters, and not right and wrong. This is the path Saruman takes. Likewise, if there is no right or wrong—if all choices are equally good—then choice itself and our free will to make choices become less important; it is not the choosing that matters but only the outcome. But in Tolkien's Middle-earth, there is objective morality. There is a standard for judgment. As a result, moral decisions are important.

7

Hope and Despair

I have already mentioned two questions that must be dealt with in Tolkien's work. One is the question of the nature of the One Ring: its power and its evil. The other is the nature of Gandalf himself: his power and his purpose. A third topic that should also be a part of any discussion of Tolkien's works is that of hope and despair. Now, many of the comments one could make here, though true and important, would also be somewhat obvious: comments to the effect that hope is very important and is shown to be a virtue, while despair is the tool of the Enemy and has deadly consequences. Nonetheless, hope and despair play important roles in Tolkien's writings, and so at least some comment needs to be made about them as they relate to the central themes of this book: free will, objective morality, and the importance of moral victory over military victory.

We should begin with definitions. The word *hope*, like many of Tolkien's favorite words (*free, doom, freedom, steward*, etc.), comes from Old English. It is derived from the Anglo-Saxon word *hopian*. Some think of hope as little more than wishful thinking without any necessary grounding in reality, but it is more than that. Hope is a *belief* that something desirable may actually happen. It is not just a groundless wish, but an expectation of an event with some *confidence in its possibility*. Tolkien gives a definition of hope through the mouth of Andreth, a wise-woman of the First Age of Middle-earth. Hope, she explains, is "an expectation of good, which though uncertain has some foundation in what is known" (MR, p. 320). There are, of course, many levels of confidence that one may have in that expectation, ranging from a "fool's hope" to a solid confidence, but there must be at least some belief that the desired outcome is possible. For example, it might be very nice if somebody came along and gave me several million dollars, but I can't say that I have any *hope* of that happening. This is illustrated by the fact that when one has no realistic expectation of the desired outcome and yet looks for it anyway, then what one has is not even called "hope" but rather "hope against hope."

Despair, on the other hand, is a lack of hope. More than that, it is an *utter* lack of hope: a loss of every shred of belief that the desired outcome may come about. Despair is the antithesis of hope. "Despair," as Gandalf tells the Council of Elrond, "is only for those who see the end beyond all doubt." (Interestingly enough, considering Tolkien's preference for Anglo-Saxon words, our modern word *despair* comes not from Old English, but from Old French *desperer*, which is from the Latin *sperare*, meaning "to hope," prefixed by *de-* to indicate an *un-hope* or *anti-hope*.) One resounding theme in Tolkien's works is that when people lose hope—when they give in to despair—they lose the ability, or strength, or motivation to choose good over evil. Thus, if our moral choices are of great importance, then so is our hope. It is therefore not surprising that hope—along with faith and love—is one of the three great virtues of 1 Corinthians 13. And, of course, *hope* is a verb as well as a noun; it is something we do as well as have.

Gandalf, the Enemy of Sauron

To see the importance of hope in (and to) Middle-earth, we need look no further than Gandalf. What is Gandalf's task? As we saw earlier, he encourages and challenges each person to

do what he can—to use what strength he has—to fight against
the work of Sauron. Tolkien describes this also in a passage
in "Of the Rings of Power and the Third Age," which his son
Christopher included in *The Silmarillion:*

> But afterwards it was said among the Elves that [the Istari,
> whom men called Wizards] were messengers sent by the Lords
> of the West to contest the power of Sauron, if he should arise
> again, *and to move Elves and Men and all living things of good
> will to valiant deeds.* (TS, p. 372, emphasis mine)

In other words, as we saw, Gandalf was not there to do Men's
work for them, but to move them to do the work themselves.
He is there to help each person grow and develop. Círdan,
Lord of the Havens, understood this and gave to Gandalf the
Elven-ring Narya, one of the three rings of power, to aid him
in that purpose, saying: "For this is the Ring of Fire, and here-
with, maybe, thou shalt rekindle hearts to the valour of old in
a world that grows chill" (TS, p. 378). Círdan doesn't say that
with Narya Gandalf himself will perform mighty deeds, but
rather that he shall be an instrument in rekindling or moving
the hearts of others to great deeds.

So how does Gandalf accomplish that? How does he rekindle
hearts in a world grown chill? In part he does it by helping
Men (as well as Hobbits, Dwarves, and Elves) to see the moral
importance of their choices and, in part, by giving them wisdom
to make those choices, but a primary way that Gandalf works
is simply by bringing hope. He brings hope to the gathered
leaders at the Council of Elrond, telling them that their path
is not one of despair, but rather one of hope, and that what
appears to be folly is only a cloak that will hide that hope from
the Enemy. He brings hope to the Fellowship that sets out from
Rivendell. "So great was Frodo's delight at this announcement
[that Gandalf would join the Fellowship] that Gandalf left the
window-sill, where he had been sitting, and took off his hat
and bowed" (FOTR, p. 286). How important is Gandalf to the
Fellowship's hope? When he falls in Moria, the eight remaining
companions lose much of theirs. "Farewell, Gandalf!" Aragorn

cried at his death. "What hope have we without you? We must do without hope" (FOTR, p. 347). And when he returns, the hope of the remaining members of the Fellowship is renewed many times over. "No, my heart will not yet despair," Pippin says. "Gandalf fell and has returned and is with us" (ROTK, p. 39). The list could go on. The effect is the same wherever Gandalf goes. He rekindles the valor of Rohan by bringing hope to King Théoden and, through the king, to all his people. "It is not so dark here," realizes Théoden, once Gandalf has come and released him from Saruman's spell. As Pippin suggests, "No stroke would have been struck in Rohan . . . but for Gandalf" (ROTK, p. 39). And Gandalf brings hope to Minas Tirith, as can be seen when he walks the walls with Prince Imrahil. "Wherever [Gandalf] came men's hearts would lift again, and the winged shadows pass from memory" (ROTK, p. 98). No matter how dark and desperate the times are, Gandalf never abandons hope. Only once, when he hears from Faramir that Frodo has taken the path toward Cirith Ungol, does his heart *almost* fail him. Yet even then, he finds a reason for hope. "And yet in truth," he says, "I believe that the news that Faramir brings has some hope in it" (ROTK, p. 88).

By contrast, the Nazgûl bring with them the power of despair, and it is more deadly than any other weapon they wield. Gandalf describes the Lord of the Nazgûl as a "spear of terror in the hand of Sauron, shadow of despair" and, later, as the "Captain of Despair" (ROTK, p. 92). When the winged shadows of the Nazgûl pass, those nearby "are stricken with a passing dread," and the less stout-hearted quail and weep (ROTK, p. 89). When the Lord of the Nazgûl is killed by Éowyn, the hearts of those in Minas Tirith are "lifted up in such a hope as they had not known since the darkness came out of the East" (ROTK, p. 132). Thus the greatest conflict between Gandalf and the Nine is not the confrontation at the gates of Minas Tirith (which never resolves into battle), nor is it Gandalf's forays out onto the fields to rescue Faramir and his men. Rather, it is the fight for the hearts of the defenders: the battle over whether they will despair or hold on to hope. For where the Nazgûl go, despair comes. "For yet another weapon, swifter than hunger, the Lord of the Dark Tower had: dread and despair" (ROTK pp. 96–97). And though Gandalf brings hope with him wherever *he* goes, he is only one, while the Nazgûl are nine. When Gandalf leaves any place of defense, "the shadows [close] on men again, and their hearts [go] cold." And without the hope that Gandalf brings, "the valour of Gondor wither[s] into ash" (ROTK, p. 98). Without hope, there is not strength to resist evil.

Even Denethor, at some level, understands this: "In what is left, let all who fight the Enemy in their fashion be at one, and keep hope while they may, and after hope still the hardihood to die free" (ROTK, p. 87). Unfortunately, even as Théoden moves from despair to hope, Denethor falls from hope to despair. In the same breath in which he counsels his people to keep hope, he is already looking ahead to what he sees as an inevitable loss of hope. He is already thinking about death. "The fool's hope has failed," he says (ROTK, p. 97). The comment is meant to disparage Gandalf, but it is a moment more revealing of Denethor's faults than of the wizard's. Later his despair is complete. "For thy hope is but ignorance," he tells Gandalf. "Against the Power that now arises there is no victory" (ROTK, p. 129). That Denethor's fall is a fall *into evil* cannot be denied. However, his evil is not, like Saruman's or Wormtongue's, an *intentional* act of treachery. He does not make any pact with Sauron, nor does he *desire* for Gondor to fall to Mordor. To the end of his life, he sees Sauron as the Enemy. Yet in his fall from hope, Denethor does do great wrong; he inadvertently chooses the very way of the Enemy whom he despises. He not only gives up commanding the defenses of the city, but seeks to take his own life and the life of his son. "Better to burn sooner than late," he cries, "for burn we must" (ROTK, p. 98). In looking at the world through the Enemy's eyes—the view shown to him through the palantír—Denethor comes to see defeat and burning as inevitable. He loses all hope, and that is the heart of his fall, for despair is ever the tool of Sauron.

As an aside, we might also step back and view hope from the reader's viewpoint, in addition to the viewpoint of the characters within the story. From the perspective of the narrative itself, the presence or absence of hope is very important.

For example, that Tolkien leads the readers to see the great importance of the hope inspired by Gandalf adds greatly to the trauma that we feel when Gandalf himself nearly loses hope at the news from Faramir that Frodo had set off with Gollum toward Cirith Ungol:

> As his story was unfolded . . . Pippin became aware that Gandalf's hands were trembling as they clutched the carven wood. White they seemed now and very old, and as he looked at them, suddenly with a thrill of fear Pippin knew that Gandalf, Gandalf himself, was troubled, even afraid. (ROTK, p. 85)

The point, of course, is that if Gandalf is troubled and afraid, then we all should be—not merely the other characters in the story, but the readers also. How afraid? It is the only point of the story when we hear Gandalf confess, "There never was much hope. . . . Just a fool's hope, as I have been told." And a moment later he adds, "Just now, Pippin, my heart almost failed me." (ROTK, p. 88). This is one way the author keeps the narrative tension so alive, and makes the hearts of the readers nearly fail with Gandalf's.

Ultimately, however, Denethor is wrong in calling Gandalf's hope a "fool's hope." Though Gandalf himself repeats Denethor's words, and acknowledges the great odds against them, he still holds to that hope. For in some important way, he does not truly believe it is a fool's hope only. His hope is never merely a matter of wishful thinking, but as we saw earlier it is a hope based in the truth. Yet in *truth* Faramir's message has *hope* in it, he tells Pippin. It is as though, despite whatever bad news comes his way, Gandalf *chooses* not to despair. *Hope* for him really is a verb. How does he do this? And why? Unlike Denethor, Gandalf refuses to see the world only as Sauron would have us see it. In his wisdom, he sees other forces at work. As he tells Pippin:

> "For it seems clear that our Enemy has opened his war at last and made the first move while Frodo was still free. So now for many days he will have his eye turned this way and that, away

from his own land. And yet, Pippin, I feel from afar his haste and fear. He has begun sooner than he would." (ROTK, p. 88)

Gandalf sees the bigger picture (a mark of wisdom). His hope is not a hope that denies reality but one that sees more of reality. In particular, he sees the spiritual plane as well as the material. Indeed, Gandalf's wisdom and his hope are closely united. And so convinced and so convincing is he in that hope that the Captains of the West are willing to follow him. "I do not bid you despair, as [Denethor] did, but to ponder the truth in these words," he tells them (ROTK, p. 154). And if the wisdom of Gandalf is not enough to convince the reader that there is a real hope, then the outcome of the story should convince us in hindsight.

Hope, Free Will, the One Ring, and Éowyn

Returning then briefly to the nature of the One Ring, I claimed earlier that the essential power of the Ring is the power to dominate other wills. It is the power to rule and enslave: the power to take away freedom. Gandalf's task, by contrast, encourages people to use their freedom. His task is to train and instruct those in Middle-earth that they may use their native strength to oppose Sauron's evil. There is, however, another way we could describe the essential power of the Ring. We might also say that the power of Sauron—which must be closely tied to the power of his Ring—is the power to bring despair. By contrast, the power of Gandalf, the "enemy of Sauron," is the power to bring hope. This is essentially what I have claimed over the previous few paragraphs. This is not a contradiction to the earlier claim that the power of the Ring is the power of domination. Despair and slavery go hand in hand, just as hope and freedom do. We might even say that despair is the central weapon by which Sauron dominates other wills, while hope is the essential tool that brings real freedom. Domination is the purpose of the Ring, and despair is the means by which that domination is accomplished.

This is shown to us, for example, in the illnesses of Éowyn and Théoden, discussed earlier in this book. As Éowyn is a complex character, so is the "illness" she suffers and from which she is eventually healed. Earlier we noted that Éowyn's illness is in some way the opposite of Théoden's: while he is afraid of death and thereby suffers shame, she is afraid of shame and seeks glory in death. Ultimately, however, the two illnesses are rooted in the same source, namely, a loss of hope. Théoden and Éowyn both have fallen to despair. Théoden is lost in darkness, unable to see the light. He is so hopeless that he is paralyzed; his inaction is a fundamental loss of his free will to act and is brought about by his despair. This is why Wormtongue encourages Théoden's feelings of hopelessness, so that he will remain inactive and continue to choose *not* to choose. Éowyn's case is similar. She is, as Merry observed, "seeking death, having no hope" (ROTK, p. 116). In her own words, she stands "upon some dreadful brink," and it is "utterly dark in the abyss" before her feet (ROTK, p. 240). The fact that despair is at the heart of Éowyn's illness can be seen in the words of Aragorn in the Houses of Healing when he calls her back to wakefulness. "I have, maybe, the power to heal her body, and to recall her from the dark valley. But to what she will awake: hope, or forgetfulness, or despair, I do not know. And if to despair, then she will die" (ROTK, pp. 144–45). How important is hope? Without it, Théoden is paralyzed. Without it, Éowyn will die.

At the surface, Théoden's healing comes when he discovers that he is not as weak as he thought. At a deeper level, however, it comes when Gandalf reveals the truth and restores his hope. *It is not so dark there. He has allies he does not even know about.* It is not so much Théoden's strength that enables him to find hope, but rather it is his renewed hope—captured in the beautiful moment in front of Edoras when "suddenly through a rent in the clouds behind them a shaft of sun stabbed down"—that enables him to find strength.

Likewise, Éowyn's healing is revealed *on the surface* when she renounces her pursuit of glory in battle. Yet the source of her healing is much deeper. It is truth and hope, which begin

to be restored in the Houses of Healing. In part it is the truth
about herself, revealed to her by Faramir, which "at last she
understood." But it is also truth about hope, or truth that
renews and restores hope. She comes to realize what Tolkien
writes in his essay "On Fairy-Stories," that universal final defeat
is not the ultimate truth about the universe, but rather "Joy
beyond the walls of the world" (FS, p. 153). Where Éowyn, in
her despair, sees a "Darkness Unescapable," Faramir speaks
to her of a "hope and joy" that cannot be denied. "White Lady
of Rohan," he tells her, "in this hour I do not believe that any
darkness will endure" (ROTK, pp. 240–41). Thus is Éowyn's
hope reborn, and this is both the means and the end of her
healing. As he did with her uncle Théoden, Tolkien symbolizes
Éowyn's renewed hope and healing with the imagery of a shaft
of light piercing the dark clouds:

> And so they stood on the walls of the City of Gondor, and a great
> wind rose and blew, and their hair, raven and golden, streamed
> out mingling in the air. And the Shadow departed, and the Sun
> was unveiled, and light leaped forth; and the waters of Anduin
> shone like silver, and in all the houses of the City men sang for
> the joy that welled up in their hearts from what source they
> could not tell. (ROTK, p. 241)

The shadow—the power of Sauron to bring despair, and thus
to enslave—departs. The sun is unveiled and leaps forth. Hope
is restored, and when hope returns the hearts of men and
women are filled with a new strength to do what it is they are
called to do.

8

Themes of Salvation

At this point, as the title of this chapter suggests, we are ready to touch on a dangerous subject—dangerous for a writer discussing Tolkien's work, that is, because it approaches ground that might be called *religious*. J. R. R. Tolkien largely avoided anything explicitly religious in his own fiction. He gives three criticisms of Arthurian legend that make it inadequate as a mythology for England (Letters, p. 144). The first is that it is not English enough; though associated with the soil of Britain, it is not associated with the English people, culture, language, etc. Second, its fairy elements (in Tolkien's opinion) are too lavish, incoherent, and repetitive. His third criticism, and his most important—what he called its "fatal error"—is that Arthurian legend contains too much *explicit* religion: religion in the same form as in the primary world. (In the final chapter we will deal more with *why* explicit religion is a problem in myth and fantasy. For now we need only note that Tolkien was critical of the presence of too much explicit religion in Arthurian legend. Thus, a critic must follow a careful path in observing meanings within Tolkien's own work that bear what one might call a religious significance.) In a similar vein, Tolkien had a well-known dislike for allegory, and probably especially for religious allegory. "But I cordially dislike allegory in all its manifestations," he writes in his "Foreword to the Second Edition," "and always have done so since I grew old and wary enough to detect its presence" (FOTR, p. 7).

So certainly we would not want to imply anything explicitly allegorical in *The Lord of the Rings;* to do so would be to contradict the author of the work we are seeking to elucidate. And yet, though he disliked allegory, Tolkien felt—as he goes on to say in the foreword—that his works should have "applicability to the thought and experience of readers." His stories are full of meaning, and furthermore, much of that meaning relates directly to themes that are theological, philosophical, and even religious in nature. As Tolkien writes in the same letter in which he criticizes Arthurian legend for its explicit religion, he affirms that myth and fairy-stories "must contain elements of moral and religious truth (or error)." In writing this, Tolkien is suggesting that there is an objective truth in the universe, even with respect to religion. Religious claims may be true or false. Not only that, but myth *must* contain elements of that truth (or attempts at it). However, the religious elements should not be "in the known form of the primarily 'real' world" (Letters, p. 144). In other words, Tolkien's works may be replete with important philosophical and religious themes and reflections, but we should not expect to find them (usually) expressed in the same language and terminology, or with the same external practices, as in our primary world.

As Tolkien himself suggests toward the end of his essay "On Fairy-Stories," part of the danger of the subject we explore in this chapter does not stem from its lack of importance, but rather from it being too important.[1] It was vitally important to Tolkien, anyway, and that alone makes it worth exploring in his writing. Furthermore, the subject of this chapter flows naturally from the discussions earlier in this book, which them-

---

1. Toward the end of this essay, Tolkien addresses the "Christian Story" contained in the "Gospels." Before doing so, he comments, "It is a serious and dangerous matter. It is presumptuous of me to touch upon such a theme; but if by grace what I say has in any respect any validity, it is, of course, only one facet of a truth incalculably rich" (FS, p. 155).

selves—if I have reasoned correctly so far—are fundamental to the understanding of the story and are fully woven into its fabric. For Tolkien's writing, as we have now seen, clearly denies the materialist presuppositions that lead to determinism. In the worldview reflected in the mythology of Middle-earth, people are more than physical beings. And if more than physical, then what do we call that "more"? The usual word to use is *spiritual:* Man and Elf both are creatures of spirit as well as of body. Tolkien writes in his commentary on "Athrabeth Finrod Ah Andreth" in *Morgoth's Ring:* "There are on Earth 'incarnate' creatures, Elves and Men: these are made of a union of hröa and fëa (roughly but not exactly equivalent to 'body' and 'soul')" (MR, p. 330).

While the natures of the bodies and spirits of Elves and Men differ slightly, as we saw from *The Silmarillion,* it is clear that both races have a spiritual nature in addition to the physical. Men have mortal bodies that die, but their spirits live on and "leave the world," eventually to take part in the Second Music of the Ainur. Elves do not die a natural death (of illness or old age), but their bodies may be slain, and if this happens their spirits are gathered to the halls of Mandos. The point is that in both cases, with Elves and Men, their nature is more than physical, and individuals continue on as *self-aware individuals* even after bodily death. But if their spiritual natures are eternal, while their physical (or bodily) natures are mortal and finite, then it would be reasonable to conclude that our spiritual natures are the more important—infinitely more important, in fact, to the degree that they last infinitely longer. If this is true, it relates to our earlier observation that moral victory is more important than military victory. Why? Because the moral life is the spiritual life—or at least it shows the quality (good or evil) of that spiritual life. Moral victory is more important precisely because it is of a spiritual kind, whereas military victory is of a bodily kind, and spiritual natures are the more important because they are eternal. What we really begin to see, in fact, is that there are two aspects of the created world: a spiritual plane and a physical plane. Both are real, and they are interrelated; what happens on the spiritual plane affects what happens on the physical, and vice versa. The moral battles can be said to take place on the spiritual plane, while the physical battles are on—well, the physical plane. One of the greatest marks of wisdom in Middle-earth can be understood as an eternal perspective: a realization that reality includes both of these planes, and that the spiritual one is the more important.

This spiritual reality also relates to objective morality, and the fact that the choices of Man, Dwarf, and Elf are subject to *judgment*. What does it mean to be judged? With respect to our moral battles, does judgment have to do with the definition of victory? Many of the answers become clearer in an exploration of the notion of "salvation" in *The Lord of the Rings*. Indeed, the very concept of spiritual (moral) victory that is at the heart of Tolkien's writing may be defined by this word, *salvation*.

The Salvation of Boromir

As I said, writing about salvation in *The Lord of the Rings* is a dangerous task—dangerous in part because it has clear religious connotations. In particular, the notion of salvation is fundamentally important to the Christian faith (including both Catholic forms of Christianity, such as was practiced by J. R. R. Tolkien, and Protestant forms) and thus a discussion of salvation is likely to tread religious ground. It is also dangerous in the specific examples that follow because the words *salvation* (or *saved*) and, its opposite, *damnation* are not the words Tolkien uses in his fiction to describe this spiritual victory. Nonetheless, he uses many similar words and concepts—for example, *cured* and *escaped* and their opposite, *fallen*—that imply a spiritual salvation. They merely do so without using the explicit form of religion in our own world (although at times, as we shall see, Tolkien comes very close to that form).

To start with, salvation implies being saved *from* something, presumably from something bad. If we are speaking of bodily salvation, then the ultimate salvation is that which is from death. If we are speaking of spiritual salvation, then the objective reality of good suggests a salvation from evil. That is the starting point for Boromir, as Frodo realizes after his attempt to take the Ring by force: "Boromir has fallen into evil," Frodo contemplates, as he tries to decide his course (FOTR, p. 418). This is, of course, a statement about objective morality. It also must be a statement about spiritual (and not physical) reality, because at the time Frodo is saying this, nothing physically bad has yet happened to Boromir. So for Boromir to be saved, he must be saved spiritually from this evil.

This is precisely what happens, although Boromir himself might not realize it. We see this in his dying words, as well as in Aragorn's reply to those words:

> "Farewell, Aragorn! Go to Minas Tirith and save my people! I have failed."
> "No!" said Aragorn, taking his hand and kissing his brow. "You have conquered. Few have gained such a victory. Be at peace!" (TT, p. 16)

This is a short passage, and yet it speaks more to the central ideas of this book than almost any other. Boromir sees himself as having failed. And in every physical and military way, he has failed. He fails in his task to bring Aragorn and the Sword-that-was-Broken back to Minas Tirith. He fails to bring Isildur's Bane back to his father. Indeed, he fails to return to Minas Tirith at all. In short, he fails to do anything to save Gondor from military defeat. (Or at least at the time of his death, this would seem to be the case.) He even fails in the last thing he attempts: to save Merry and Pippin from capture by the Orcs. From a physical or bodily viewpoint, he suffers the greatest possible failure: he dies. So in the material plane, Boromir's final words are true.

Yet Aragorn contradicts him. "No!" he says emphatically. He tells Boromir that he has "conquered," that he has won a "victory." Of what victory does Aragorn speak? Not a military victory, but a moral one; not a bodily victory, but a spiritual one. Whereas Boromir is speaking about the material plane, Aragorn is speaking of the spiritual plane. Now one might suggest that Aragorn's words are little more than comforting sounds for a dying man, devoid of any more significant meaning. (I have heard this said on more than one occasion.) This is worth considering. Suppose for a moment we were to ignore how important words are to Aragorn, and to suggest that he is of a kind that would speak falsely in order to make somebody feel better—an assumption that altogether misses the mark with Aragorn. Even then, the point that Boromir, in his death, has won an important victory could still be made from the words of Gandalf and Faramir. As Gandalf says, when he hears how Boromir has fallen:

> "It was a sore trial for such a man: a warrior, and a lord of men. Galadriel told me that he was in peril. But he escaped in the end. I am glad. It was not in vain that the young hobbits came with us, if only for Boromir's sake." (TT, p. 99)

And Faramir, in discussing his brother's death with Frodo and Sam, comments:

> "Now I loved him dearly and would gladly avenge his death, yet I knew him well. . . .
> ". . . Whether he erred or no, of this I am sure: he died well, achieving some good thing. His face was more beautiful even than in life." (TT, pp. 277–78)

Whatever motive we may place on Aragorn's words, we cannot say that Gandalf is merely comforting a dying man, since his words are spoken several days later. Yet he says Boromir has "escaped." Likewise with Faramir, who is painfully honest about his brother's faults and yet sees from his brother's face that in his death he has moved from the "evil" that Frodo has seen in him to "some good thing."

So we must agree that Boromir, in some important spiritual sense, has "conquered," "won a victory," and "escaped," having achieved "some good thing." We will use the term *salvation* to refer to this spiritual victory. What is the essence of this salvation? What does Boromir do to achieve it? The answer is actually fairly simple. First and foremost, Boromir acknowledges his evil and apologizes for it. "I tried to take the Ring from Frodo," he confesses. "I am sorry." This path to what Aragorn describes as a victory strongly corresponds to the Christian notion of salvation, which comes through repentance of sin. "Repent and believe" is the essential response called for by the gospel. (See, for example, Mark 1:15.) In that sense, Aragorn's words can be used as a central piece of evidence supporting the thesis that in Tolkien's work *moral victory is more important than military victory.*

There is one other thing we might associate with Boromir's victory, though it represents perhaps more of a stretch and is not immediately clear from this passage alone. From the start, Boromir has a strong dependence on his own strength and importance, and upon military might (his own, that of Gondor, etc.). In giving his life to save the Hobbits, he is giving up his own quest to save Gondor. He is acknowledging that the fate of Gondor is no longer in his hands—much as Gandalf does when he sacrifices himself on the Bridge of Khazad-dûm. This, too, might be associated with the gospel that people can be saved by faith in God's work and not by their own strength or actions. (See, for example, Eph. 2:8–9.) In any case, Boromir is seen to have been saved from a great evil, and that salvation is something that happens on the spiritual and moral plane. And since that salvation is an important thing to Aragorn, Gandalf, Faramir, and—through them—to Tolkien, it may also be to Tolkien's readers.

The Salvation of Sméagol

Gollum-Sméagol also makes for an interesting study, in part because there are so many passages in *The Lord of the Rings* dealing with what might be called his salvation (including much of book 4, beginning with "The Taming of Sméagol"), in part because—unlike with Boromir—Gollum's salvation is never achieved, and also in part because Tolkien has shared some of his own thoughts about Gollum's salvation in his personal letters.

As mentioned, there are numerous references throughout *The Fellowship of the Ring* and *The Two Towers* to Gollum's "cure." Gandalf in particular, on several occasions, speaks of Gollum's cure. Even before Frodo leaves the Shire, he says:

> "But that, of course, would only make the evil part of him [Gollum] angrier in the end—unless it could be conquered. Unless it could be cured." Gandalf sighed. "Alas! there is little hope of that for him. Yet not no hope. No, not though he possessed the Ring so long, almost as far back as he can remember." (FOTR, p. 64)

And a short time later, for extra emphasis, Gandalf adds:

> "I have not much hope that Gollum can be cured before he dies, but there is a chance of it. . . . In any case we did not kill him: he is very old and very wretched. The Wood-elves have him in prison, but they treat him with such kindness as they can find in their wise hearts." (FOTR, p. 69)

Cured is a different word than *saved*, of course, and usually refers to a physical illness rather than a spiritual condition. The word *conquered* more often refers to an enemy but also is used of physical diseases such as cancer. In this case, however, there is no particular medical problem that Gollum suffers. Rather, we see that it is a moral condition of evil—or "the evil part of him"—that needs a cure. That the "treatment" is "kindness" also suggests that the illness is not physical at all, but spiritual. This treatment of kindness suggested by Gandalf is also later administered by Frodo and is at the center of the taming of Sméagol. One part of Frodo's kindness is treating Gollum with dignity and trust, which includes the simple act of calling him by his given name: Sméagol.

We also must note that as little *hope* as Gandalf sees for Gollum's cure, there can be no question that he *desires* that cure and still works toward it with some shred of hope. He shows noticeable sympathy for the creature, lamenting that his tale is "a sad story" (FOTR, p. 63) and sighing about how deeply he has fallen into evil. As Legolas shares at the Council of Elrond, "Gandalf bade us hope still for his cure, and we had not the heart to keep him ever in dungeons under the earth, where he would fall back into his old black thoughts" (FOTR, p. 268). Admittedly, there are not many others who share Gandalf's vision for Gollum's salvation. At the start, not even Frodo does. To the contrary, he wishes Gollum dead. By the end of the book, however, Frodo shows mercy to Gollum and works toward his cure. It is Frodo's kindness to him—*good Master, nice Master, kind Master*—that leads to the whole inner debate between the Sméagol-side and the Gollum-side, and to the change that takes place in him. It is a change that Tolkien illustrates in several ways, and which Frodo is aware of. After the famous debate between the two voices in "The Passage of the Marshes," "Gollum welcomed [Frodo] with dog-like delight. He chuckled and chattered, cracking his long fingers, and pawing at Frodo's knees. Frodo smiled at him" (TT, p. 242). Initially, Frodo may only be using Gollum as a guide, out of necessity. By the time they reach Faramir, however, it is clear both that Frodo has grown considerably in his understanding and pity for the poor creature, and also that he truly desires his salvation. This is especially evident in Frodo's anguish at the Forbidden Pool, when in order to save Gollum's life he has to lure him away from the water to be captured. "His heart sank . . . what Frodo did would seem a treachery to the poor treacherous creature. It would probably be impossible ever to make him understand or believe that Frodo had saved his life." He knows from the start that Gollum will feel betrayed, and guesses (correctly) the damage that sense of betrayal will do to Gollum's repentance process. Thus, when it is over, Frodo is "feeling very wretched," and tells Sam, "I hate the whole business" (TT, p. 297).

In the end, despite the incident at the Forbidden Pool, Gollum comes very close to the salvation that Gandalf and Frodo seek and hope for him. In one of the most poignant passages of *The Lord of the Rings,* Tolkien shares this moment with the readers:

Gollum looked at them. A strange expression passed over his lean hungry face. The gleam faded from his eyes, and they went dim and grey, old and tired. A spasm of pain seemed to twist him, and he turned away, peering back up towards the pass, shaking his head, as if engaged in some interior debate. Then he came back, and slowly putting out a trembling hand, very cautiously he touched Frodo's knee—but almost the touch was a caress. For a fleeting moment, could one of the sleepers have seen him, they would have thought that they beheld an old weary hobbit, shrunken by the years that had carried him far beyond his time, beyond friends and kin, and the fields and streams of youth, an old starved pitiable thing. (TT, p. 324)

The interior debate, we may guess in hindsight, is whether or not to go through with his plan of leading Frodo to Shelob. We may also guess that Sméagol (that is, the Sméagol side of Gollum) is on the verge of winning this debate. The "gleam," a sign of his sneaking slyness, fades from his eyes. The pawing becomes "almost . . . a caress"—a sign of love and affection—and for "a fleeting moment" he is no longer the slinking, stinking Gollum of secret caves but the Hobbit-like creature he once was, associated with "friends and kin, and the fields and streams of youth." Unfortunately, the fleeting moment of near-salvation slips away. For Sam, who does not take part in administering the treatment of kindness, also does not see the results of that treatment. Mistaking this moment of sorrow, compassion, and near-repentance on the part of Gollum for mere "pawing at his master," Sam continues with his unkind and untrusting treatment. As a result, "Gollum withdrew himself, and a green flint flickered under his heavy lids. Almost spider-like he looked now, crouched back on his bent limbs, with his protruding eyes. The fleeting moment had passed, beyond recall" (TT, p. 324). Gollum has come so near to salvation, but has turned away in the end. Suddenly, the imagery associates him more with Shelob-kind than with Hobbit-kind.

Just how important salvation is to Tolkien is illustrated by a letter he wrote in 1963 describing this scene:

Sam was cocksure, and deep down a little conceited. . . . He plainly did not fully understand Frodo's motives or his distress in the incident of the Forbidden Pool. If he had understood better what was going on between Frodo and Gollum, things might have turned out differently in the end. For me perhaps the most tragic moment in the Tale comes . . . when Sam fails to note the complete change in Gollum's tone and aspect. "Nothing, nothing," said Gollum softly. "Nice master!" His repentance is blighted and all Frodo's pity is (in a sense) wasted. (Letters, pp. 329–30)

This is quite a telling statement that among all the episodes in three volumes, Tolkien would refer to Gollum's failure to come into his cure as "the most tragic moment in the Tale." It speaks volumes about what is really important to the author. He says almost the same thing—though more briefly—in another earlier letter to his son Christopher written in 1945 while *The Lord of the Rings* was still in progress: that he was "most moved" by "the tragedy of Gollum who at that moment came within a hair of repentance—but for one rough word from Sam" (Letters, p. 110). In short, it is not only Gandalf who seeks and hopes for salvation, but Tolkien himself.

This also contributes to our understanding of why Gandalf restricts his own use of power in the war against Sauron, but seeks rather to encourage each person in Middle-earth to use his own strength. If the path toward (or away) from salvation relates to moral choices (and not to physical or material victory), and if salvation truly is the highest and most important end, then it will avail nothing for Gandalf to do the work of others for them; with regard to salvation, the laboring itself—that is, the choice to do good—is as important as the result of that labor. So Gandalf seeks for each person to make good choices, even when he could accomplish the outcome of those choices more quickly himself. Or, looking at this from the point of view of those whom Gandalf is helping, the way to escape judgment is not to abdicate choices and responsibility to the wizard, but rather to make good choices.

Saruman, Denethor, and Damnation as Un-Salvation

Indeed, Tolkien shows Gandalf as having a desire for the salvation of all in Middle-earth, no matter how far they may have fallen. As we saw, Gandalf rejoices at Boromir's "escape" even though it comes about only at Boromir's death, for what was accomplished on the spiritual plane is more important than what was lost on the physical plane. Likewise, he seeks and hopes for Gollum's cure. He is also chiefly responsible for bringing about Théoden's awakening, which we saw in the first chapter with respect to the vivid portrayal of Théoden's death and the battle between Éowyn and the Nazgûl.

Gandalf hopes even for the cures of Saruman and Wormtongue. "Dangerous, and probably useless; but it must be done," he says, as he readies for his conversation with Saruman after the fall of Isengard to the Ents (TT, p. 181). Why does it *have* to be done? Gandalf's words to Saruman give us some hints. "I do not wish to kill you, or hurt you, as you would know, if you really understood me. And I have the power to protect you. I am giving you a last chance" (TT, p. 188). Despite the evil that Saruman has done to Gandalf, and indeed to all of Middle-earth, Gandalf does not intend any retribution. Instead he offers kindness: an opportunity for freedom, and a chance to turn (as Boromir does) away from the evil he has chosen. It seems even that Gandalf feels a moral *duty* to offer Saruman "a last chance," even though the attempt is "dangerous." A last chance at what? At salvation. "You have become a fool, Saruman, and yet pitiable. *You might still have turned away from folly and evil,* and have been of service. But you choose to stay and gnaw the ends of your old plots" (TT, p. 188, emphasis mine). Gandalf's language, here, has strong Christian connotations. The word *repent*, which is at the core of the "gospel message" preached by Christ and is also the word used by Tolkien to describe what is happening to Gollum, simply means to "turn away from evil." Thus Gandalf could equally have said to Saruman, "You might still have repented." This is particularly significant in light of two other aspects of these words, relating back to earlier chapters of this book. In Gandalf's reference to "folly and evil," we see yet again the objective nature of morality; Saruman is not free to define his own good and evil, but rather there is an objective good and evil above and beyond both Gandalf and Saruman, to which Gandalf may refer. We also see again the emphasis of Saruman's free will to "choose" and the importance of the moral choice to turn away from evil or, in Saruman's case to "choose to stay and gnaw the ends of [his] old plots."

As for Gandalf's desire to see that repentance and salvation, Gandalf's words to Pippin as he departs from this encounter reinforce what we have already seen: "But I had reasons for trying; some merciful and some less so. . . . What will become of him? I cannot say. I grieve that so much good now festers in the tower" (TT, p. 190). Yes, Gandalf has personal motives for seeking Saruman's repentance: Saruman is still powerful and knowledgeable, and could be of great help in the war against Sauron. But Gandalf also has compassionate motives. He grieves that Saruman turns away from salvation. Indeed, we might well conclude that to Gandalf, this salvation from evil—a spiritual salvation that comes not from physical might or military victory, but from repenting of the evil and choosing the good—is the highest and greatest end for all in Middle-earth. As he says to Denethor, he pities even Sauron's slaves.

That Frodo really learns the virtue of mercy is shown as much (or more) in Saruman's case as it is in Gollum's. With Gollum, it may be easier for Frodo to feel pity, because Gollum is so weak and miserable and also so similar to the Hobbits in his origins. Also, as a Ringbearer, Frodo knows the torment that Gollum has experienced, and in clinging to a hope for Gollum he is thereby also clinging to some hope for himself. But Saruman has no such excuse. He is of a wise and powerful order, and also he is never burdened with the One Ring (much though he desires it). Furthermore, the evil Saruman does to Frodo strikes much closer to home. Indeed, it literally does strike *home*. When they finally meet near the end of the trilogy, Saruman is coming out of the home that once belonged to Bilbo and Frodo. Nor does Saruman ever take even the smallest steps toward a repentance—not even a repentance that is later blighted, like that of Gollum. Nonetheless, Frodo follows Gandalf's path and offers Saruman yet another chance at being "cured." "He is fallen, and his cure is beyond us; but I would still spare him, in the hope that he may find it" (ROTK, p. 299). This not only sheds added light on the desire of the more noble characters to help others find their cure—this spiritual salvation of which I wrote—but it also suggests that one of the reasons that mercy is so important, and shown to be so virtuous, is that mercy leaves open the door to salvation. Once a sentence of death has been carried out, there is no longer the possibility of repentance.

At this point, one must wrestle with the reality that salvation has an opposite, or alternative, which is damnation. This, at least, is what Tolkien believed to be the truth about the primary reality of this world, as is illustrated in the letter we quoted earlier: "There are persons who yield to temptation, reject their chances of nobility or salvation, and appear to be 'damnable.'" And as unpopular a notion as this is in modern times, it is also the reality in Middle-earth. Indeed, our earlier observations on moral responsibility and judgment at least suggest the possibility of damnation in Tolkien's writing, for judgment means nothing if there are not consequences to our choices: good consequences for good choices, and evil consequences for evil. Even our affirmation of free will suggests the possibility of damnation, for if created beings are to be truly free, then they cannot be *forced* to follow their Creator, and damnation is nothing but the natural eternal consequence of rejecting that Creator. Of course, the fact that salvation is a possibility but not a necessity, as has been shown in this chapter, affirms something like damnation as the alternative: the "un-salvation."

We see several hints of this final judgment in *The Lord of the Rings*. We see it in the imagery surrounding the deaths of Denethor and Gollum, two characters who fail to come to salvation and who both perish in their evil. Both of them end in flames—a *consummation* of their wickedness in both the literal and figurative meaning of that word—described with imagery that evokes the damnation of their souls. In the case of Denethor, he "leaped upon the table, and standing there wreathed in fire and smoke he took up the staff of his stewardship that lay at his feet and broke it on his knee. Casting the pieces into the blaze he bowed and laid himself on the table" (ROTK, p. 130). Gollum ends in the greatest flames in Middle-earth: the fires of Mount Doom. Both of these scenes bring up unmistakable images of the flames of hell, which is the scene of eternal damnation.

Equally interesting are the words of Gandalf when he faces the Lord of the Nazgûl at the gates of Minas Tirith: "Go back to the abyss prepared for you! Go back! Fall into the nothingness that awaits you and your Master. Go!" (ROTK, p. 103). The imagery of these words clearly calls up the notion of damnation, not only for the Nazgûl but also for his master, Sauron. Though once a man, the Lord of the Nazgûl has long ago ceased to be of human kind but is of the spirit realm. In the Bible, the *abyss* is another name for hell, the place where evil spirits in rebellion against God will be sent. It is a place of damnation. In Luke 8:31, the legion of demons possessing the man of the Gerasenes pleads with Jesus "that he would not command them to go into the abyss." It is not only evil spirits who are sent to the abyss, however. Later, in the parable of the sheep and the goats, Jesus speaks of the final judgment of the goats (those who did not serve God) in words that should strike a familiar chord with anybody who has just read the words of Gandalf. "Then he shall say to them also that shall be on his left hand: Depart from me, you cursed, into everlasting fire, which was prepared for the devil and his angels" (Matt. 25:41).

The point here is not to dwell on damnation. Tolkien's writing certainly does not. The focus is rather on salvation. Nevertheless, we must acknowledge that just as salvation is a real possibility in Tolkien's world, so is the alternative. For free will beings in a moral universe, having a choice between salvation and damnation seems inevitable. However, when a being follows a path toward damnation, and seems to receive it as a punishment, there is no gloating, only sorrow. Gandalf grieves at the demise of Denethor, his face "grave and sad" (ROTK, p. 132). Frodo shows similar sadness at the death of

Gollum—"Let us forgive him," he says (ROTK, p. 225)—and even later at the failure of Saruman to turn from his evil. Salvation is not only a possibility; it is the hope for everybody in Middle-earth.

Bilbo and Frodo: Mercy for the Merciful

The possibility of one's own damnation is yet another reason that mercy is so important in Middle-earth. Not only might the showing of mercy lead to the salvation of others—of the recipients of that mercy—but it may be the most important instrument in the salvation of the one showing the mercy. This seems to be the case with both Bilbo and Frodo. Before Gandalf comments about the effect on Gollum of Bilbo's mercy, and the possibility of Gollum's cure, he discusses the effect of that mercy on Bilbo himself:

> "Pity? It was Pity that stayed his hand. Pity, and Mercy: not to strike without need. And *he has been well rewarded*, Frodo. Be sure that *he took so little hurt* from the evil, and *escaped in the end*, because he began his ownership of the Ring so. With Pity."(FOTR, pp. 68–69, emphasis mine)

Again, Tolkien does not use the word *salvation*—he avoids such religion-laden vocabulary—but Gandalf is certainly speaking of something on the moral (rather than physical) plane, and he uses three different phrases that all suggest something similar to salvation. Bilbo is "well rewarded." What reward can be greater than salvation and the gift of heaven? This is an illustration of one of the principles of Jesus' teaching: "Blessed are the merciful: for they shall obtain mercy"(Matt. 5:7). Or, looking at the passage in terms of the opposite possibility, Gandalf sees that Bilbo "took so little hurt" from evil and that he "escaped." In fact, Bilbo is one of only two bearers of the One Ring who ever freely relinquish the Ring. (The other being Sam, who possesses the Ring for only a fraction of the time that Bilbo does.) We can only guess what might have happened had Bilbo not begun his ownership of the Ring with an act of mercy, but we can "be sure" that things would have gone worse for him. Indeed, we need look only as far as Gollum, who begins his ownership of the Ring with murder. We can also be sure that Gandalf cares at least as much for Bilbo's salvation as he does for Gollum's.

Frodo's case is not very different. Here, I will rely on Tolkien's own explanation of the situation. In a letter describing what happens at the Crack of Doom, he writes: "But at this point the 'salvation' of the world and Frodo's own 'salvation' is achieved by his previous *pity* and forgiveness of injury. . . . By a situation created by his 'forgiveness,' he was saved himself, and relieved of his burden" (Letters, p. 234). Up to this point, I have claimed that Tolkien, without explicitly using the word *salvation*, nevertheless uses the *language* and *imagery* associated with the Christian concept of salvation. Here in this letter, however, Tolkien himself explicitly uses the word. Interestingly enough, he uses it two different times to mean two different things. With respect to "the world," Tolkien is probably using the word to mean something more akin to military victory: namely, salvation from the dominion of the Dark Lord Sauron. The peoples of Middle-earth have been saved from slavery. But with respect to Frodo, the word has a double meaning. Frodo is physically saved; what he could not do himself, Gollum does for him, and had he not shown mercy, then Gollum would not have been alive to do what he does. But Frodo is also spiritually saved from his burden, enslavement to the evil of the Ring, and here it is not the outcome of the act of mercy (the fact that Gollum is still alive) but rather the *showing* of mercy itself that keeps Frodo from sinking even further under the dominion of the Ring.

Thus in this subject of salvation are tied up the notions of moral victory, free will, objective morality, and judgment. Even hope is involved here, for as Tolkien illustrates through Gandalf, the greatest hope one can have for oneself or for others is the hope of salvation. Frodo follows a path toward salvation in his moral choices to do right, even when it is inconvenient or dangerous. Yet ultimately his salvation comes by mercy, when he is unable to complete his task and Gollum does it for him. Indeed, it comes through mercy in two ways: the mercy Frodo has consistently shown to Gollum, and the mercy shown to him by the higher Authority who intercedes and brings about the destruction of the Ring when Frodo fails. "Blessed are the merciful," Jesus taught, "for they shall obtain mercy" (Matt. 5:7).

9

The Hand of Ilúvatar

Even the casual reader of J. R. R. Tolkien is likely to observe a significant difference between the narrative tone of *The Hobbit* and that of *The Lord of the Rings*. While the former is a light-hearted fairy tale that could well be labeled as children's literature, the latter is a heroic romance more akin to an epic. The difference between *The Lord of the Rings* and *The Silmarillion* is even more striking, although those who knew Tolkien and his goals would not be surprised by this difference. In Tolkien's 1951 letter to Milton Waldman of Collins—a letter of some 10,000 words already mentioned earlier in this book—he recounts his desire to "make a body of more or less connected legend, ranging from the large and cosmogonic, to the level of romantic fairy-story" (Letters, p. 144). These three works—*The Hobbit, The Lord of the Rings,* and *The Silmarillion*—represent three distinct parts of that range (though not a continuum): the light-hearted fairy tale, the epic romance, and the large and cosmogonic myth.

This book has focused on the middle, in part because it *is* the middle (and thus provides the common ground that allows us to see something of the whole range), in part because it is the longest, and in part because at the time of this writing it is the most widely popular, partly thanks to the release of Peter Jackson's film trilogy. Nonetheless, we have seen something of both ends. We have explored *The Silmarillion* and found in the roots of this work some deeper and clearer answers to various questions raised in *The Lord of the Rings*. And we have turned to *The Hobbit* to see that some of the profound ideas explored in more depth in the other books are so important to Tolkien that they can be found even within the most lighthearted of the works.

As we approach the end of this book, and get closer to the roots of some of the themes we have explored, we begin to draw more heavily from *The Silmarillion* and the roots of Middle-earth. Yet we see that hints of these deeper ideas—whether by the design of the author or not—can be found even in *The Hobbit*. And our starting point is to notice that even within *The Hobbit* there is a marked change in narrative tone between the start of the book and the end. Indeed, the change within *The Hobbit* is almost as significant as the change from *The Hobbit* to *The Lord of the Rings,* except that the change within *The Hobbit* happens gradually. If we were to pick a specific place where this change *begins* to occur, it would be from the moment the reader first meets Elrond in Rivendell. A full articulation of all aspects of this shift in tone is beyond the scope of this book, but it can be illustrated it in a few ways.

A Deepening of Voice

One way we see the change in tone is in the songs and poetry. The first song we read in *The Hobbit* is that of the Dwarves at the "unexpected party." This song begins:

> Chip the glasses and crack the plates!
> Blunt the knives and bend the forks!
> That's what Bilbo Baggins hates—
> Smash the bottles and burn the corks!

(TH, p. 19)

It is a lighthearted piece—almost a child's rhyme—with a sing-song rhythm and no particularly profound meaning. In fact, it might be argued that it has *no meaning at all*, which is to say the Dwarves do not *mean* the words they are singing, since they actually do "none of those dreadful things" (TH, p. 20). They sing the song only to mock and tease their anxious host. Now contrast this with the last poem of the book, found in the final chapter:

> Roads go ever ever on,
> Over rock and under tree,
> By caves where never sun has shone,
> By streams that never find the sea;
> Over snow by winter sown,
> And through the merry flowers of June,
> Over grass and over stone,
> And under mountains in the moon.
>
> Roads go ever ever on,
> Under cloud and under star,
> Yet feet that wandering have gone
> Turn at last to home afar.
> Eyes that fire and sword have seen
> And horror in the halls of stone
> Look at last on meadows green
> And trees and hills they long have known.
>
> (TH, pp. 252–53)

The difference between the somber, contemplative tone of this poem and the mocking, humorous tone of the earlier one is striking. Indeed, not only *might* this later poem fit comfortably in the context of *The Lord of the Rings*, but a version of it is sung in the trilogy—twice! And far from being without significance, its final lines touch on those things that are most important in life, in a way reminiscent of the dying words of Thorin: "If more of us valued food and cheer and song above hoarded gold, it would be a merrier world" (TH, p. 243). When Bilbo finishes this poem, the wizard says to him "My dear Bilbo! Something is the matter with you! You are not the hobbit that you were.'"

We can almost hear Tolkien's own voice saying, "My dear me, this is not the Story it once was."

But does this contrast between songs really illustrate a change in narrative tone? One might suggest that the latter poem is intentionally given a more somber tone *only* to illustrate the change that comes over Bilbo from the start of the Quest to the end, and that it is not reflective of any *overall* change in narrative voice. Certainly we must acknowledge, as Gandalf does, that Bilbo has changed over the course of the book from the innocent Hobbit who tries to "good morning" a wizard to the one who has lived through the deaths of Thorin, Fili, Kili, and many worthy Elves. We could also point out that it is the Dwarves who sing the former song, while the latter is sung by a Hobbit, and thus the difference between the songs might only serve to illustrate the differences in character between two of the races of Middle-earth, not a difference between the start of the book and the end. Both of these observations would be well taken, except that the same point could also be illustrated with contrasts between several other pairs of songs and poems. Furthermore, these contrasts in poems are only a few among many examples of the dramatic change in voice, and when all of the different aspects are taken as a whole, they are hard to ignore.

Consider, for example, the song sung early on when Thorin's company first approaches Rivendell. The song begins:

> O! What are you doing,
> And where are you going?
> Your ponies need shoeing!
> The river is flowing!
>   O! tra-la-la-lally
>   here down in the valley!

(TH, p. 48)

This is the third song or poem appearing in the story, and the last before we meet Elrond. Of particular importance is the fact that it is not a song sung by Dwarves, but by *Elves!* To put it very plainly, this is not a song we could really imagine being sung by the Elves of Rivendell in *The Lord of the Rings*. It is another song of teasing, with a refrain of nonsense syllables, much more akin to the early song of the Dwarves than to anything we would later come to associate with the nobility, splendor, wisdom, or grace of the Elven race. I don't think I put it too strongly if I say that it is entirely out of character for those of the high House of Elrond. Of course at the time this song appears, we haven't met Elrond yet!

By contrast, consider the first song or poem recited *after* the appearance of Elrond. This song comes shortly after the departure of the company from Rivendell, and it is the Dwarves who sing it:

> The wind was on the withered heath,
> but in the forest stirred no leaf:
> there shadows lay by night and day,
> and dark things silent crept beneath.

> (TH, p. 112)

This song has a much more serious and somber tone than the tra-la-la-lally rhyme. The imagery is more mythic in scope: "shadows," "tide," "heavens cool," and "wide seas." It also has nature imagery—leaved forests, hissing grasses, rattling reeds—that one might rather associate with Elves. It even ends with a reference to the stars, which are also an Elven love. The point simply is this: in this contrast the more serious song is sung *by the Dwarves* and comes *after the departure from Rivendell,* while the sillier song is sung *by the Elves* and occurs before the meeting with Elrond. Indeed, after the meeting with Elrond the Elven songs also take a more serious tone. Consider the striking *similarity* between the first line of that last Dwarvish song, with its wind/heath[er] imagery, and the second line from the last Elven poem to appear in the book: "The wind's in the tree-top, the wind's in the heather" (TH, p. 251). The common theme in the contrasts between the poems has naught to do with races, but with where the poem falls with respect to the meeting with Elrond.

Admittedly, not every poem in the book adheres strictly to this general pattern. Another "tra-la-la-lally" song, for example, is

repeated at the end of the story when Bilbo returns to Rivendell.
One might think that Tolkien has returned to the pre-Elrond silli-
ness. Yet even the post-Elrond "tra-la-la-lally" song is much more
serious than the earlier one, and deals with ultimate values:

> Though sword shall be rusted,
> And throne and crown perish
> With strength that men trusted
> And wealth that they cherish,
> Here grass is still growing,
> And leaves are yet swinging,
> The white water flowing,
> And elves are yet singing
> > Come! Tra-la-la-lally!
> > Come back to the valley!

(TH, p. 249)

This is a song that reflects on the vanity of the mortal pursuits
of power and treasure, and on the timelessness of nature. Other
than the shared refrain, it is a different song entirely than the
one that makes fun of the wagging beards of the Dwarves.

Another significant difference between the tone of the book
before and after Elrond's entrance can be seen in the monsters
faced by Bilbo.[1] There are five significant groups of enemies in
The Hobbit that might be deemed "monsters"[2]: the three trolls,
the goblins, Gollum, the spiders, and Smaug. (We might add the
wolves to this list or simply lump them in with the goblins.) Of
these, only the trolls come before Elrond, and these three trolls
are as out of place in Middle-earth as the "tra-la-la-lally" song
is out of place in Rivendell. They have common English names:
Tom, Bert, and William. They speak with cockney voices. And
they border on being silly. They come from the world of children's

---

1. Some of the ideas in this and the next two paragraphs were influenced by a
lecture by Keith Kelly: "Beneath the Shadow: Heroism and Despair in *The Lord of the
Rings*," given at Middlebury College on January 9, 2003.

2. I use the term *monsters* here in keeping with Tolkien's own term from his semi-
nal essay "Beowulf: The Monsters and the Critics." The term was used to describe
the collection of evil creatures faced by Beowulf: Grendel, Grendel's mother, and the
dragon Beowulf.

nursery stories, not from the heroic landscape of Middle-earth. We see nothing of their kind in *The Lord of the Rings*. (The cave-trolls encountered in Moria are of another kind altogether.) Even if we did see their kind later, we could not really imagine Elrohir, or Elladan, or the Glorfindel who faces the Nazgûl near the end of the first book of the trilogy, or for that matter any of Elrond's folk as we know them from *The Lord of the Rings*, "hurrying along for fear of the trolls"—not if the trolls were Tom, Bert, and Bill! Tolkien, when he later realized where *The Hobbit* had taken him, even regretted the choice of their names.

Here it must also be pointed out that the Hobbits themselves and their beloved Shire are also anachronistic; they don't fit into the heroic world created in *The Silmarillion* any more than Tom, Bert, and Bill do. Indeed, their presence in Middle-earth is quite by accident. But it is a wonderful accident—what Tolkien might call a *eucatastrophe*—that may be the most important ingredient in making *The Lord of the Rings* the successful work that it is. For part of the wonder of the Hobbits' existence in Middle-earth is precisely their anachronistic nature: the fact that we see regular people placed in heroic situations, situations that require heroic actions, such as the facing of heroic monsters. However, an exploration of the nature of the Shire and its inhabitants in the setting of Middle-earth, as enjoyable as it would certainly be, would take us far afield from the topic of this book.

Returning to the monsters, those we meet *after* Elrond are much more worthy enemies than the three trolls, with natures more fitting to the heroic world of Middle-earth. We can consider them each in turn. Though in stature and origin he is akin to Hobbits, Gollum is actually a considerably more frightening "monster." He is certainly more crafty and intelligent than the trolls, as he proves in the riddle game. He also speaks riddles taken from a heroic age: riddles that Tolkien borrowed and adapted from Old English and Old Norse and other medieval poetry. In other words, while the trolls belong in the nursery, Gollum belongs in a medieval heroic poem. Likewise, as we discover at the end of the book, the goblins are vicious enemies, nothing less than the Orcs of *The Silmarillion* and *The Lord of the Rings*. They are motivated by vengeance and hatred, not by the desire for a good leg of mutton. Likewise, the spiders of Mirkwood, though lesser in size and power than the great spider Shelob who appears at the end of *The Two Towers*, are akin to her and to Ungoliant, the horrific spider-beast that destroys the two trees of Yavanna and nearly devours the Silmarils. As for dragons, they are the archetypal monsters of the heroic world. Smaug is of the same type as Glaurung, the bane of Túrin. It is as if, once we meet Elrond, we have suddenly stepped into an older, larger, more heroic world, including the appropriate villains. In fact we have, and the narrative tone changes to reflect that.

Even the Quest itself takes on a much greater significance after the meeting with Elrond. Initially, the Quest is a private affair of Thorin, centered upon personal revenge on the dragon Smaug and upon recapturing the treasure of Thorin's ancestors. Gandalf's comment at the unexpected party, regarding the possibility of a direct approach to Smaug's front gate, gives insight into how insignificant Thorin and company are: "That would be no good, not without a mighty Warrior, even a Hero. I tried to find one; but warriors are busy fighting one another in distant lands, and in this neighbourhood heroes are scarce, or simply not to be found" (TH, p. 27). To the reader it is a humorous comment, giving a glimpse of Gandalf's lighter side, but to the characters themselves—Thorin especially—it is a condescending and even insulting statement. Gandalf is stating outright that none of them are heroes. Furthermore, in telling the Dwarves that the real heroes and warriors are all off doing *more important things*, Gandalf is also letting them know that *their* quest is *not* so important: certainly not important enough to warrant the time of a hero.[3] Gandalf makes a similar comment later in the conversation with respect to the

3. Gandalf himself must certainly be considered a hero, and he does offer them his time and aid on the Quest. However, we must note that even Gandalf leaves the Company at a critical moment to take care of more important "pressing business" of his own (TH, p.120). It is also the case that Gandalf was not motivated by revenge or treasure; the aid he gave to Thorin seemed to come rather from old friendship to Thorin's father, and from promises made long before. And I think a strong case could be made that Gandalf's real motivation for the Quest was both to help the Dwarves grow, from being exposed to Bilbo's values, and to help Bilbo grow by freeing him from the constraints of his small world. In other words, Gandalf was concerned with the character development of all parties that would result from the *process* of the Quest, rather than in any stated *goal* of the Quest.

Necromancer: "Here is an enemy quite beyond the powers of all the dwarves put together, if they could all be collected again from the four corners of the world. . . . The dragon and the Mountain are more than big enough tasks for you!" (TH, p. 30).

It is after the meeting with Elrond that this quest for dragon's gold does take on greater significance than Gandalf hints at with the Dwarves—and likely more than the author himself initially supposed. Elrond, for example, has motives much different than the Dwarves' when he gives them his help as they pass through Rivendell:

"For if he did not altogether approve of dwarves and their love of gold, he hated dragons and their cruel wickedness, and he grieved to remember the ruin of the town of Dale and its merry bells, and the burned banks of the bright River Running." (TH, p. 52)

In any case, at least the unintended consequences of the Quest become more important than earlier imagined. The discovery of the One Ring, the death of Smaug, and the Battle of Five Armies all turn out to be important events in the history of Middle-earth. As the narrator tells us when Bilbo departs with the elf-host, "the northern world would be merrier for many a long day. The dragon was dead, and the goblins overthrown, and [the Elves'] hearts looked forward after winter to a spring of joy" (TH, pp. 246–47). None of this was in the mind of Thorin—nor was it, we might guess, in the mind of Tolkien—when Thorin set out from Hobbiton with his company of fourteen.

The common theme in all of the changes we have just discussed is Elrond. Before we meet Elrond, the story seems to be one thing. After we meet Elrond, it changes to something else. Not that the change is immediate. As T. A. Shippey explains, Tolkien could be quite stubborn even with his bad ideas.[4] Nor is it a complete change in direction. It is more a deepening, a sending down of roots—a movement from children's story to something bordering on the heroic romance genre of *The Lord*

4. This particular wording comes from a personal conversation with T. A. Shippey, by phone, on February 2, 2003. However, similar ideas are suggested in his books.

of the Rings. The shift starts in chapter 3, "A Short Rest," when we meet Elrond, but it takes time to really set in. It seems to complete about two chapters later when Bilbo acquires the Ring and meets Gollum. Thus, the goblins of chapter 4, for example, have not yet become the goblins of the Battle of Five Armies in chapter 17. This explains why many readers associate the shift more with the appearance of Gollum or the discovery of the Ring than with the appearance of Elrond. Also, Tolkien's revisions both before the first edition and the substantial revisions between the first edition and the second edition obscure the exact moment in which the shift occurs. Nonetheless, the shift in narrative voice cannot be doubted, and the beginning of that shift can be traced to Elrond.

Attaching a Leaf

Why, then, is this meeting with Elrond so important? And why does it spawn such a significant shift in the tone and voice of the narrative? Much of the answer to this lies in the genesis and roots of *The Hobbit*. For many years before Tolkien began writing this story, he had been working on a deep and profound mythology for his created world of Middle-earth. Some of his surviving stories date back to late 1915. Though at the time he was very private about his writing, there is evidence that he had been working on what was later to become *The Silmarillion* from as early as 1914. Certainly by the 1920s he had done a significant amount of work on the languages and early histories of Middle-earth. Surprisingly, however, when he began *The Hobbit* he didn't realize that this story would eventually fit into the larger (and much more serious) framework that he had already devoted so much time to! *The Hobbit* begins with a voice much more akin to that of *Farmer Giles of Ham* than to that of *The Silmarillion*.

The situation can be explained using imagery from Tolkien's short masterpiece "Leaf by Niggle." Imagine a painter who has a broad canvas on which he is painting a Tree. Imagine further that he has been working on this Tree for many years; it is his passion and life's interest. Imagine also this painter has several smaller canvases on which he paints leaves. He has quite a collection of them. Some of these leaves remain works of art in their own right. With others, however, the painter realizes some time after he begins them that they really are leaves belonging to his Great Tree, and so he attaches them to that other, broader canvas. This is precisely what happened with *The Hobbit*. Some readers are under the impression that Tolkien began with *The Hobbit*, and then later went back and added the histories that were to become *The Silmarillion*, but it was the other way around: the myths and histories of Middle-earth had been around for a long time, and *The Hobbit* merely got added onto them like a small leaf glued to the giant mural of the Tree. At what exact point Tolkien "realized" that this new story involving Bilbo Baggins was part of his other canvas, I don't know for sure, but the evidence we've been looking at in this chapter suggests that it happens when the company meets Elrond at Rivendell. In any case, Elrond is the obvious connection to the preexisting myth. He is:

> one of those people whose fathers came into the strange stories before the beginning of History, the wars of the evil goblins and the elves and the first men in the North. In those days of our tale there were still some people who had both elves and heroes of the North for ancestors, and Elrond the master of the house was their chief. (TH, pp. 50–51)

Readers of *The Silmarillion* will realize at once that those "people who had both elves and heroes of the North for ancestors" refers to the offspring of Beren and Lúthien, and of Tuor and Idril, from which spring not only Elrond's line but the line of the kings of Númenor and thus Aragorn himself. The great hidden kingdom of Gondolin—the tale of which is told in *The Silmarillion*—is also mentioned by name; it is from there, we learn, that Gandalf's and Thorin's swords come. In short, it is right here, when Bilbo meets Elrond, that we are suddenly plunged more fully into the thematic depth and importance of Middle-earth.

It is even interesting to note that the narrator's comment *in those days of our tale* follows immediately after a reference to *the strange stories before the beginning of History*. It would seem, therefore, that the phrase "those days" refers to this earlier history, when Elrond's forefathers were alive. If this is the case, then the phrase "our tale" encompasses both the strange stories of Elrond's past and the current story of Bilbo's adventure, implying that it is all one tale. And it is one, though Tolkien himself didn't realize this when he began writing *The Hobbit*. We are told, for example, that Gandalf's sword Glamdring belonged to the king of Gondolin, who was Turgon, the father of Idril Celebrindal, the mother of Eärendil the Mariner, the father of none other than Elrond himself. Thus the story comes full circle, and Elrond identifies the sword of his great-grandfather and begins the living connection tying us to the past.

Aragorn's tale also comes full circle. When he sits by the fire on the edge of Weathertop in book 1 of *The Lord of the Rings* and sings to the four Hobbits the tale of Beren and Lúthien Tinúviel, he is singing his own song about a mortal man who falls in love with an Elf maiden and goes through many perils and hardships to earn the right to wed her. "Why to think of it," Sam says to Frodo on the Stairs of Cirith Ungol, "we're in the same tale still! It's going on." This is a fundamental aspect of Tolkien's work. It is one great story. We simply keep stepping into it at different spots. Time and time again Tolkien connects us with the deep past of Middle-earth's history, and yet does so in a way that relates that history to the present situation. "Don't the great tales never end?" Sam goes on to ask. "No," Frodo replies, "they never end as tales" (TT, p. 321).

And it is as Tolkien brings Thorin and company into contact with this deeper and richer preexisting history, embodied in Elrond, that their quest—which in and of itself is not of great significance to any but themselves—suddenly takes on more importance. In fact, it is much more important than Tolkien himself realized when he began writing *The Hobbit*. But once this story begins to be intertwined with the existing landscape and history that was so dear to Tolkien's heart, it naturally takes on much greater importance to the author. This later realization accounts for numerous changes Tolkien made to the book after its first edition. One can only wonder why he didn't make more changes.

The Presence of the Authority

Now if the story and characters of *The Hobbit* suddenly find themselves entering a world and history both deeper and more important than the one Tolkien thought they were in when he began writing the book, it should not be surprising to find that the narrative also begins to take up themes that are more important. At the start of *The Hobbit*, for example, the author is concerned with such things as the invention of golf. In a line that is more cute than profound, we learn that Bullroarer Took, in the Battle of the Green Fields, knocked the head of the goblin-king clean off, whereupon after "it sailed a hundred yards through the air and went down a rabbit-hole, and in this way the battle was won and the game of Golf invented at the same moment" (TH, p. 24). By the end of the story, however, we have begun at least to encounter issues of much greater import: themes such as the objectivity of moral law, the importance of free will, the role of fate, the value of life and friendship, and even salvation. That is, we begin to see the moral, philosophical, and theological themes that become much more prevalent in *The Lord of the Rings* (and which are the focus of this book).

One thing we begin to get hints of in *The Hobbit* is something mentioned in the introduction to this book: that reality consists not only of a physical plane—a seen world—but of a spiritual plane—an unseen world—as well, and that this spiritual plane is vitally important. Indeed, the spiritual and physical planes are intimately related: what happens on the spiritual plane impacts what happens on the physical, and the decisions made on the physical plane have spiritual import. In a few critical places in *The Hobbit*, Tolkien shows the contrast between temporal (physical) values and eternal (spiritual) values, and challenges his readers to begin to understand the world through the eternal values. This is seen especially in Thorin's sad downturn, where we witness in him the destructive nature of greed. In his parting speech to Bilbo, he glimpses in the face of death the realization of what is really important.

> "Farewell, good thief," he said. "I go now to the halls of waiting to sit beside my fathers, until the world is renewed. Since I leave now all gold and silver, and go where it is of little worth, I wish to part in friendship from you, and I would take back my words and deeds at the Gate." (TH, p. 243)

First, Thorin is professing a belief that the end of his bodily life does not mean the end of his spiritual existence. His bodily life is temporal, but his spiritual life is eternal. His spirit will have a time of waiting and then (so he believes) a new incarnation in a renewed world. And gold and silver, though they have worth in the physical plane, have no value in the spiritual plane, while friendship, by contrast, does have spiritual worth and significance. It is sad that Thorin must face death—that is, he must come face-to-face with the reality of his finite existence in the material plane and his eternal existence in the spiritual plane—before he contrasts temporal values with eternal values and realizes the greater importance of the latter.

Another place we gets hints, later in *The Hobbit,* of something going on in the spiritual plane is in the long-standing battle against the evil embodied in the Necromancer. We see this at the edge of Mirkwood when Gandalf leaves Thorin's company in order to play some role in this battle. We learn in the final chapter of the book not only that Smaug is defeated but that the Necromancer is "at last driven . . . from his dark hold in the south of Mirkwood" and that as a result the land would "be freed from that horror for many long years." We also learn that this is not merely a physical war against a bodily enemy, but rather a battle against a spiritual evil that has gone on for many lives of men and whose end, Elrond guesses, "will not come about in this age of the world, or for many after" (TH, p. 250).

Perhaps the most important spiritual idea that Tolkien gives a glimpse of in Bilbo's story is the presence of some sovereign or divine hand of authority at work in the events of the world. The hint of this is expressed by Gandalf in the penultimate paragraph of the book: a paragraph that may be the most important of *The Hobbit* when it comes to understanding Tolkien's Middle-earth:

> "Then the prophecies of the old songs have turned out to be true, after a fashion!" said Bilbo.
> "Of course!" said Gandalf. "And why should not they prove true? Surely you don't disbelieve the prophecies, because you had a hand in bringing them about yourself? You don't really suppose, do you, that all your adventures and escapes were managed by mere luck, just for your sole benefit? You are a very fine person, Mr. Baggins, and I am very fond of you; but you are only quite a little fellow in a wide world after all!" (TH, p. 255)

At one level, this passage could be compared with the realization that comes to Théoden when he first sees Ents: that the world is much bigger than he imagined and, therefore, that his own little problems are somehow less significant. Or, rather, that the significance of his problems must be understood in the context of the bigger problems of the world around him. Bilbo, like Théoden, is "only quite a little fellow in a wide world."

There is much more than this at work in this passage, however. We first note that Gandalf is not at all surprised that the prophecies should be fulfilled. The very fact that Tolkien includes prophecies, and that they come true, suggests in Middle-earth some reliable foreknowledge of future events. Gandalf himself trusts the source of this foreknowledge, and he is not alone. When Boromir arrives at the Council of Elrond and shares the prophecy that came to him in a dream—*"There shall be shown a token / That Doom is near at hand"*—nobody at the Council doubts the significance of those words; the importance of prophecy is taken for granted (FOTR, p. 259). Now, prophecy may spring from impersonal fate, but at least it raises the possibility that there is some sort of plan with a purpose. In the Christian worldview of Tolkien's Catholicism, for example, prophecy does not come from an impersonal source but from the Creator of the world whose plans are communicated through the prophecy. It is out of trust in the Creator that one would also trust the prophecy. And so the presence of trustworthy prophecy may be a first piece of evidence, even within *The Hobbit*, that there is a hand of authority at work in Middle-earth.

Admittedly, the reference to "prophecy" might be interpreted in many ways, some of which could spring from a nonmonotheistic notion of fate, such as that held in Greek mythology or in Tolkien's own beloved Germanic legend. But there is more than just this one hint of such an authority. For Gandalf goes on to challenge Bilbo's belief that all his adventures and escapes were *managed by mere luck*. Throughout the story there have been many references to luck and to its importance in bringing Bilbo and the Dwarves to the successful completion of his quest. Gandalf himself has spoken of luck on numerous occasions, as has the narrator. Apart from the deeper consequences of the quest that the author wouldn't know about until it stumbled its way into Middle-earth, *luck* (meaning an impersonal chance) is the appropriate word. However, here at the end of *The Hobbit*, after it has completed its transition from being a children's story to playing a part of the broad heroic landscape of Middle-earth, Gandalf says something much more important. In one blow, with the mere use of the word *mere*, he lays to rest all notions that the course of events is determined by "luck"—if by the word *luck* we mean a blind, purposeless chance. For in his appeal to prophecy, Gandalf is referring to a power behind the luck, so that however lucky (or unlucky) certain events appear, it is not "mere luck." More importantly, Gandalf's reference to the events being *managed* implies the presence of a *manager!* In other words, there is some hand at work in all of the events of the story, leading the events (and the characters) to their prophesied (and planned or managed) conclusion. This manager, then, has both the *desire*—the care and concern for Middle-earth and its people—to act, and also the *power* (or authority) to bring about his purposes (though to characters within the story who are merely experiencing something beyond their control and their ability to understand, his actions may appear as luck).

Given how powerful and wise Tolkien portrays Gandalf to be, one might think that Gandalf himself is the author's manager. He certainly seems to know more than any of the others, as is evident in the final moments leading up to the Battle of Five Armies. However, it cannot be the case that Gandalf is the manager responsible for all of the supposedly "lucky" events, for not only is he absent from many of them, he also is as surprised as any of the Dwarves by Bilbo's reappearance after his finding of the Ring, and again by Bilbo's survival of the Battle of Five Armies. Furthermore, Gandalf is as helpless as Bilbo and the Dwarves when the company is caught by the Orcs in the burning trees in the chapter "Out of the Frying-Pan into the Fire." He is really frightened and expects to die.

At this point we must note that while Gandalf affirms the presence of a managing hand at work in the events of the world, and simultaneously affirms the validity of prophecy and of certain predestined events, he also affirms the reality of free will. He admits that even little Bilbo, by his choices and actions, had a hand in bringing about the prophesied events: events that within the manager's purposes are much more significant than any of Thorin's company expected. In other words, Bilbo's free will—emphasized several times and most especially in his choice to continue down the tunnel to Smaug's lair—is not an illusion, but is somehow used by the manager to bring about the very events that were fated and foretold by prophecy. If we return to *The Silmarillion,* we must understand this in the context of Ilúvatar's gift of freedom. Ilúvatar can use for his own ends the good choice of Bilbo to show mercy to Gollum as well as the evil choices of Fëanor bound up in his oath, and yet in both cases the individuals are still free to act.

Of course, even at the end, *The Hobbit* remains a more light-hearted work than its sequel, and many of these deeper matters are only suggested in a way peripheral to the story. Gandalf's concluding words to Bilbo, though they carry the added weight of being concluding words, are really the only significant reference we see in *The Hobbit* to any sort of God, or Creator, or Divine Hand: anything that Tolkien would refer to as the Authority (with a capital *A*). Had Bilbo's story never found its way into Middle-earth, we might not have seen even that glimpse of greater theological concerns in *The Hobbit*. When we move to the deeper heroic work of *The Lord of the Rings,* however, we begin to see many more examples of Authority: this Managing Hand at work in the history of Middle-earth. We see examples in how the Wise of Middle-earth speak of Frodo's role: Gandalf refers to him as having been "chosen" (FOTR, p. 70); Elrond speaks of him as having been "appointed" (FOTR, p. 284); and even Frodo sees himself as having been chosen, though he wonders why. But just as events being *managed* implies the existence of a manager, Frodo having being *chosen* and *appointed* implies that there is a Chooser and Appointer. And both Gandalf and Elrond make it clear that this Chooser is neither of them but a much higher Authority. Aragorn uses a word even more laden with spiritual connotation when he says to Frodo, "It has been *ordained* that you should hold it for a while" (FOTR, p. 260, emphasis mine). The term *ordination* usually implies a spiritual calling from a Supreme Being.

Elrond also hints at this Authority when he welcomes the visitors to the Council:

> "That is the purpose for which you are called hither. Called, I say, though I have not called you to me, strangers from distant lands. You have come and are here met, in this very nick of time, by chance as it may seem. Yet it is not so. Believe rather that it is so ordered that we, who sit here, and none others, must now find counsel for the peril of the world." (FOTR, p. 255)

Though no Authority is explicitly named, Elrond suggests one in several ways in this passage. He speaks of each person present as having been *called* but denies being the one who called them. A "calling," like an ordination, has connotation of a spiritual purpose and vocation. The phrase "by chance as it may *seem*" is a clear implication that it is not by chance at all, but by some greater intentional purpose that only seemed like chance. Then we get another reference to the strangers being "ordered" to have been there. In fact, we see a pattern here that no explicit subject is given for any of these verbs: *chose, called, managed, ordained,* and *ordered.* Yet for all of them, a higher Authority is suggested and implied. It is also clear that this Authority is actively involved in the affairs of Middle-earth.

Those who have read *The Silmarillion* know the name of this Authority: it is Eru Ilúvatar, the Creator of Middle-earth in Tolkien's mythology. Or at the very least it is lesser authorities (the Valar) working on behalf of Ilúvatar. Why Tolkien did not give more explicit details in *The Lord of the Rings* as to the name and nature of this Manager-Ordainer-Chooser-Caller-Prophesier, but left all references to Ilúvatar vague and indirect, is an interesting and important question to which we shall return in the final chapter. But first we must explore the importance of this presence in Middle-earth and in *The Lord of the Rings.*

The Purpose of the Authority

Though Ilúvatar is not mentioned by name in *The Lord of the Rings,* the evidence of his presence and of his concern for the peoples of Middle-earth is significant to the tale and to the characters within it. Among other things, awareness of the great purpose of the Authority, and of the scope of his concerns, becomes at times a source for hope in that it gives a very different perspective to some of the troubles encountered by the characters. This hope is vitally important, as we saw in the earlier chapter "Hope and Despair."

Not surprisingly, it is in Gandalf that we see this understanding most clearly manifested. He is able to see beyond one day and one battle; one victory or one defeat: *And for my part, I shall not wholly fail of my task, though Gondor should perish, if anything passes through this night that can still grow fair or bear fruit and flower again in days to come.* Thus he is able to expand the vision of many of those with whom he comes into contact, such as Théoden, whose healing was discussed earlier: *For not only the little life of Men is now endangered, but the life also of those things which you deemed the matter of legend. You are not without allies, even if you know them not.* It is a scene in Minas Tirith, as we approach the siege, where Gandalf's awareness of the spiritual plane is most clearly and beautifully captured:

> Pippin glanced in some wonder at the face now close beside his own, for the sound of that laugh had been gay and merry. Yet in the wizard's face he saw at first only lines of care and sorrow; though as he looked more intently he perceived that under all there was a great joy: a fountain of mirth enough to set a kingdom laughing, were it to gush forth. (ROTK, p. 31)

As mentioned at the start of the introduction to this book, this scene takes place at one of the darkest points in the story. Sauron's darkness is coming upon the land. Frodo has been captured. The terrible siege of Minas Tirith is about to start, and there is no sign of Aragorn or the Rohirrim or Faramir. Denethor is showing signs of the evil coming upon him. And on the outside, Gandalf himself is showing the great burden upon him. Yet beneath that terrible weight, there is a spiritual side to the wizard. That spiritual side shows in the incredible joy—a joy that is inexplicable from the point of view of the current *physical* reality of his situation. This joy can be explained in no other way than that Gandalf has a deeper understanding of the *spiritual* reality beyond what is visible. Indeed, the imagery here of Gandalf's fountain of mirth is very biblical. As Jesus told the woman at the well: "But the water that I will give him shall become in him a fountain of water, springing up into life everlasting" (John 4:14).

In a personal letter quoted earlier in this book, Tolkien explains a little bit more of Gandalf's spiritual understanding and the fact that the wizard dwells in part in the spiritual plane. Writing of Gandalf's sacrifice at Khazad-dûm, Tolkien explains how the wizard's understanding of Ilúvatar's purposes enables him, or frees him, to do what he does:

> For in his condition it was for him a sacrifice to perish on the Bridge in defense of his companions, less perhaps than for a mortal Man or Hobbit, since he had a far greater inner power than they; but also more, since it was a humbling and abnegation of himself in conformity to "the Rules": for all he could know at that moment he was the only person who could direct the resistance to Sauron successfully, and all his mission was vain. He was handing over to the Authority that ordained the Rules, and giving up personal hope of success. . . .
>
> . . . In the end before he departs for ever he sums himself up: "I was the enemy of Sauron." He might have added: "for that purpose I was sent to Middle-earth." But by that he would at the end have meant more than at the beginning. He was sent by a mere prudent plan of the angelic Valar or governors; but Authority had taken up this plan and enlarged it, at the moment of its failure. "Naked I was sent back—for a brief time, until my task is done." Sent back by whom, and whence? Not by the "gods" whose business is only with this embodied world and its time; for he passed "out of thought and time." (Letters, pp. 202–203)

Here, Tolkien explains the Authority and his purpose, and how it exceeds even the understanding of the Valar, the angelic beings who govern Middle-earth from Valinor. Gandalf's return is akin to a resurrection—though not quite the same thing, since the wizard is not of mortal kind, but is one of the Maiar, the lesser angelic beings who serve the Valar. Tolkien makes his intention clear in this letter: that it is Ilúvatar and not the Valar who send Gandalf back. For it is the Authority's purpose to rescue Middle-earth from Sauron. As mentioned earlier, he has both the desire and the power. So he completes his plan by sending Gandalf back, at the very moment of Gandalf's failure. Yet even as we get a glimpse of Ilúvatar's plan, we also see Gandalf's faith in that Authority, and his understanding of the Authority's plan—that its scope far exceeds his own personal definition of "success." In Gandalf's limited knowledge (limited compared to

that of Ilúvatar, not to that of mortal beings of Middle-earth),
there is nobody else capable of doing what he can do. It would
be easy for him to believe that the entire resistance to Sauron
depends on his own strength. But he knows the Authority and
has faith in him, and this knowledge broadens his vision so that
he can see that even he, Gandalf, is not responsible for the fate
of Middle-earth. Thus, he subordinates his own mission and
purposes. In many ways, this discussion of Gandalf's faith and
knowledge relates to the reality behind the prophecies that we
looked at earlier. In knowing something of Ilúvatar's purposes,
Gandalf is able to have faith that the plan will be accomplished
and the prophecies fulfilled. Interestingly enough, far from
making Gandalf care less about the little individuals of Middle-
earth—Hobbits, for example!—his understanding of Ilúvatar's
bigger purposes gives him a greater care for each individual.

Even Sam, in his simple understanding, takes courage from
the little glimpse he gets of the larger reality of Ilúvatar's plans.
In another of the most beautiful passages of the trilogy, we
read of Sam's thoughts:

> Far above the Ephel Dúath in the West the night-sky was still
> dim and pale. There, peeping among the cloud-wrack above a
> dark tor high up in the mountains, Sam saw a white star twinkle
> for a while. The beauty of it smote his heart, as he looked up
> out of the forsaken land, and hope returned to him. For like a
> shaft, clear and cold, the thought pierced him that in the end
> the Shadow was only a small and passing thing: there was light
> and high beauty for ever beyond its reach. His song in the Tower
> had been defiance rather than hope; for then he was thinking of
> himself. Now, for a moment, his own fate, and even his master's,
> ceased to trouble him. (ROTK, p. 199)

What exactly does Sam see? Just a single star. Nor is there any
deep philosophical dialogue about the meaning of that star.
Rather, it is one simple thought, reaching him at a level much
more intuitive and visceral than intellectual: *The Shadow is only
a small and passing thing: there is light and high beauty for ever
beyond its reach.* Like Sam himself, the thought is simple, but

also profound. For it tells him that even if he fails in his quest, it will not mean that evil will triumph forever. The scope of Ilúvatar's plan is much broader than that. And in light of the greater scope, his own troubles are put in a new perspective. Like Théoden, he moves from *thinking of himself* to thinking of others. In other words, he moves from selfishness to unselfishness. And the less he focuses on himself, Tolkien is saying, the less his own fate troubles him. And hope returns to him.

The Power of the Authority

Now it is not only the abstract notion of some broader *plan* of the Authority that gives hope (both to the characters within the story and to its readers); the evidence of the Authority's *power* at work in practical and visible ways provides an even greater hope. Again, though the Authority is not explicitly named, evidence of the workings of the Authority's power in *The Lord of the Rings* is significant even if not abundant. Consider the finding of the One Ring. As Gandalf tells Frodo, "it was the strangest event in the whole history of the Ring so far: Bilbo's arrival just in time, and putting his hand on it, blindly, in the dark" (FOTR, p. 65). This comment alone does not necessarily point to Ilúvatar's power at work. In the context of *The Hobbit*, it might be seen merely as one additional lucky event in a long chain of lucky events. In this case, however, the event—the finding of that "tiny ring of cold metal" in the midst of all the vast underground chambers and tunnels—seems rather far-fetched even for Bilbo's luck. Suppose a whole army of Hobbits was sent underground beneath the mountains and told to look for the Ring. We would still have to say their chances of finding it were rather slim. How many readers have ever dropped a ring or similar object in the safe confines of their living room and been unable to find it? Now add the fact that Bilbo isn't even looking for the Ring at the time he discovers it. He just places his hand down in exactly the right place where it has been dropped on the hard floor of the tunnel, and not six inches to one side or another. This is so astronomically unlikely that the word *luck* cannot even describe it. Indeed, though the reader is told, for example, that the riddle game is won by "pure luck," the finding of the Ring is one place in *The Hobbit* where Tolkien specifically does not use the word *luck* (TH, pp. 65–74). If not luck, then what is behind this event? It is hinted in the hindsight offered by *The Lord of the Rings* that this event was the result of a higher power. Gandalf explains this to Frodo:

> "There was more than one power at work, Frodo. The Ring was trying to get back to its master. . . .
>
> Behind that there was something else at work, beyond any design of the Ring-maker. I can put it no plainer than by saying that Bilbo was *meant* to find the Ring, and *not* by its maker. In which case you also were *meant* to have it. And that may be an encouraging thought." (FOTR, p. 65, emphasis Tolkien's)

This is as close as Gandalf comes to explaining to Frodo the theology of Middle-earth. Those who have read *The Silmarillion* first can more fully grasp what Gandalf is speaking of. Up to this point, he has been telling Frodo about the power of Sauron. Now suddenly he speaks of *another* Authority or power at work: one, we are led to understand, that is greater and higher than the Dark Lord. It is this *other* Authority that overrules the will of the Ring to return to its master, and the will of the master to recover the Ring, and instead leads the ring to Bilbo, and thence to Frodo. For that other Authority has its own purpose, in which the Ring is meant to go to Frodo (and not to Sauron, its maker), and it *acts in power* to bring this purpose to fulfillment. In fact, in part 3 of Appendix A to *The Lord of the Rings,* it is hinted by Gandalf that the entire Quest of *The Hobbit* was brought about by similar involvement of this Authority, at work in a seeming "chance-meeting," at an inn in Bree, between Gandalf and an important dwarf named Thorin (ROTK, pp. 359–60). The meeting, however, was no more "chance" than was the Council of Elrond. In any case, when the characters of Middle-earth can see that there is a caring and powerful Authority at work in the events of Middle-earth, it is indeed an encouraging thought: one that creates a sense of hope.

At times this Authority grants an apparently supernatural power to those serving him. Gandalf, as an angelic being—one of the Istari—naturally possesses some of this power. We see it manifest in a few places, most notably when he opposes evil beings of similar power, such as the winged Nazgûl attacking Faramir's retreating forces, or the Balrog of Moria at Khazad-dûm:

> "You cannot pass," [Gandalf] said. . . ." I am a servant of the Secret Fire, wielder of the flame of Anor. You cannot pass. The dark fire will not avail you, flame of Udûn. Go back to the Shadow! You cannot pass." (FOTR, p. 345)

This passage is interesting to note with respect to Gandalf's power, because Tolkien (through Gandalf) gives his readers a hint of the source of this power. What is meant by "servant of the Secret Fire" and "wielder of the *flame of Anor*"? The flame of Anor may refer to Narya, the Ring of Fire, one of the three Elven-rings. We learn at the end of the trilogy that Gandalf is the *wielder* of Narya, which had been given him earlier by Círdan. However, there is no explicit connection between Narya and Anor; the name *Anor* is just a derivative of *Anar*, the Elven name for the sun. So if "the flame of Anor" refers to Narya, why is that particular name used for Narya here and nowhere else? Whether the *flame of Anor* refers to Narya or not, one guess as to the significance of that title is that it is the Valar who put Anor (the sun) in the sky, and who govern its course.[5] The Valar originally set the sun above Middle-earth to help thwart Melkor's evil deeds done in darkness. Anor is drawn on its path by Arien, a "spirit of fire whom Melkor had not deceived nor drawn to his service" (TS, p. 114). Melkor feared Arien and Anor "with a great fear, but dared not come nigh her" (TS, p. 117). We also might simply note that the realm of the sun is in the heavens, and so the flame of Anor would seem to be a

5. See chapter 11 of *The Silmarillion*.

reference to the heavens, or to heaven, or to the supernatural power of heaven set against Melkor's own dark powers.

Of equal or greater interest is the reference to the "Secret Fire." Again, readers of *The Lord of the Rings* might guess that this also is a reference to Narya, which, as mentioned, is the Ring of Fire. Narya certainly gives Gandalf power. However, it doesn't quite make sense for Gandalf to claim that he is a servant of a ring; Narya would have been something he wielded rather than served. It is more likely that the "Secret Fire" is another name for the Imperishable Flame. In the fourth paragraph of the Ainulindalë, the tale of the creation and the Music of the Ainur, which is the opening part of *The Silmarillion,* there is a reference to the "secret fire" (though as here, with lowercase *s* and *f*); and again in the first paragraph of the Valaquenta, the second part of *The Silmarillion,* there is another reference to the "Secret Fire" (this time capitalized). In both cases it seems to be another name or description for the Flame Imperishable. But the Secret Fire, or Flame Imperishable, is with Ilúvatar (TS, p. 4)—that is, in heaven. Thus, this is another reference to the power of heaven.

In fact, the imagery of the Secret Fire may be even more specific than this. Clyde Kilby, who spent the summer of 1966 working with Tolkien at Oxford, helping him get *The Silmarillion* in order for publication, wrote, "Professor Tolkien talked to me at some length about the use of the word 'holy' in *The Silmarillion.* Very specifically he told me that the 'Secret Fire sent to burn at the heart of the World' in the beginning was the Holy Spirit" (Ki, p. 59).[6] Thus, the creation passage in *The Silmarillion* with its reference to the "Secret Fire" is akin to Genesis 1:2: "And the earth was void and empty, and darkness was upon the face of the deep; and the spirit of God moved over the waters." This makes the words of Gandalf even more telling. They may mean, quite plainly: "I am a servant of the Holy Spirit." Udûn, by contrast, is a region of Mordor and a synonym for hell. (See the index at the end of *The Lord of the*

---

6. This observation was mentioned as a footnote in a previous chapter, in the context of discussing the source of creativity.

Rings.) Thus Gandalf makes it clear that the battle between himself and the Balrog is in reality a battle between heaven and hell—or specifically between a servant of Ilúvatar and a servant of Morgoth, Ilúvatar's enemy. Furthermore, as Gandalf indicates, since Ilúvatar is the more powerful, he has the confidence to face this enemy. Readers of this passage who are familiar with the biblical narrative will recognize his words as not unlike those spoken by David to Goliath: "And David said to the Philistine: Thou comest to me with a sword, and with a spear, and with a shield: but I come to thee in the name of the Lord of hosts, the God of the armies of Israel, which thou hast defied" (1 Sam. 17:45). As with David, whose confidence comes from his trust in God, Gandalf's confidence, or hope, comes from his hope in Ilúvatar's power. In any case, from the letter we quoted earlier we see that the power given to Gandalf after his return is a supernatural power enhanced by what Tolkien's narrator calls the Authority so that he can do the work that the Authority sent him to do. This is a message of hope for Sauron's enemies: such a power is being used on their behalf against their enemy.

It is more surprising, perhaps, to see supernatural power at work not through a wizard but through the Hobbit Sam, a lowly gardener from the Shire. Yet this seems to be what happens when he faces Shelob:

"Galadriel!" he said faintly, and then he heard voices far off but clear: the crying of the Elves as they walked under the stars in the beloved shadows of the Shire, and the music of the Elves as it came through his sleep in the Hall of Fire in the house of Elrond.
Gilthoniel A Elbereth!
And then his tongue was loosed and his voice cried in a language which he did not know:
A Elbereth Gilthoniel!
o menel palan-diriel
le nallon sí di'nguruthos!
A tiro nin, Fanuilos! . . .
As if his indomitable spirit had set its potency in motion, the glass blazed suddenly like a white torch in his hand. It flamed

like a star that leaping from the firmament sears the dark air
with intolerable light. (TT, pp. 338–39)

We might see this display of power merely as Sam's unconscious
memory recalling words he heard months earlier in the Shire,
or as the potency of Galadriel herself at work through her star-
glass, given as a gift to Frodo, or even as some latent power
at work in Sam's *indomitable spirit*. All these ideas are present
in the passage, but there are two additional things suggesting
this miraculous display of power is of a supernatural source,
coming from a higher Authority at a time of great need. Some
readers may recognize this passage as resonating with the New
Testament narrative of the coming of the Holy Spirit on the
apostles at the day of Pentecost. (See Acts 2:1–4.) When the
Holy Spirit comes—not insignificantly, in the visible form of a
flame—Jesus' apostles receive the supernatural power to speak
in languages that they do not know. Many other miraculous
powers also follow in the coming days: the power to heal, *and
even power to drive out evil spirits*. This is precisely the manifestation of power we see in Sam. First he speaks words he
does not understand in a language he does not know. They are,
of course, words of great power! Then he drives out Shelob,
the evil being. It is probably not coincidental that the passage
speaks of Sam's indomitable *spirit* rather than his body or even
his will, for with such a reference Tolkien leads the readers
at least to be thinking about the spiritual reality rather than
the physical.

     Additionally, we must consider the name upon which Sam
now calls for help. It is not Galadriel, the powerful Elven queen
whom he has met and would have reason to recall, but who
is nonetheless a being of flesh more akin to him than to the
Valar. Rather it is the Vala Elbereth. Elbereth, which means
"Star-Queen," is another name for Varda, the queen of the Valar
and spouse of Manwë the king. Of her we read, "The light of
Ilúvatar lives still in her face. . . . Elbereth [the Elves] name her
. . . and they call upon her name out of the shadows of Middle-
earth, and uplift it in song at the rising of the stars" (TS, pp.
18–19). She is also called Gilthoniel, meaning "Star-Kindler," a

title of praise and adoration used only of Elbereth, who made the stars. When Frodo strikes the Black Rider at Weather-top, Aragorn comments, "More deadly to him was the name of Elbereth" (FOTR, p. 210). Indeed, in the light of Tolkien's Catholicism, we cannot help but see in the honoring of Elbe-reth some reflection of the veneration of Mary. Thus, though he does not understand it himself, Sam is praising the Queen of Angels and calling upon her for aid. So his vague memory, the potency of the star-glass, and his indomitable spirit are not *sources* of this power, but rather *vehicles* through which the greater power is at work.

Thus, Tolkien lets his readers see both Gandalf and Sam as instruments through whom the Authority demonstrates his power in *The Lord of the Rings*. However, the most important demonstration of the power of Ilúvatar does not involve any physical being within Middle-earth at all. Rather, it is the battle of the winds that takes place high above Middle-earth in *The Return of the King*. This battle is the turning point in the siege of Minas Tirith, for the reversal of winds blows back the black clouds of Mordor and lets the sun shine once again. So impor-tant is it that it is noticed in all of the separate threads of the nar-rative going on at this point, and it is used to tie all the threads together. It is noticed by Merry as he travels with Théoden and Éowyn: "Then suddenly Merry felt it at last, beyond doubt: a change. Wind was in his face! Light was glimmering. Far, far away, in the South the clouds could be dimly seen as remote grey shapes, rolling up, drifting: morning lay beyond them" (ROTK, p. 112). It is noticed by Pippin and Gandalf as they make their way back from Gandalf's confrontation at the gate: "They felt the wind blowing in their faces, and they caught the glimmer of morning far away, a light growing in the southern sky" (ROTK, p. 127). Gimli recalls it as he and Legolas recount to Merry in the House of Healing something of their strange tale with Aragorn. "Hope was indeed born anew. . . . a change coming with a fresh wind from the Sea. . . . And so it was, as you know, that we came in the third hour of the morning with a fair wind and the Sun unveiled" (ROTK, p. 153). Perhaps the clearest expression of the spiritual significance can be seen in Sam and Frodo's part of the story.

> There was battle far above in the high spaces of the air. The billowing clouds of Mordor were being driven back, their edges tattering as a wind out of the living world came up and swept the fumes and smokes towards the dark land of their home. Under the lifting skirts of the dreary canopy dim light leaked into Mordor like pale morning through the grimed window of a prison.
>
> "Look at it, Mr. Frodo!" said Sam. "Look at it! The wind's changed. Something's happening. He's not having it all his own way. His darkness is breaking up out in the world there. I wish I could see what is going on!" (ROTK, p. 196)

It is significant that Tolkien uses the word *battle* to describe what is happening. The first thing he shows us here is that the change in winds is not just a coincidence, or good luck, but yet another part of the great war going on in Middle-earth. The imagery that follows is equally significant. Though the winds certainly are a part of the physical universe, the phrase "far above in the high spaces of the air" carries the suggestion of heaven. That is, this is a war going on in heaven, or in the spiritual realm. Certainly no physical being within Middle-earth accomplishes this; these are the winds of Manwë, or of Ilúvatar himself. Ilúvatar's power is at work to rescue the people of Middle-earth. Sauron may be powerful, and his power brings terrible despair to his enemies, but there is one who is infinitely more powerful than Sauron. Thus, Sauron does not have it all his own way. His darkness does not go unopposed. Tolkien shows his reader that the power that is against Sauron is the power that controls the winds and the airs. This, as is evident in Sam's words, is a source of tremendous hope to the people of Middle-earth.

Free Will and the Hand of the Authority

That the hand of Authority intervenes in the affairs of Middle-earth on behalf of those who serve him—whether through Gandalf, or through Galadriel's glass, or through battles in the heavens, or through what appear to be lucky events—is, as we saw, a source of hope. Ilúvatar's intervention does not remove the significance of the choices made by the Children of Ilúvatar, but in many ways it can redeem those choices. Or, to put this another way, the characters are responsible only for their own choices and not for the outcome of those choices; they are responsible for the means, while the ends are in Ilúvatar's hands.

We see this principle at work in countless ways throughout *The Lord of the Rings*. Earlier in this book, we saw that so many choices made by the wise and noble are not aimed at military victory. We now observe that by the power of Ilúvatar many of these choices result in a greater good than was imagined by those making the choices. Among these, one of the best examples is Aragorn's choice to pursue the Orcs across Rohan to rescue Merry and Pippin. As noted earlier, of the three courses of action considered by Aragorn, this one makes the least sense from a strategic standpoint. The fate of Middle-earth lies with the actions unfolding to the east, as Frodo and Sam make their way toward Mordor. Gondor lies to the south, and there, it would seem to Aragorn at the time, also lies the hope of Middle-earth as well as Aragorn's own heart. To the west are only two seemingly insignificant Hobbits. Aragorn, however, feels a moral duty to go west and rescue the Hobbits, rather than let them suffer torture. In doing so, he guesses (wrongly, as it turns out) that he may be taking himself out of the battle for Middle-earth. Yet this choice proves pivotal, as Gandalf explains:

> "You chose amid doubts the path that seemed right: the choice was just, and it has been rewarded. For so we have met in time, who otherwise might have met too late. But the quest of your

companions is over. Your next journey is marked by your given word." (TT, p. 104)

Gandalf does not say that Aragorn's choice was strategic, or even wise, but rather that it was *right* and *just*—words in which the idea of moral goodness is implicit. Likewise, Aragorn's next choice is not determined by strategic planning or military foresight, but morally by his *given word*, meaning that holding to the virtue of honesty is more important than good strategy—a point made several times in chapter 3 of this book. Yet the Authority is able to take these choices and *reward* them, making them bear fruit that may be unintended but that is good. Indeed, had Aragorn not followed Merry and Pippin, his help might never have come to Rohan, in which case King Théoden might never have been healed. And had Rohan fallen, then its help would not have reached Minas Tirith, but instead a whole new host of enemies. Nor would Aragorn have followed the Paths of the Dead. In short, it is likely that Gondor would have fallen had Aragorn chosen to go directly to Minas Tirith to try to rescue it. As a consequence of the fall of Gondor, the diversionary assault upon the Black Gates would never have taken place, and it is possible that Frodo might also have failed.

The same may be said of the decision to include Merry and Pippin in the Fellowship—another decision made, at least on the surface of things, on the basis of friendship and not for any demonstrable strategic advantage or military wisdom. "I think, Elrond," Gandalf advises as they are planning the membership of the Fellowship, "that in this matter it would be well to trust rather to their *friendship* than to great *wisdom*" (FOTR, p. 289, emphasis mine). Yet as Gandalf discovers in hindsight, at a much later point in the story:

> "It was not in vain that the young hobbits came with us, if only for Boromir's sake. But that is not the only part they have to play. They were brought to Fangorn, and their coming was like the falling of small stones that starts an avalanche in the mountains." (TT, p. 99)

Of course what looks like hindsight may well have been foresight on Gandalf's point, but if so he was able to offer no concrete reasoning for that foresight other than the value of friendship. Yet as we see, even the downfall of Isengard is brought about because of the presence of the Hobbits.

Indeed, even *the work of the Enemy* can be used by the Authority to accomplish something good. This is one of the central themes of *The Silmarillion*. Ilúvatar says to Melkor:

> "And thou, Melkor, shalt see that no theme may be played that hath not its uttermost source in me, nor can any alter the music in my despite. For he that attempteth this shall prove but mine instrument in the devising of things more wonderful, which he himself hath not imagined." (TS, p. 6)

Later he says of the race of Men: "These too in their time shall find that all that they do redounds at the end only to the glory of my work" (TS, p. 38). This theme might be seen as reflecting a Christian principle that the apostle Paul expresses in Romans 8:28: "And we know that to them that love God all things work together unto good: to such as, according to his purpose, are called to be saints." It is a principle illustrated wonderfully in *The Lord of the Rings* in the story of Merry and Pippin. For it is important not only that these two Hobbits are a part of the Quest—a decision of their own and of Elrond's—but that their enemies the Orcs capture them. They do not go to Fangorn of their own will; they are *brought* there. Brought by whom? By the Orcs, yes. But if we carry over our understanding from *The Silmarillion,* the hand of Ilúvatar is also involved in making use of this.

For most of the characters in the story, there is no indication of any knowledge of or faith in Ilúvatar. For the wisest of the wise, however—especially Gandalf, Elrond, and Galadriel, but at times also Aragorn and Faramir and a few others—there is often seen an explicit faith in the higher Authority. It is faith in the power and purpose of the Authority that enables them to do what is morally right rather than what appears to hold the most promise. It is faith that enables Gandalf to be full of joy even when all is dark. And from Gandalf, Elrond, and Galadriel, this vision of faith often passes to others, whether it is Gandalf (and later Aragorn) comforting Frodo with the thought that he was *meant* to find the Ring, or Elrond telling the strangers at the Council that they were *called,* or Galadriel telling the companions toward the end of their stay in Loth-lórien: "Sleep in peace! Do not trouble your hearts overmuch with thought of the road tonight. Maybe the paths that you each shall tread are already laid before your feet, though you do not see them. Good night!" (FOTR, p. 384). The message is similar: There is a hand of Authority at work in the world, guiding the events and preparing the paths so that his purposes are fulfilled. Those who follow him need concern themselves only with doing what is right, and not in the results of those decisions. *It is not their part to master all the tides of the world,* Gandalf tells them, *but to do what is in them for the succor of those years wherein they are set, uprooting the evil in the fields that they know, so that those who live after may have clean earth to till. What weather that will be is not theirs to rule.*

What better example is there than the final success of Frodo's quest? The list is long of those who, somewhere along the way, show mercy to Gollum and spare his life, doing what they think is right even though it seems to be a risky thing. And their mercy is rewarded, despite the failure of Frodo at the very end. One word for this is *grace.* Another—a word coined by Tolkien that he associates with grace—is *eucatastrophe.*

10

ilúvatar's Theme
and the Real War

In his brilliant essay "On Fairy-Stories," Tolkien makes several comments about the goals and purposes of myth and fairy-story—a category that includes what we now call fantasy literature. Of the mythical and fairy-tale setting, he writes: "They open a door on Other Time, and if we pass through, though only for a moment, we stand outside our own time, outside Time itself, maybe" (FS, p. 129). And a little later in this essay, he adds, "The peculiar quality of the 'joy' in successful Fantasy can thus be explained as a sudden glimpse of the underlying reality or truth" (FS, p. 155). Fantasy literature—at least the higher and better literature of that kind, of which Tolkien's writing is the prime example—transports us outside our own time (and space). Or at least it opens the door that we may travel there ourselves. And once there, in other time and space, we look at something that is timeless, and we are able to see truths, or Truth, that we might not see within the context and confines of our own limited perspective. If the fantasy is written well—if it is "successful," to use a term from Tolkien's essay—then it gives a glimpse of the *underlying reality or truth,* and because

199

that truth is seen apart from our own particular and peculiar time, we are able to see its universality rather than merely associating it with one time and place. For as we have seen illustrated in numerous ways in *The Lord of the Rings*, *The Hobbit*, and even in the essay "On Fairy-Stories," Tolkien did believe that Truth is absolute and objective, and not relative to time or space: that there is an underlying truth that we can (and ought to try to) see.

In his book *The Orphean Passages*, Walter Wangerin Jr. expresses in slightly different words something of what I think Tolkien is saying in his essay:[1]

> In order to comprehend the experience one is living in, he must, by imagination and by intellect, be lifted out of it. He must be given to see it whole; but since he can never wholly gaze upon his own life while he lives it, he gazes upon the life that, in symbol, comprehends his own. Art presents such lives, such symbols. Myth especially—persisting as a mother of truth through countless generations and for many disparate cultures, coming therefore with the approval not of a single people but of *people*—myth presents, myth *is*, such a symbol, shorn and unadorned, refined and true. And when the one who gazes upon that myth suddenly, in dreadful recognition, cries out, "There I am! That is me!" then the marvelous translation has occurred: he is lifted out of himself to see himself wholly.

Wangerin's "mother of truth" is Tolkien's "underlying reality or truth," which myth (and fairy tale and fantasy) is the ideal vehicle for revealing. It is not just some distant inapplicable truth that we see, but a truth that speaks to our own situation. As Tolkien also writes, in describing the recovery that fairy stories can bring us, "We should meet the centaur and the dragon, and then perhaps suddenly behold, like the ancient shepherds, sheep, and dogs, and horses—and wolves. This recovery fairy-stories help us to make" (FS, p. 146). The glimpses of the fantastic in the realm of Faërie can help us see

1. Walter Wangerin Jr., *The Orphean Passages* (Grand Rapids: Zondervan, 1986), pp. 14–15.

in a new light that which is common and part of our primary world. In fact, we even see ourselves more clearly—we see the truth about ourselves in *dreadful recognition*—in a way we might not otherwise see.

My goal in writing this book has been to suggest some of the "underlying reality or truth" into which Tolkien gives us a glimpse. One need not, by any means, agree with Tolkien's understanding of truth in order to enjoy and appreciate his work. That is, one needn't believe that his idea of truth is *The Truth,* or even that there is such a thing as truth. Yet whether or not one agrees with Tolkien's views of truth and reality, it is tremendously helpful, and perhaps indispensable, to at least understand what those views are if one is to understand what Tolkien was seeking to accomplish in his work. Then again, it just may be—and this is my own view here—that part of the reason for the phenomenal success of *The Hobbit* and *The Lord of the Rings* is that the books really do have the ring of truth through all of their important particulars. Further, even readers who do not give intellectual assent to those truth claims that are fundamental to Tolkien's work (when they are spelled out as in this book) may be subconsciously drawn to the work as being true. Whatever the readers may think of the underlying reality and truths into which Tolkien is giving us a glimpse, they are not trivial truths but ones dealing with the fundamental questions of our existence as humans. As Tolkien also wrote in that essay, the "electric street-lamp"—along with many things that seem so important in the world of supposedly realistic fiction—"may indeed be ignored, simply because it is so insignificant and transient. Fairy-stories, at any rate, have many more permanent and fundamental things to talk about" (FS, p. 149). I hope the reader will agree that the themes we have discussed in this book do deal with *permanent and fundamental things.* This is by no means a boast about any particular virtues in this book, but rather about the significance of J. R. R. Tolkien's writing.

If Tolkien's theistic Christian worldview is in any sense correct—if the Christian expression is the underlying truth about the world—then the most permanent and fundamental thing we might wish to talk about is Ilúvatar himself: Eru, the One, Father of All, both the Author of Middle-earth and the Authority over it. (Again, even if some readers don't believe this view to be true, they still might wish to talk about Ilúvatar for the purpose of understanding Tolkien's writing!) Indeed, as Tolkien also wrote of myth and fairy, "Something really 'higher' is occasionally glimpsed in mythology: Divinity, the right to power (as distinct from its possession), the due of worship; in fact 'religion'" (FS, p. 124). These words are certainly a true description of what may be found in Tolkien's own writing. Thus, for example, amidst the many glimpses of the corruption of the earthly (or Middle-earthly) desire for the power of domination are also numerous *glimpses* of real *divinity, the right to power*. This is not the only truth we are given glimpses of in Tolkien's writing. Many aspects of his books reflect elements of underlying truth, as we have been exploring throughout this text. However, if Tolkien is correct about the reality of divinity, then this existence and importance and power of the Authority—the "due of worship," the "something really higher"—is a truth worth exploring.

These strong theological underpinnings of Tolkien's work, especially with respect to salvation, as discussed earlier, and to the hand of Ilúvatar, discussed in the previous chapter, raise several more questions: Do *The Silmarillion, The Hobbit,* and *The Lord of the Rings* comprise a Christian mythology? If so, how? And if not, why not?

Not a Christian Myth?

My answer to this last question, "Do *The Silmarillion, The Hobbit,* and *The Lord of the Rings* comprise a Christian mythology?" is a firm and definite "yes and no." I would feel guilty giving such a vague, equivocal answer, except that I think Tolkien's own answer to this question would also be "yes and no," depending on how the question is meant and the context in which it is asked. As we approach the end of this book, let us now explore both what Tolkien said *about* his great trilogy, *The Lord of the Rings,* and also a few more aspects of the works themselves that illustrate these points, and see how both answers may seem to be correct in certain contexts.

I will begin by answering, "No. *The Lord of the Rings* is not a Christian mythology." A starting point for this answer is what Tolkien himself wrote about his own works, in what has become the well-known "Foreword to the Second Edition." Of the origins of *The Silmarillion,* he writes, "it was primarily linguistic in inspiration" (FOTR, p. 5), and of *The Lord of the Rings* he adds:

> The prime motive was the desire of a tale-teller to try his hand at a really long story that would hold the attention of readers, amuse them, delight them, and at times maybe excite them or deeply move them. . . .
>
> As for any inner meaning or "message," it has in the intention of the author none. It is neither allegorical nor topical. (FOTR, p. 6)

In other words, if by saying that Tolkien's Middle-earth mythology in general, and *The Lord of the Rings* in particular, is a Christian mythology one meant that Tolkien had some hidden agenda leading him to write a cleverly disguised bit of Christian propaganda, or even a Christian allegory, then I would have to disagree. Indeed, on the evidence of Tolkien's own writing about his writing, I would have to say that this idea is altogether misguided. At the least, Tolkien had a well-known distaste for allegory. "I cordially dislike allegory in all its manifestations, and always have done so since I grew old and wary enough to detect its presence" (FOTR, p. 7). Put another way, the stories of Middle-earth are not written as Sunday school lessons. In the stated intention of the author, they are on the one hand linguistic explorations and on the other stories intended to amuse, delight, and move the reader. This is not to say that these goals are somehow *un*-Christian. Christian theology says much about delight, and about the value of art and creativity, and about language. We merely observe that there is nothing *uniquely* Christian about either linguistic exploration or about telling a good story.

Another bit of support for answering "no" is simply to show how important mythologies *other* than the Christian mythology were as inspirations for Tolkien's writing. In particular, there is a strong influence of pagan Germanic mythology in *The Hobbit* and *The Lord of the Rings*. No one who knew Tolkien personally would be surprised to hear this, whether they had read his books or not. Tolkien was deeply in love with this early northern mythology and appreciated its richness and depth. In "On Fairy-Stories" he writes:

> I had no desire to have either dreams or adventures like Alice [in Wonderland], and the account of them merely amused me. I had very little desire to look for buried treasure or fight pirates, and Treasure Island left me cool. . . . But the land of Merlin and Arthur was better than these, and best of all the nameless North of Sigurd of the Völsungs, and the prince of all dragons. (FS, pp. 134–35)

We see this influence everywhere in Middle-earth. Not only are the names of the Dwarves (and the wizard) in *The Hobbit* taken directly from Snorri Sturluson's *Prose Edda*—an important piece of twelfth-century Icelandic writing that is a centerpiece in Norse mythology—but the story is based largely on the poem *Beowulf*. Indeed, *Beowulf* almost has to be seen as the most important narrative source for *The Hobbit*. There are at least three Beowulf figures in *The Hobbit*. On the surface, Thorin Oakenshield is the obvious example. The parallels between Thorin and the character Beowulf are numerous. Like Beowulf, Thorin is the descendant of the great kings of old, who leads a group of fourteen companions (if you count Gandalf) on a quest in which they face several monsters, culminating with the dragon who is woken to a rage by a thief. The dragon is slain, but Thorin also dies and is buried with his great sword and with treasure taken from the worm's hoard.

Beorn is even more of a Beowulf figure than Thorin, as the similarity in their names suggests. Beowulf possesses superhuman strength—the strength of thirty men, we are told by the poet—and is invincible in battle until he faces the dragon at the end of his life. Likewise, Beorn is a bear-man, whose superhuman strength and prowess are clearly visible at the Battle of Five Armies.

> He came alone, and in bear's shape; and he seemed to have grown almost to giant-size in his wrath.
> The roar of his voice was like drums and guns; and he tossed wolves and goblins from his path like straws and feathers. . . .
> . . . so that nothing could withstand him, and no weapon seemed to bite upon him. (TH, p. 244)

Beorn's house closely resembles a medieval Germanic mead hall, right down to the beverage served there; it is described as "a wide wall with a fire-place in the middle," where they "sat long at the table with their wooden drinking-bowls filled with mead" (TH, pp. 105, 112). Tolkien's illustration of Beorn's house (found in some editions of *The Hobbit*) could easily be a drawing of a mead hall and is highly similar to a mead-hall drawing in Gordon's *Introduction to Old Norse*.[2] Given Tolkien's philological interest, it is certainly significant that while Beorn is himself a bear-man, or were-bear, Beowulf's name *means* "bear"—though in a roundabout way: *Beowulf* is translated literally to "bee-wolf," but a wolf is another name for a thief, hence a bee-wolf is a bee-thief, or honey-thief, or bear.

Even Bilbo is a kind of Beowulf figure, though the alliteration in their names is likely an accident. Bilbo lacks Beowulf's superhuman strength, but he gains through the Ring some measure of superhuman abilities. By the end of the quest it is he, and not Thorin, who is the real leader of the company. It is also Bilbo, and not Thorin, who aids Bard in slaying the dragon. Finally, Bilbo is himself a bee-thief like Beowulf—though with a little twist typical of many of Tolkien's philological jokes. Rather than being a thief *of* bees as Beowulf the bear is, Bilbo is a thief (a burglar to be exact) who is a bee (he carries a Sting).

2. The similarity between Tolkien's drawing and Gordon's illustration was pointed out to me by Prof. Jonathan Evans of the University of Georgia.

Recall also the tale of Éowyn, Théoden, and the people of Rohan discussed earlier in this book. They are clearly modeled after the Anglo-Saxon people; their values, customs, and ceremonies are those of pagan Germanic prehistory. We should also note that the Elvish language (though not the Elves themselves) is modeled after Old Finnish. Even *The Silmarillion* provides an example. Though Middle-earth is very clearly a monotheistic world—Eru means "the One"—once we get beyond the short creation story of *The Ainulindalë*, we see much more of the Valar (the gods) than we do of Ilúvatar (the God), and thus in many ways the remainder of the book reads more like Norse mythology than it does like the book of Genesis in the Bible. The point here is that the story—by which I now mean the plot, the characters, the setting, and the language of both *The Hobbit* and *The Lord of the Rings*—has far more *visible* elements that are identifiable with pagan Germanic mythology than with the Christian myth.[3]

In answering the question of whether the Middle-earth mythology is Christian we also must recognize the fact that there is almost no explicit reference to religion anywhere in *The Lord of the Rings*. Though there are veiled references to a higher Authority—many of which have been discussed earlier—there is only one place where we see anything remotely resembling a religious practice, and that is when Faramir and his men face the west in a moment of silence before their meals: a custom that brings to mind the practice of prayer. Faramir says, "We look towards Númenor that was, and beyond to Elvenhome that is, and to that which is beyond Elvenhome and will ever be" (TT, pp. 284–85). This strongly echoes Christian prayer, especially the Gloria Patri: *who was and who is and who ever shall be.* But though the phrase "that which . . . will ever be" certainly brings to mind the divine—the Eternal Omnipotence—there is no explanation beyond that, and only if one has read *The Silmarillion* would one recognize this last phrase as a reference to Ilúvatar.

3. Note that while *Beowulf* itself is almost certainly the product of a Christian society, it is still largely pagan in its narrative detail and framework.

The Missing Piece

Finally, the ultimate reason to say "no" to categorizing the Middle-earth mythology as Christian is both the simplest and the most profound: there is no Christ in these stories! Christianity rests fundamentally on a set of historical events: the birth, life, death, and especially the resurrection of Jesus the Christ. At a real moment in the earth's history, God the Son was incarnate; he became a man and lived on the earth. As is written about Jesus in the Gospel of John, "He was in the world: and the world was made by him: and the world knew him not. . . . And the Word was made flesh and dwelt among us" (John 1:10, 14a). Paul the apostle, the first international missionary of Christianity in its infancy, also understood clearly the significance of the historical incarnation and resurrection when he wrote:

> Christ died for our sins, according to the scriptures: And that he was buried: and that he rose again according to the scriptures: And that he was seen by Cephas, and after that by the eleven. Then was he seen by more than five hundred brethren at once:
> And if Christ be not risen again, then is our preaching vain: and your faith is also vain. . . . And if Christ be not risen again, your faith is vain: for you are yet in your sins. (1 Cor. 15:3–6a, 14, 17)

In short, the story of Christ may be a beautiful story, but in the Christian understanding it won't bring salvation unless it really happened as a historical event—unless God the Creator entered his creation at a particular moment in its history. Faith in this story, if it is not historically true, is futile and worthless. According to Paul, this historicity is of *first importance* to Christianity.

J. R. R. Tolkien also understood the importance to Christianity of the incarnation as a real historical event in addition to its status as a powerful myth. He writes, toward the end of "On Fairy-Stories":

But this [Gospel] story has entered History and the primary world; the desire and aspiration of sub-creation has been raised to the fulfillment of Creation. The Birth of Christ is the eucatastrophe of Man's history. The Resurrection is the eucatastrophe of the story of the Incarnation. This story begins and ends in joy. It has pre-eminently the "inner consistency of reality." There is no tale ever told that men would rather find was true, and none which so many sceptical men have accepted as true on its own merits. (FS, p. 156)[4]

Emphasizing the reality of the incarnation, Tolkien uses the term *history* twice, and also twice uses the word *true* to refer to the actuality of the events of the Gospel story within history. Even the term *eucatastrophe*, which Tolkien coined, implies a real event: that is to say, an event with a real, sudden, and dramatic impact. Thus, the power of the Gospel story, which Tolkien describes earlier in that paragraph as containing "a fairy-story of a larger kind which embraces all the essence of fairy-stories," goes beyond words to the underlying truth, which in this case is the reality of history. The story itself is beautiful, containing "many marvels—peculiarly artistic, beautiful, and moving: 'mythical' in their perfect self-contained significance." However the chief part of the power and beauty of that story—as Tolkien writes, the ultimate "fulfillment" of the creative art at work in story itself—comes from the fact that this story has entered the history of the primary world.

It is interesting to note here that Tolkien doesn't say the story originated in history, or that it describes history, but rather that it *entered* history, implying that the story preexisted that history. As he writes in the next paragraph, "This story is supreme; and it is true. Legend and History have met and fused." If Tolkien is correct, then the Gospel story is the truth from which all story truths are measured. But no such Gospel is present in *The Lord of the Rings*, or even in *The*

---

4. Earlier in this essay, Tolkien defines *eucatastrophe* as "the joy of the happy ending," or a "sudden and miraculous grace." Literally, the eucatastrophe is the good catastrophe. It is a sudden joyous turn of events "never to be counted on to recur": the "consolation" that is the "true form" and "highest function" of fairy tale (FS, p. 153).

Silmarillion: the story that Tolkien believes has entered the earth's history has not entered the history of his Middle-earth. Yet if the historical presence of that story is critical to the Christian mythology—as Tolkien understood that it is—and if it doesn't exist in Tolkien's mythology, then in what sense can Tolkien's mythology be Christian?

Now one might claim that in fact there are Christ-figures in Middle-earth. If by "Christ-figure" one is referring to characters who imitate Christ in significant ways—by living out the definition of Christian charity, by embodying mercy, truth, wisdom, humility, and faith, and more specifically by giving their lives for the sake of others—then it is easy to agree with this statement: there are characters in Tolkien's writing who are Christlike. Indeed, there are numerous such figures. Gandalf is wise and merciful, committed to truth, and full of faith. At Khazad-dûm, he sacrifices his life for his companions. In this way he is a "Christ-figure." Of greatest importance, he not only dies but is resurrected, passing from death back into life. Aragorn also makes Christlike sacrifices; though his heart longs to go to Minas Tirith, where he might take up the throne of Gondor and earn the right to wed Arwen, he instead sacrifices his goals and ambitions (or so it seems to him at the time) for the sake of the Hobbits Merry and Pippin. Like Christ, Aragorn also is a healer, calling back Éowyn even from death, and Faramir and Merry as well, and later on, Frodo and Sam. And he, too, experiences a sort of resurrection in entering the Paths of the Dead and coming back out again into life. It is also interesting to compare Aragorn's experience with the apostle Paul's description of Christ, who when he ascended from the depths led a host of captives, including the spirits of the dead whom he had rescued from their torment.

Likewise, Frodo, when he takes upon himself the Quest to Mount Doom, is offering his life in Christlike sacrifice for the sake of all the free peoples of Middle-earth. Frodo could certainly be seen as fitting the prophet Isaiah's depiction of the promised Christ: "There is no beauty in him, nor comeliness: and we have seen him, and there was no sightliness, that we should be desirous of him" (Isa. 53:2). Which is to say that

Frodo had no great physical stature that would have made him one of the great of Middle-earth. His experience at the Tower of Cirith Ungol furthers this image. Richard Purtill points out, "His physical sufferings parallel those of Christ: he is imprisoned, stripped of his garments, mocked, and whipped" (Pu, p. 57). And though he does not actually die a physical death and return to life, he is thrice brought back from the *verge* of death: once from the blade of the Nazgûl when he was well on his way to becoming a wraith, once from the sting of Shelob when even Sam had given him up for dead, and once by Aragorn at the end of the Quest. In this last instance we read that he went "to the very brink of death ere [Aragorn] recalled [him]" (ROTK, p. 234). At the conclusion of the trilogy, we see just how real his sacrifice is, for like Christ he always carries the scars of his death wounds (on his hand!), and he is never able to really return to his life again.

Even Boromir, in the final moments of his life, is a sort of Christ-figure in that he gives up his life defending the Hobbits. Yet none of these characters are Christ, for none of them are the incarnate God, and neither is any of them perfect. Christ is the ultimate fulfillment and embodiment, in both the mythic sense and in the primary historical sense, of the completeness of God's love, truth, wisdom, mercy, and ultimately of self-sacrificial giving. He is the perfect sacrifice given for the sins of all mankind. That element is left out of Tolkien's Middle-earth. Gandalf comes the closest to this, but though he is a Maia (or "incarnate angel," as Tolkien ventured to write in a letter) who "passes the test, on a moral plane anyway (he makes mistakes of judgement)" (Letters, p. 202), he is not Ilúvatar incarnate. Though he loves words and takes on flesh, he is not the Word made flesh. And the Christian understanding of the importance of the cross depends both on Jesus' divinity—that he is the Creator and not part of the creation—and on his perfection. In fact, to deal with these sacrifices within Tolkien's story by labeling the characters involved as "Christ-figures," and then subsequently dismissing them as if that "Christ-figure" label says all that needs to be said, diminishes both their sacrifices and the sacrifice of the real Christ. (Such a simplifying label also gets at why Tolkien disliked allegory and was wary of explicit religion in fairy tale and myth.) Jonathan Evans explained well one of the shortcomings of such oversimplifications, in a lecture given at Middlebury College in January 2003:

> The idea of symbolic sacrificial death to save someone or every-one is too universally encountered to permit a narrow definition of one of them as a pattern for all of them. Not that the pattern isn't there: but the way specific instances of this motif are related is probably not one of a simple transference of the pattern from one to another. Like triads, redemption through death and resurrection is a pattern of meaning so deeply inscribed into the nature of things that they will appear in many narratives otherwise unconnected in the literature and mythology of many cultures in many times and places.

These examples of Christlikeness may point back to a Christ, but to find that Christ we must look into the primary world, and into Tolkien's Christian (and specifically Catholic) faith, for we will not find that Christ in Middle-earth.

So if we return to my early chapter on salvation, we real-ize that something is missing there too. As I claimed, Tolkien certainly uses Christian *imagery* of salvation—though he does so by relying on words like *cured* rather than *saved*—and like the Christian Gospel writers, he even ties the spiritual notion of salvation to repentance, especially in the case of Boromir. But the *means* of salvation is never spelled out. In the Chris-tian faith, one is saved through faith in Jesus Christ: faith that he died on a cross to pay the penalty for sin, and that he was raised again from the dead. That is, salvation is not earned by anything the individual does, but rather it comes by God's grace, which is worked out through the death (a real, physical death, occurring within our history) and resurrection of the Christ; Jesus had to die a real death in order to pay for our sins, and in his rising from the dead, death itself is conquered. But this saving faith (or belief) in the Christ cannot be at work in the world of Middle-earth, because there is no Christ in Middle-earth in which to have faith! And since this incarnation of the

Creator within his creation is so important to Christianity, as is his sacrificial death to pay for our sins, it must be argued that any mythology that does not include the death and resurrection of a Christ is therefore not finally a "Christian mythology."

Sorrow and Loss

This last point connects to another aspect of Tolkien's Middle-earth that I have always found very curious. It is hard to read either *The Silmarillion* or *The Lord of the Rings* and not come away with a profound sense of sorrow and loss. Galadriel captures this pathos early on in the trilogy, when she welcomes the Fellowship to Lothlórien with the strangely solemn comment, "For ere the fall of Nargothrond or Gondolin I passed over the mountains, and together through ages of the world we have fought the long defeat" (FOTR, p. 372). This sense of sorrow abounds wherever the reader turns. Consider, for example, our last encounter with the Ents.

> Treebeard's face became sad. "Forests may grow," he said. "Woods may spread. But not Ents. There are no Entings." . . .
>
> . . . "It is long, long since we met by stock or by stone, *A vanimar, vanimálion nostari!*' he said [to Celeborn and Galadriel]. "It is sad that we should meet only thus at the ending. For the world is changing: I feel it in the water, I feel it in the earth, and I smell it in the air. I do not think we shall meet again." (ROTK, p. 259)

This is a clear picture of loss: no Entwives; no Entings; no future. Tolkien leaves the reader with the knowledge that the Ents are doomed to disappear from Middle-earth, and with them something good and wonderful is forever lost. Likewise, we also learn from Celeborn that his own doom is to be parted from Galadriel, while Galadriel's doom is to see—with the destruction of the One Ring—the subsequent loss of all that she had worked for in Lothlórien. Nor are these isolated examples. Rather, as I said earlier, this tone pervades the story. There is also the grievous parting of Arwen from Elrond, her father. "None saw her last meeting with Elrond her father, for they went up into the hills and there spoke long together, and bitter was their parting that should endure beyond the ends of the world" (ROTK, p. 256). Galadriel, Elrond, and Gandalf also depart from Middle-earth forever, leaving it a lesser place. The result of the war proves much as Théoden guessed it would when he asks Gandalf: "May it not so end that much that was fair and wonderful shall pass for ever out of Middle-earth?" To which Gandalf replies, "The evil of Sauron cannot be wholly cured, nor made as if it had not been. But to such days we are doomed" (TT, p. 155).

We might sum up much of this sadness simply by pointing out that *The Lord of the Rings* does not end with the victory celebration and wedding at the Field of Cormallen but with parting at the Grey Havens: "Frodo dropped quietly out of all the doings of the Shire, and Sam was pained to notice how little honour he had in his own country" (ROTK, p. 305). For in the end, Frodo is "too deeply hurt"; he "tried to save the Shire," and it is saved, but not for him. He left "filled with a sadness that was yet blessed and without bitterness" (ROTK, p. 309). It is not that *The Lord of the Rings* is all sadness. There are frequent glimpses of joy. But the joy is a distant, veiled joy, whose source we are not given to see clearly. It is like the passage, discussed earlier, when Sam sees the star from the Land of Shadow, "and hope returned to him. For like a shaft, clear and cold, the thought pierced him that in the end the Shadow was only a small and passing thing: there was light and high beauty for ever beyond its reach." And yet the next moment he is back in Mordor, and the suffering resumes, and light and high beauty are lost and never explained.

The Silmarillion is an even more deeply sorrowful piece. It is centered upon the curse of Fëanor and the evil that arises because of it, yet all of Middle-earth is caught in that web of deceit and destruction. Every major Elven kingdom fails and falls: Hithlum, Lothlann, Nargothrond, Doriath, and lastly, Gondolin. Likewise, nearly all of the great Elven lords are killed: not only the sons of Fëanor, but also Fingolfin, Finrod, Turgon, Thingol, and many others. The tales of Húrin and his son Túrin are especially tragic. Tolkien writes, with profound understatement, "It is called the Tale of Grief, for it is sorrowful" (TS, p. 243). Even the victory of the Valar over Morgoth at the end of the *Quenta Silmarillion* brings little joy. Two of the three Silmarils are lost, and a dark shadow is cast by the last evil act of Fëanor's sons, who hold to their father's wicked oath and slay the guards in the camp of Eönwë, Manwë's herald, in a final effort to possess the jewels. Thus, of Manwë's victorious forces returning to Valinor, we read: "Their joy in victory was diminished, for they returned without the Silmarils from Morgoth's crown, and they knew that those jewels could not be found or brought together again unless the world be broken and remade" (TS, p. 315).

The depths of sorrow, even in victory, are expressed in the final lines of the *Quenta Silmarillion:*

> "Yet the lies that Melkor, the mighty and accursed, Morgoth Bauglir, the Power of Terror and of Hate, sowed in the hearts of Elves and Men are a seed that does not die and cannot be destroyed; and ever and anon it sprouts anew, and will bear dark fruit even unto the latest days." (TS, pp. 315–16)

The sadness of this ending should not come as a surprise, though. That *The Silmarillion* (as well as *The Lord of the Rings*) will be so filled with sorrow is foretold early in the *Ainulindalë* in a description of the battle being waged between the Theme of Ilúvatar and that of Melkor. Ilúvatar's Theme, we are told, is "deep and wide and beautiful, but slow and *blended with an immeasurable sorrow,* from which its beauty chiefly came" (TS, p. 5, emphasis mine). The sorrow in these books truly is immeasurable! And yet, as the author claims, there is beauty in it. There is tragedy in the tale of Húrin, but there is great joy also when Húrin finally comes before the throne of Melian and by her power is released from the lies of Morgoth and is his thrall no longer. There is great beauty in the forgiveness of Fingon for Maedhros, and in his memory of their former friendship, which prompts him to heal the feud that divides their people. There is beauty in the valor of Fingolfin, even when he falls crushed beneath the left foot of Morgoth. There is beauty in the self-sacrificing loyalty of Finrod to Beren. Indeed, all of the examples of beauty are made all the more poignant because they are surrounded by such tragedy. It is not idly that Tolkien begins the tale of Beren and Lúthien with the words: "Among the tales of *sorrow and of ruin* that come down to us from the darkness of those days there are yet some in which *amid weeping there is joy* and under the shadow of death light that endures" (TS, p. 195, emphasis mine).

As Tolkien suggests in *The Ainulindalë,* for many of his readers the beauty of the stories does come from their sorrow. But where does this sorrow come from? The sadness of *The Silmarillion* and *The Lord of the Rings*—and even of *The Hobbit,* which ends with the deaths of Thorin, Fili, and Kili—can be seen in part as echoing the sadness of Norse mythology that Tolkien found so moving. Here the gods themselves are doomed to disaster, and with them is doomed all the earth. Glory is not to be found in the hope of the hero, or in the hero's final victory, but rather in the hero's willingness to continue to fight the battle *even though he knows he is fated to die in the end.* There is something of this type of sorrow present, and perhaps even more of the sorrow of the Old Testament (at least as it is understood from a Christian perspective). Or rather, the two sorrows go hand in hand. Specifically, the pervasive sadness comes from the absence of Christ and thus an absence of a *means* for redemption and salvation; there is, in the body of Tolkien's Middle-earth writing, the *knowledge* that such redemption is *necessary*—that is, there is an understanding that the Christian hope lies in a *historical* incarnation of the Creator—but no such Christ has come to Middle-earth.

Professor Shippey has mentioned this pervading sense of sadness both in his writings on Tolkien and in lectures. I asked him what he made of it.[5] His reply was very interesting, and it enlightens some of what I have just written. His sense is that both Tolkien and his good friend C. S. Lewis, while being drawn to the stark beauty of early Germanic paganism, were also concerned

5. T. A. Shippey, personal communication and correspondence.

with the way that England was "slumping back" toward this paganism. They saw England moving away from the specifics of Christianity toward a vague deism, and as devout Christians they worried about that move. What they desired, according to Shippey, was a sort of mediation. They wanted to show the beauty and the splinter of truth in paganism, without adopting it. They wanted to present the people of the pagan Germanic north as doing the best they could under the circumstances, but also to show that without the revelation of Christianity they couldn't help but be sad. Thus, these people were not to be blamed, but rather pitied; there is no happy ending without divine intervention. "A point I would make at length if I ever had to comment on the subject is how horrible paganism was in reality," Shippey went on. "Tolkien occasionally showed signs of impatience with sentimental neo-paganism of the kind now thoroughly familiar." He then concluded, "I think he wondered what it would have been like for a decent honest sort of man, an Englishman in fact, indeed someone like him, living in a pagan world before Christ. Sad, that's the word!"

Returning to the pre-Christian sorrow of the Old Testament, we see that the Old Testament holds the *promise* of the coming Messiah, but none of these promises are yet fulfilled; they are still centuries away when the Old Testament ends. The stories of the patriarchs—of Abraham, and Isaac, and especially of Jacob—are stories of deception, loss, and unfilled promises. None of them makes a permanent home in the Promised Land. As for the nation of Israel, it goes from captivity to captivity: from slavery in Egypt to slavery in Babylon, with numerous captivities in between, such as the frequent periods of subjugation to the Philistines during the time of the judges and the reign of King Saul. In all of the centuries of Israel's history recounted in Judges, Samuel, Kings, and Chronicles, there are only a few brief lifetimes of glory and victory, such as during the reigns of King David and King Solomon. Even the years of David's reign have significant tragedies, including the rebellion and subsequent death of David's own son Absalom. Most of the heroes of faith of the Old Testament die without seeing their hope fulfilled. There is ever a sense that they are strangers in the world. As the author of the New Testament book of Hebrews writes of these heroes:

> All these died according to faith, not having received the prom-ises but beholding them afar off and saluting them and confess-ing that they are pilgrims and strangers on the earth. . . . And all these, being approved by the testimony of faith, received not the promise. (Heb. 11:13, 39)

What separates the New Testament from the Old? In the Chris-tian understanding, it is fundamentally this: the coming of the Christ: the incarnation of God the Son: the entering of the Creator into his creation: the fulfillment of the plan of salvation, so that salvation is not merely a word or idea or plan, but an actuality. That is also what separates a Christian understand-ing from the mythology of Middle-earth. To quote once again from Richard Purtill:

> If *The Silmarillion* seems to end on a somewhat dark and despairing note, it is because Tolkien has not allowed himself to introduce any hint of the true Hope of the World. Partly, this is his personal reticence; partly it is his artistic purpose. But the Christian hope is in Tolkien's own heart and is hidden in the heart of his work. (Pu, p. 101)

A Christian Myth?

To some it might seem odd, after the declarations of the past few paragraphs, to turn around and suggest that Tolkien's Middle-earth mythology is, after all, a Christian mythology. Yet in many other ways it is. Depending on what is meant by the question of whether Tolkien's mythology is a Christian one, the answer might be "yes." Again, to understand this, we should begin with Tolkien's own words, once again taken from a letter written in 1953:

> *The Lord of the Rings* is of course a fundamentally religious and Catholic work; unconsciously so at first, but consciously

in the revision. That is why I have not put in, or have cut out, practically all references to anything like "religion," to cults or practices, in the imaginary world. For the religious element is absorbed into the story and the symbolism. However that is very clumsily put, and sounds more self-important than I feel. For as a matter of fact, I have consciously planned very little; and should chiefly be grateful for having been brought up (since I was eight) in a Faith that has nourished me and taught me all the little that I know. (Letters, p. 172)

According to Tolkien himself, his trilogy is not merely peripherally Christian, but *fundamentally* so. Not only fundamentally so, but *consciously* so. Indeed, this seems so obvious to the author that he can only say "of course" to the suggestion. All that he knows—and thus all that he is able to put into his stories—has been nourished by his Christian faith. In explaining this, Tolkien also answers a question we posed earlier. Why are the references to the Authority—that is, to Ilúvatar—so vague and veiled in *The Lord of the Rings*? We now see part of the answer. It is not, according to Tolkien, because the work is not Christian, but rather because the work is so *thoroughly* Christian. Among other things, therefore, any visible element of the *practice* of religion would be too great a temptation (for readers, not for the author) to view the work as an allegory. In that way, it would interfere with the deeper and more profound Christian themes by trivializing them; not to mention that it likely also would cost Tolkien numerous readers who do not share his Christian faith! When readers suspect allegory, they either quit reading (as Tolkien likely would have done) or start chasing exact parallels—*this* equals *this*, and *that* equals *that*—and proceed as if the story can be reduced to mathematical equations rather than appreciating what is actually there. By contrast, the fabric of reality is far more complex, far richer and more wonderful than a formulaic representation of one idea by one narrative symbol. Tolkien, therefore, instead of letting the Christian *element* remain on the surface, where it might easily be dismissed with little thought—by those who agree with it as well as by those who disagree—lets his faith be *absorbed* into the story and the symbolism. It is there to be pondered, thought about, and reflected upon: to bring new insights with each subsequent reading.

Absorbed into the story, Tolkien says. In what ways? In all the ways we have been discussing in this book: in the Christian understanding of objective morality and moral responsibility; in the Christian importance of hope; in ideas of human worth, nobility, and purpose having their source in a divine Creator; in Christian notions of stewardship; in the understanding of human creativity as also having its source in a Creator; in Christian notions of salvation; in acknowledgment of the reality of the spiritual plane as well as the physical; and especially in the ever present hand of Authority at work within his creation. In a letter written in 1958, Tolkien suggests that most of the biographical information one might learn about him would not significantly aid one in understanding his writing (including *The Lord of the Rings*). Most facts about him would be completely useless. Some pieces of information, such as his tastes in languages, might have some relation to his writings but would require significant unraveling to figure out exactly what that relationship was. However, a few facts about him are actually quite significant in understanding his work. Of these he mentions only three, of which the "more important" is his Christian faith: "And there are a few basic facts [about myself], which however drily expressed, are really significant. . . . I am a Christian (which can be deduced from my stories), and in fact a Roman Catholic" (Letters, p. 288). There are two important points to be made here. The first is Tolkien's claim that knowing the "fact" of his Christian faith is "really significant" and "important" in explaining his works. The second important point is Tolkien's belief that his Christianity is evident in his writings, or *deducible from his stories,* as he puts it. On the latter point, he may be mistaken; many fans of his writing seem to be oblivious to the fact of his Christianity—though my own guess is that this is largely due to a lack of knowledge of just what the tenets of the Christian faith are. As to the former point, I think Tolkien is absolutely correct that an understanding of his Christian beliefs is tremendously important to understanding his works. A significant part of this book has been to explain how those beliefs are manifest in various ways in the Middle-earth mythology. But isn't that an argument that the mythology can and ought to be understood, at some level, as being Christian?

Returning for a moment to the influence of northern mythologies, we do see the presence and influence of many pagan Germanic values throughout these tales, as we noted earlier, but we also see the author understanding, presenting, and ultimately judging those values from a Christian perspective. In *The Hobbit*, we see both the values of the mead hall—"food and cheer and song," or simply friendship and fellowship—and the code of the warrior, whose glory comes from amassing treasure and defeating and subjecting enemies in war. What we see is reminiscent of how the *Beowulf* poet starts his poem:

> Yes, we have heard of the glory of the Spear-Danes' kings in the old days—how the princes of that people did brave deeds.
> Often Scyld Scefing took mead-benches away from enemy bands, from many tribes, terrified their nobles. . . . He lived in comfort for that, became great under the skies, prospered in honors until ever one of those who lived about him, across the whale-road, had to obey him, pay him tribute. That was a good king. (B, p. 1)

However, the perspective Tolkien brings to these values is that of the Christian: the perspective that there is an objective morality and a spiritual reality that make moral victory more important than military victory. It is a worldview that includes, among other things: a belief in life after death, a belief in a day of judgment, and a belief that reality includes both a spiritual plane and a material plane. This perspective leads one to view the world with eternal rather than temporal values. As we saw in the previous chapter, Tolkien uses the words of Thorin to present that perspective:

> "Since I leave now all gold and silver, and go where it is of little worth, I wish to part in friendship from you, and I would take back my words and deeds at the Gate. . . .

. . . If more of us valued food and cheer and song above
hoarded gold, it would be a merrier world." (TH, p. 243)

In the face of the Eternal, Thorin is able to see in a new light
what he previously valued. Gold and silver have temporal worth.
Friendship has eternal worth. And so Thorin repents of his
earlier words and deeds. So while Tolkien's writing upholds
from the Christian worldview the mead-hall values of "food and
cheer and song," it shows the vanity of the warriors' pursuit
of glory and riches. Likewise, in an earlier chapter we saw the
Anglo-Saxon warrior's glory epitomized in Théoden, especially
at his death, and yet even as Tolkien presents this glory he also
lets us see it from another perspective, which in that case is
through the eyes of Merry.

If we turn from *The Hobbit* and *The Lord of the Rings* to
The Silmarillion, we see even more clearly Tolkien's Christian
faith woven through the fabric of the tale, or *absorbed in its
symbolism*. Whereas references to the Authority are veiled in
The Lord of the Rings, and religious practices are almost completely expunged, *The Silmarillion* is fully and overtly theistic.
Ilúvatar is explicitly present, personally and directly and also
through his angelic servants, the Valar. It is Ilúvatar himself
who throws down Númenor and sunders the seas:

> Then Manwë upon the Mountain called upon Ilúvatar, and for
> that time the Valar laid down their government of Arda. But Ilú-
> vatar showed forth his power, and he changed the fashion of the
> world; and a great chasm opened in the sea between Númenor
> and the Deathless Lands, and the waters flowed down into it,
> and the noise and smoke of the cataracts went up to heaven, and
> the world was shaken. And all the fleets of the Númenóreans
> were drawn down into the abyss, and they were drowned and
> swallowed up for ever. (TS, pp. 344–45)

A full exploration of *The Silmarillion* would be beyond the
scope of this book (whose title suggests a focus on *The Lord
of the Rings*). However, there are three aspects of that work
that must be discussed in the context of this book, for they

suggest a profoundly Christian understanding of the mythology of Middle-earth, and they relate to comments made in the previous section.

The first aspect is that while nearly all references to religious practices were "cut out" from *The Lord of the Rings,* they play a central role in the *Akallabêth: The Downfall of Númenor,* which is part 4 of the published version of *The Silmarillion.* The worship of Ilúvatar is the central element of the *Akallabêth* (which mirrors the history of Israel from the kingdom of David onward, told in the books of Kings and Chronicles, ending with the fall of Israel to Babylon). At the start of the great kingdom of Númenor, we read:

> But in the midst of the land was a mountain tall and steep, and it was named the Meneltarma, the Pillar of Heaven, and upon it was a high place that was hallowed to Eru Ilúvatar, and it was open and unroofed, and no other temple or fane was there in the land of the Númenóreans. (TS, p. 322)

The decline of the kingdom is then intimately linked to the loss of faith in Ilúvatar, to the cessation of his due worship, and to the persecution of those faithful to him. Tolkien chronicles this downfall by coming back at key times to the state of this temple. We later read that "after the days of Tar-Ancalimon the offering of the first fruits to Eru was neglected, and men went seldom any more to the Hallow upon the heights of Meneltarma in the midst of the land" (TS, p. 329). This is the first major step in the decline of Númenor. Under the kingship of Tar-Palantír, there is a brief period of restoration, but then the kingdom grows even worse, until by the end we read that "the Meneltarma was utterly deserted in those days; and though not even Sauron dared to defile the high place, yet the King would let no man, upon pain of death, ascend to it, not even those of the Faithful who kept Ilúvatar in their hearts" (TS, p. 336). Instead, a temple is built to Morgoth, and people begin to worship the Dark Lord. Then the downfall is complete: "And men took weapons in those days and slew one another for little cause" (TS, p. 338). Though the military might of Númenor actually reaches a peak in these days, the internal state of the kingdom is abysmal, and its final end approaches quickly. Thus the fate of Númenor parallels the state of Ilúvatar's temple and of the Faithful who worship him. When Ilúvatar is worshiped properly, Númenor prospers in the way it ought to prosper. When worship of Ilúvatar ceases, and his people are persecuted, Númenor declines and becomes like the worst of the heathen kingdoms of Middle-earth. It is difficult, then, to see Tolkien's *Akallabêth* as anything other than a deeply religious work. In many ways it mirrors the Bible narrative of the downfall of Israel under the kings who succeed David and Solomon, leading up to the fall of Israel into captivity to Babylon. If the *Akallabêth* is not a Christian mythology, then at the very least it is a profoundly Christian understanding of a pre-Christian time.

In fact, the reasons for labeling even *The Lord of the Rings* a "Christian work" are plentiful enough that we must return to the final and most important reason we saw for answering "no" to the question at the start of this chapter. Our last and most significant reason for saying that Tolkien's mythology is not a Christian mythology was that there is no incarnation: there is no Christ, or divine Savior, in Middle-earth. Here I address a second aspect of *The Silmarillion*—or rather, *The Silmarillion* as it might have been. There is a very interesting dialogue scene buried in *Morgoth's Ring: The Later Silmarillion, Part One*, which is the tenth volume of the *History of Middle-earth*, written by J. R. R. Tolkien and edited posthumously by his son Christopher. According to Christopher's notes, there is a strong indication that his father viewed this particular dialogue (which is now called the "Athrabeth Finrod Ah Andreth"), as well as an essay discussing the scene, as *finished* and as a part of the canon of what he intended to go into the published version of *The Silmarillion*. According to these notes, the story itself was to have been included in *The Silmarillion* proper, and the essay included in an appendix. So what is this scene? In "Athrabeth Finrod Ah Andreth," the great King Finrod Felagund, lord of the realm of Nargothrond (and the brother of Galadriel), is having a conversation with a wise woman named Andreth. Finrod, who is of the race of Elves, and Andreth, of the race of Men, are trying to understand the differences between their races and what hope each race has separately or together. Andreth mentions an old belief that one day Ilúvatar himself will enter into his creation: "They say that the One will himself enter into Arda, and heal Men and all the Marring from the beginning to the end" (MR, p. 321). Finrod and Andreth then have a discussion about this ancient belief, during which Finrod comments that it seems right to him for an artist to enter his creation, and that if any artist could and would do it, it would be Ilúvatar. Moreover, Finrod believes that such an incarnation is actually the only hope that Elves and Men have for the healing of the hurts of Morgoth. Thus Finrod concludes:

> "If Eru wished to do this, I do not doubt that he would find a way, though I cannot foresee it. For, as it seems to me, even if He in Himself were to enter in, He must still remain also as He is: the Author without. And yet, Andreth, to speak with humility, I cannot conceive how else this healing could be achieved. Since Eru will surely not suffer Melkor to turn the world to his own will and to triumph in the end. Yet there is no power conceivable greater than Melkor save Eru only. Therefore Eru, if He will not relinquish His work to Melkor, who must else proceed to mastery, then Eru must come in to conquer him. . . . If any remedy for [Melkor's evil] is to be found, ere all is ended, any new light to oppose the shadow, or any medicine for the wounds: then it must, I deem, come from without." (MR, p. 322)

Tolkien seems to have viewed the coming of the Christ as somehow inevitable in Middle-earth. Through the voice of Finrod, he describes the incarnation as necessary: as the only hope for Middle-earth, the only way "healing could be achieved," the only way to prevent Morgoth from *triumphing in the end*, the only possible *remedy* for Morgoth's evil. No other solution to the fundamental problem of evil is conceivable—none except for the incarnation of the Creator Ilúvatar. "Surely" Eru will do it, Finrod reasons; he "must."

The fact that Tolkien wrote such a scene, describing the incarnation of the Creator within his creation, illustrates both how thoroughly Tolkien's Christian faith is ingrained in his mythology and his realization of just what it is that would need to happen in his world for it to fully reflect his deep and profound Christian joy. Tom Shippey even suggests that a dialogue between Gimli and Legolas at the start of "The Last Debate" might actually be about the "Incarnation, the Coming of *the Son of Man*" (Sh, pp. 218–19). The conversation has to do with the hope of Men and the seed of Men. Shippey examines Gimli's pessimistic response that all that Men do will "come to naught in the end but might-have-beens" (ROTK, p. 149), and he notes that Gimli's comment "would be entirely true without qualification, in the Christian view, if fallen humanity had not been rescued by a Power from outside, a Power beyond humanity which nevertheless became human" (Sh, p. 219). As Finrod tells Andreth, the coming of Ilúvatar into his creation is the *only* hope. Since that hope has not yet been fulfilled, and indeed is not even widely known among the peoples of Middle-earth, it is not surprising that the stories are so full of sorrow and sadness; Melkor's evil is still, ultimately, without a cure.

To return to our question, we might now answer that Tolkien's Middle-earth mythology is certainly not un-Christian; neither is it fully Christian. Rather it is a Christian understanding of a pre-Christian time. It is undeniably a work coming from a fully Christian mind, and yet it does not describe a fully Christian world. In that way, it is not unlike *Beowulf.* However, the Christian understanding of truth and reality seems (at least to me) to be far more deeply woven into the fabric of the Middle-earth legendarium than into the poem *Beowulf.*

The Theme of Ilúvatar

The third aspect of *The Silmarillion* that reflects its Christian underpinnings brings us to the conclusion of this book, for it gets at a root issue in understanding *The Lord of the Rings* and indeed all of Tolkien's Middle-earth mythology. In Tolkien's mythology, the original fall (the rebellion of some of the created order against the Creator) begins before the physical earth is even made, affecting the earth before any of the Children even appear. In the account of the creation of Middle-earth (TS, pp. 3–13), Ilúvatar begins a great theme of music that his first created beings, the Ainur, are to take part in, "each with his own thoughts and devices." However Melkor, to whom "had been given the greatest gifts," in seeking "to increase the power and glory of the part assigned to himself" begins to weave into his music an aspect of discord that is seemingly in opposition to the Theme of Ilúvatar in which the other Ainur are partaking. The result is discord, and before long some of the Ainur begin to follow Melkor rather than Ilúvatar. There is, as it were, a rebellion in heaven. Here, rather than stopping Melkor's music altogether or expelling him, Ilúvatar begins a second Theme. Against this second Theme, Melkor also rebels with discord. So Ilúvatar begins yet a third Theme. Here we get to one of the most important moments in the creation, around which all of the events in the coming history of Middle-earth revolve:

> And it seemed at last that there were two musics progressing at one time before the seat of Ilúvatar, and they were utterly at variance. The one was deep and wide and beautiful, but slow and blended with an immeasurable sorrow, from which its beauty chiefly came. The other had now achieved a unity of its own; but it was loud, and vain, and endlessly repeated; and it had little harmony, but rather a clamorous unison as of many trumpets braying upon a few notes. And it essayed to drown the other music by the violence of its voice, but it seemed that its most triumphant notes were taken by the other and woven into its own solemn pattern. (TS, p. 5)

In this imagery, Tolkien gives us a history of Middle-earth. Indeed, the music is the history of Middle-earth—so Ilúvatar tells the Ainur. This is where all the stories come from: *The Silmarillion*, *The Hobbit*, and *The Lord of the Rings*. They are about the rebellion of Melkor, and his desire to destroy the works of Ilúvatar. More importantly, however, they are about how Ilúvatar responds to Melkor by taking the most triumphant notes of his enemy and weaving them into his own solemn pattern. In other words, Ilúvatar's plans are not thwarted by

Melkor's evil. The Creator is able to foresee everything that Melkor is going to do in opposition to him, and to work his own plans so that they encompass even the actions done by his enemy in rebellion.

In doing this, Tolkien is working out in his writing a great principle of Christianity. The apostle Paul, whom I have already quoted, is one of the most important figures in understanding Christianity. In a letter Paul writes to the first-century Christian church in Rome, he encourages the recipients of the letter by telling them that God is able to take all things—even those things intended for evil—and work them out so that they result in good (Rom. 8:28). This is at the heart of the Christian understanding of history. What was the greatest triumph of Satan, the Devil, in all of history? It was having Jesus, the Christ who was sent to save the world, nailed to a cross by the very people he had come to save. Yet God takes that most triumphant note of his enemy and makes of it his own greatest victory, for in Christ's death on the cross and his ensuing resurrection, God works out his plan of salvation: the solemn pattern that has been at work since God promised to Abraham that through his offspring all the nations of the earth would be blessed. Satan, in working to have Jesus put to death, ends up aiding in the fulfillment of the prophecy made to Adam and Eve when evil first entered into the world, that a descendant of Eve would one day deal Satan the crushing blow. That crushing blow is dealt by Jesus on the cross, when he dies for the sins of the world and then rises again from death and conquers both sin and death. This story, more than any other, is at the heart of the Christian faith that is woven into the fabric of Middle-earth. As Ilúvatar says to Melkor, none can alter the music in his despite. "For he that attempteth this shall prove but mine instrument in the devising of things more wonderful, which he himself hath not imagined" (TS, p. 6). And later he says of Men, "These too in their time shall find that all that they do redounds at the end only to the glory of my work" (TS, p. 38).

One of the most moving examples of this principle illustrated in *The Silmarillion*—at least in terms of the beauty of the imagery—comes very shortly after Ilúvatar makes this proclamation.

Ulmo, one of Ilúvatar's chief servants, and one of the most wise and powerful of the Valar, laments the destruction that Melkor is causing in the new creation.

> And Ilúvatar spoke to Ulmo, and said: "Seest thou not how here in this little realm in the Deeps of Time Melkor hath made war upon thy province? He hath bethought him of bitter cold immoderate, and yet hath not destroyed the beauty of thy fountains, nor of thy clear pools. Behold the snow, and the cunning work of frost! Melkor hath devised heats and fire without restraint, and hath not dried up thy desire nor utterly quelled the music of the sea. Behold rather the height and glory of the clouds, and the everchanging mists; and listen to the fall of rain upon the Earth! And in these clouds thou art drawn nearer to Manwë, thy friend, whom thou lovest." (TS, p. 9)

Ilúvatar doesn't merely proclaim empty words of hope to the Ainur, that the deeds of his enemies will prove but his instrument in the devising of things more wonderful; he immediately shows Ulmo how he works it out. Bitter cold immoderate, intended to destroy the works of Ilúvatar and his servants the Ainur, instead becomes a vehicle through which the beauty of snow and frost is brought to life. Heat also, intended by Melkor to dry up the waters of Ulmo, instead results in the height and glory of clouds and ever changing mists and rain. We see this principle at work time and again in Middle-earth, in *The Lord of the Rings* and elsewhere. We see it in the evil plans of Saruman; with evil intent, the Orcs capture Merry and Pippin to bring them to Isengard, and yet Ilúvatar uses this as a means both of waking the Ents and of bringing Aragorn to Rohan to arouse Théoden, Éomer, and the latent strength of the Rohirrim. Eventually, we see it even in Gollum's evil, for he becomes the instrument by which the Ring is destroyed, when Frodo becomes unable to complete his task.

Indeed, it is in understanding the Theme of Ilúvatar that much is tied together, including the importance of moral victory over military victory, and even the nature of Gandalf's power and actions. If Ilúvatar is capable of taking the most evil acts of Morgoth, the most powerful of his creatures, and bringing good out of them—even while the acts themselves remain evil—surely he can bring good from the efforts of his servants. The outcome of the war is in Eru's hands; what he desires from his servants is their love and obedience—that they do what is right—and not that they win the war for him.

The Real War

And now we have come full circle, for we are once again speaking of war. At the start of this book, I asked whether J. R. R. Tolkien glorified war and violence. I claimed that war is not what *The Lord of the Rings* is really about: that moral victory is much more important than military victory. If by "war" we mean the physical conflict between armies, then that statement is precisely what I meant. For Ilúvatar has the power, at any time, to destroy entire kingdoms if he so desires, as he does with Númenor. What, then, is the power of Sauron to him? Nothing.

But at another level, war is exactly what the story is about. Not the wars of Human, Elf, Dwarf, Ent, or Orc armies, but the war that Melkor is waging upon Eru Ilúvatar: "that about his throne there was a raging storm, as of dark waters that made war one upon another in an endless wrath." It is the conflict in which "the discord of Melkor rose in uproar and contended with [the Theme of Ilúvatar], and again there was a war of sound more violent than before" (TS, p. 5). It is not ultimately a war over land or territory, but a war over the hearts of the Children of Ilúvatar. It is, as we saw in the confrontation between Gandalf and the Balrog, a war between Heaven and Hell, between the Secret Fire (the realm of Anor) and the realm of Udûn. It is, in short, a spiritual war rather than a physical one. *The Lord of the Rings* is, in fact, a working out of another great Christian principle, expressed again by the apostle Paul: "For our wrestling is not against flesh and blood; but against principalities and powers, against the rulers of the world of this darkness, against the spirits of wickedness in the high places" (Eph. 6:12). The real battle is not against physical armies, but against spiritual enemies. The goal of these spiritual enemies is not to destroy the body but to destroy the spirit. This is why this enemy cannot be defeated using weapons of evil. This is why, as Paul explains, the Christian's real armor is truth, righteousness, peace, faith, and ultimately salvation and prayer. Frodo has a mithril coat, but he also is defended by his own mercy. Sam wears loyalty and hope. Aragorn and Faramir have the armor of truthfulness. Interestingly enough, Tolkien visualizes this spiritual battle in the physical realm in a handful of places, in order to give the readers an imaginative glimpse of it. We see it in the battle of Gandalf and the Balrog discussed earlier, as well as in the confrontation between Gandalf and the Nazgûl in front of Minas Tirith. We even see it in the confrontation between Glorfindel and the Nine outside Rivendell. Gandalf explains to Frodo, "Those who have dwelt in the Blessed Realm live at once in both worlds, and against both the Seen and the Unseen they have great power. . . . you saw [Glorfindel] for a moment as he is upon the other side" (FOTR, p. 235).

Many of the separate elements of the story come together in this understanding. What is at stake is the salvation of the Children of Ilúvatar, and therefore the moral choices of those Children are what matters. This is why Faramir would not slay even an Orc with a falsehood. The physical battle might be won in such a way, but a battle in the real war—the spiritual war—would be lost. In the spiritual battle, everybody has a part.

> "I am [still willing to help]," said Mr. Butterbur. "More than ever. Though I don't know what the likes of me can do against, against—" he faltered.
> "Against the Shadow in the East," said Strider quietly. "Not much, Barliman, but every little helps." (FOTR, p. 181)

In the dialogues between Gandalf and Denethor, it becomes clear that Gandalf understands the spiritual nature of the war, while Denethor sees only military victory or defeat. Consider that Gandalf, himself a spiritual being who took the form of flesh in order to aid the people of Middle-earth, almost never takes up arms against a fleshly foe, but reserves the full demonstration of his powers for other foes of like spiritual nature: the Balrog (itself a spirit of flame and shadow in service of Morgoth), Saruman (another of the Istari), and the Nazgûl (once a Man, but now a wraith who has entered the spirit world). As Gandalf tells Frodo shortly before the Council of Elrond, "There are many powers in the world, for good or for evil. Some are greater than I am. Against some I have not yet been measured. But my time is coming" (FOTR, p. 232). This is also why Gandalf is so concerned with the "cure" of the characters of Middle-earth (Gollum, Saruman, and Wormtongue, as well as Bilbo and Frodo) and why he always wants to give people the chance to repent; why he would rather encourage people to fight the battle themselves (that is, to choose well) than to fight the battle for them. As we saw in the earlier chapter on salvation, the outcome of the spiritual war has eternal consequences: salvation or damnation.

In this battle, the unity of those who oppose Sauron (and his master, Morgoth) is vitally important, but this is as much true because unity itself is a good thing as it is because unity will bring about a great military force. Unity is the goal, not just the means to a goal. Or, to put another way, the music of Morgoth (if it may be called music) is the sound of "discord" or disunity. For Morgoth, it is not that the disunity of his foes is merely a means to some other end; rather, the disunity of his foes is itself an end. "Folly it may seem," said Haldir, when he had to blindfold the Fellowship upon their entry into Lothlórien. "Indeed in nothing is the power of the Dark Lord more clearly shown than in the estrangement that divides all those who still oppose him" (FOTR, p. 362). Galadriel tells the Fellowship, "Your Quest stands upon the edge of a knife. Stray but a little and it will fail, to the ruin of all. Yet hope remains while all the Company is true" (FOTR, p. 372). It is not by chance that Galadriel mentions *hope* in the same breath that she speaks of the values of faithfulness and unity within the Fellowship. Hope, too, is part of the battle. Hope and despair are not simply means to some other end, but they also are the ends themselves. For Ilúvatar, the desire is for his Children to have hope; for Morgoth and his servant Sauron, they have already won a battle the moment they have brought about despair.

Every chapter in this book has had this war behind it: the reality of the spiritual as well as physical realms; the importance of the eternal as opposed to the temporal. So we end with a last question. What is the applicability of this understanding to our lives today? What is the underlying reality or truth that Tolkien would have us see? I return again to two passages I referred to earlier from the end of Tolkien's essay "On Fairy-Stories." The first paragraph comes from the section immediately before the essay's epilogue, and the rest from the epilogue itself:

> The consolation of fairy-stories, the joy of the happy ending: or more correctly of the good catastrophe, the sudden joyous "turn" (for there is no true end to any fairy-tale): this joy, which is one of the things which fairy-stories can produce supremely well, is not essentially "escapist," nor "fugitive" In its fairy-tale—or otherworld—setting, it is a sudden and miraculous grace: never to be counted on to recur. It does not deny the existence of *dyscatastrophe*, of sorrow and failure: the possibility of these is necessary to the joy of deliverance; it denies (in the face of much evidence, if you will) universal final defeat and in so far is evangelium, giving a fleeting glimpse of Joy, Joy beyond the walls of the world, poignant as grief. (FS, p. 153)

> It has long been my feeling (a joyous feeling) that God redeemed . . . men, in a way fitting to this aspect . . . of their strange nature. The Gospels contain a fairy-story, or a story of a larger kind which embraces all the essence of fairy-stories. They contain many marvels—peculiarly artistic, beautiful, and moving: "mythical" in their perfect, self-contained significance; and among the marvels is the greatest and most complete conceivable eucatastrophe [consolation]. But this story has entered History and the primary world; the desire and aspiration of sub-creation has been raised to the fulfilment of Creation. The Birth of Christ is the eucatastrophe of Man's history. The Resurrection is the eucatastrophe of the story of the Incarnation. This story begins and ends in joy. . . . There is no tale ever told that men would rather find was true, and none which so many

sceptical men have accepted as true on its own merits. . . . To reject it leads either to sadness or to wrath.

. . . The Christian joy, the *Gloria,* is of the same kind; but it is pre-eminently . . . high and joyous. Because this story is supreme; and it is true. Art has been verified. God is the Lord, of angels, and of men and of elves. Legend and History have met and fused.

. . . The Christian has still to work, with mind as well as body, to suffer, hope, and die; but he may now perceive that all his bents and faculties have a purpose, which can be redeemed. (FS, 155–56)

What Tolkien is saying, here, is that we fight the same battle in our primary world. It is not fought with swords and spears against physical foes, the armies of Sauron. Rather it is fought with our truth, righteousness, peace, faith, and prayer. It is fought as we "work, with mind as well as body." It is fought as we "suffer, hope, and die." Barliman Butterbur fights the battle as much in his Prancing Pony inn at Bree as soldiers fight it on the front lines of Gondor. The Hobbits must fight this battle in the Shire as much as the Men of Rohan fight it on their borders. Indeed, the "Scouring of the Shire" is not an appendix tacked onto the end of the story, but it is the real story; it is what the entire book is about. Gandalf is training the Hobbits so that they are prepared do in the Shire what they have seen him and Aragorn do in Rohan and Gondor. That training succeeds. They don't need Gandalf anymore. The Hobbits are all grown up. Frodo shows to Saruman the same mercy that Gandalf does.

Of course it is not just Gandalf training the Hobbits to fight this battle; it is also Tolkien training his readers. But if Tolkien is right—if the Christian story is true, as he (and so many skeptical men) have come to believe is the case—then the victory of salvation is possible. And if sadness and wrath come from rejecting that story, then salvation comes in the opposite way: from believing it. What is exciting to Tolkien is that not only may the Children themselves be redeemed, but all of their efforts, their working as well as their suffering, and even their art, may have redemptive value and may be redeemed.

Fortunately, the war is not destined to continue through eternity. Eventually the war will come to an end. At the end of Tolkien's story "Leaf by Niggle," which I mentioned earlier in the context of Tolkien's tree, the painter Niggle has gone on a journey and finally meets the shepherd, who leads him into the mountains. All of the imagery of the book leads us to believe that this journey is Niggle's death—or the life that follows his death—and that the shepherd is none other than the Great Shepherd of Christian faith, namely, Jesus. Niggle follows the shepherd into the mountains. (If one discerns the more obvious imagery of the shepherd, then understanding the mountain imagery is not difficult either). Niggle's final surviving painting—a single leaf that had hung in a museum—is lost: "For a long while 'Leaf: by Niggle' hung there in a recess, and was noticed by a few eyes. But eventually the museum was burnt down, and the leaf, and Niggle, were entirely forgotten in his old country" (TL, p. 95). Nonetheless, Niggle's creative art is ultimately vindicated in the most profound and fitting of ways. His tree is given the gift of reality; his "desire and aspiration of sub-creation has been raised to the fulfillment of Creation." I have no doubt that Tolkien had himself and his own art in his mind and hopes when he wrote this ending, and we hear the second voice say of this now living tree (and the lands surrounding it): "It is proving very useful indeed. As a holiday, and a refreshment. It is splendid for convalescence; and not only that, for many it is the best introduction to the Mountains." For countless people, *The Lord of the Rings* has provided splendid refreshment. For that, the author would be glad. But his deeper desire is that for some it would be an introduction to the mountains.